END TIMES

END TIMES

ANNA SCHUMACHER

Penguin.com
Razorbill, an Imprint of Penguin Random House

Copyright © 2014 Penguin Group (USA) LLC

Library of Congress Cataloging-in-Publication Data

Schumacher, Anna.
End times / Anna Schumacher.
pages cm. – (End times ; 1)
Summary: When life in Detroit becomes too hard to bear, Daphne flees to her Uncle Floyd's home in Carbon County, Wyoming, but instead of solace she finds tumult as the townsfolk declare that the End Times are here, and she may be the only person who can read the signs and know the truth.
ISBN 978-1-59514-749-3 (paperback)
[1. End of the world–Fiction. 2. Oracles–Fiction. 3. Family life–Wyoming–Fiction. 4. Oil well drilling rigs–Fiction. 5. Dating (Social customs)–Fiction. 6. Pregnancy–Fiction. 7. Wyoming–Fiction.] I. Title.
PZ7.S39137End 2014
[Fic]–dc23
2013047608

Printed in the United States of America

1 3 5 7 9 10 8 6 4 2

Interior design by Vanessa Han

1

DAPHNE'S MOTHER CLUTCHED HER HUSBAND'S hand, which was blue and waxy under the hospital lights. Tears ran down her cheeks, carving sooty mascara canals in skin as dingy and haggard as the cracked linoleum and seasick-green walls in the intensive care unit.

"Are you proud of yourself?" Her hair stood out in frizzy, white-streaked lightning rods from her head, as if electrified by the dark mania in her eyes. "You killed him."

Daphne didn't answer. She just stared at the slack line on the life-support machine, listened to the empty space that had been filled with her stepfather's raspy, uneven breathing just moments before.

It was over. He was gone. There would be no more sleepless nights spent smothered by the close, dark air of her tiny room in their dingy Detroit apartment, bracing herself with every footstep behind the door. He would never come to her bed again, demanding something she wasn't willing to give. She was safe—and no matter what her mother said, the world was a better place without guys like Jim in it.

A sob ripped through Myra's body. She had been pretty once, back when Daphne was little and her real father was still alive. But years of bickering with Jim, working extra jobs to supplement his meager unemployment income, and glaring at Daphne had left deep lines in her face and turned her hair dull and gray. It was hard to see any remnants at all of the woman who had once seemed made of laughter and sunshine.

"Mom . . ." Daphne struggled to find the right words as Myra collapsed on Jim's chest.

"Come back!" she wept into his neck. Her back quaked, shoulder blades cutting sharp wings in the cheap polyester of her dress.

Action had always been easier for Daphne than words. She took her mother by the arms and gently pulled her off the bed, hoping her touch would be comforting. But it had the opposite effect.

"You beast!" Myra screamed, clawing at her with ragged fingernails. Daphne felt her cheek tear open and the sting of suddenly exposed blood before she was able to grasp her mother's hands, holding them tightly in the air between them.

"You're a murderer!" Myra shrieked. "You know it and I know it and the Lord knows it."

The accusation seemed to tire her. She sank into an orange plastic chair and resumed her high-pitched wailing.

The words stung more than the cut on her cheek, but Daphne

kept her face placid, a mask. She'd learned long ago it was easier that way. "Mom, I don't know why you can't believe me. The cops, the lawyers . . . they all did. It was in self-defense."

Myra rocked back and forth, tears leaking from her eyes. "It's a pack of lies."

They'd been over the argument so many times it felt like a well-worn path through a thorny wood, a path that went in circles and never came out into the sun. But Daphne tried again anyway. Because some part of her didn't want to give up hope that her mom would someday believe her.

"They found his fingerprints on the knife handle. He was going to use it on me."

A cloud passed over Myra's face. She looked up at her daughter almost trustingly, as if Daphne was the parent and she the child. Her brittle lips opened in an empty O, and the frigid rage Daphne had carried in her chest since That Night—and practically since Jim had come into their lives—threatened to melt as her mother's eyes searched hers. Maybe this time the path would come out on the other side, into the sunlit warmth she remembered from her childhood.

But the O flattened out to a hard, mean line, and the bitter glare returned to Myra's eyes.

"Why should I trust you?" she spat. "Making up those lies about Jim, weaving your nasty little spells on him, trying to come between us. And now you have. Forever. Are you happy now?"

Daphne looked at Jim's cold face, eyes staring out into a new world neither of them could see. She looked at her mother, shivering like a Chihuahua in the sickly hospital lighting. Finally, her eyes met her own reflection in the glass partition between Jim's room and the hallway. Long, dark hair struggled to escape her ponytail, falling in messy strands around the sharp lines of her face: cheekbones two angry slashes, chin set in perpetual defiance. Fury simmered in her amber eyes. She'd hoped that maybe, just maybe, the rage would abate with Jim's death, but it was stronger than ever. Even as a corpse, he had her mother on his side.

"No," she said simply. "Of course I'm not happy."

"You never were," her mother sighed. She took a deep, ragged breath. "I wish you'd just leave. When I look at you, all I see is a killer."

A glacier of hurt expanded in Daphne's chest. "I am leaving," she said.

"Good." Myra said absentmindedly. Her hand sought Jim's again, fluttering over his blue-tinted fingernails.

"I'm going to stay at Uncle Floyd's place in Wyoming for a while," Daphne said. "To give you time to grieve."

"Wait—you're what?" Myra's head snapped up.

She knew better than to tell her mother the real reason: that lately she'd felt a pull as strong as gravity toward her father's side of the family in Carbon County. It woke her in the middle of the night with an ache in her stomach that felt stronger than longing—almost like homesickness. It was more than just the desire to escape: Something in her body was drawing her there and telling her she had to go as soon as possible.

She couldn't explain why. She hadn't been to Wyoming since she was a child, and even though she remembered liking her aunt Karen's lasagna and her cousin Janie's antics, the way the sky rolled endlessly over the mountains and how Uncle Floyd knew the name of every animal, plant, and tree, she hadn't thought about it much since. Not until that night with Jim and the knife, when it had lodged in her mind like a tumor. It had been growing ever since.

Her mother blew her nose loudly into a hospital tissue, then balled it up and threw it on the floor. "So you're just abandoning me? Now, when I'm all alone with nobody else in the whole wide world?"

"You just said you can't bear the sight of me." Daphne tried not to sound exasperated. "That every time you look at me, all you see is a killer."

"How dare you talk back to me, missy!" Myra hissed. "If you want to go, then go. But don't expect me to take you in when you inevitably come crawling back."

"Okay." It wasn't the first threat her mother had made. Ever since Jim came along, Daphne's place in their home had felt precarious, with her mom constantly hinting at throwing her out, and complaining about the expense of having an extra mouth to feed. It had gnawed at Daphne until she'd gotten her first job at the 7-Eleven when she was fourteen, lying about her age on the application to work extra hours. She'd started contributing to household expenses, but at the same time she'd kept a secret bank account: her "just-in-case" money for the inevitable day when Myra's threats became reality.

Now that day was here. It was time to go.

She knelt by her mother's chair and wrapped her arms around her tiny frame. "Take care of yourself, Mom," she said. "You'll be all right."

She wanted to say more—that in spite of everything she still loved her, that somewhere she believed Myra still loved her back—but the words wouldn't come. She hugged her mom tighter, trying to find the old scent of sunshine under the antiseptic smells of the hospital's industrial-grade cleaner and her mom's cheap shampoo.

Myra's arms stayed tight by her sides, her shoulders sharp as glass. Daphne could feel the rage trembling inside her mother's body, the hatred that Jim had wedged between them with the hungry way he'd eyed her growing body and reached for her in the cramped kitchen. It had always been there, but it was stronger now.

She stood and turned toward the door.

"Don't you *dare* come back!" her mother shouted. "I never want to see your face again!"

The words echoed down the bustling hallway of the hospital where Myra had spent the last few weeks at Jim's bedside, wondering how she could afford to keep him on life support. Daphne had stopped by nearly every day, bringing snacks from the 7-Eleven that her mother never touched, checking in with the doctors about Jim's progress, but it was obvious to everyone but Myra that he would never be more than a vegetable. Finally the money ran out, and her mother decided to pull the plug.

Daphne knew she wouldn't be back. She had a long journey ahead of her, but by the time she reached Carbon County, Wyoming, her mother's accusations and threats would be as firmly behind her as Jim's last breath. All she wanted was to put the last nine years behind her, to pretend that their relationship had ended when she was still a child with a mother who loved her. The moment she stepped onto that Greyhound, it would be over. She'd learn to remember her mom fondly from a distance, to touch her only through postcards and the occasional check when she could find work. Jim's wandering hands and eyes, her mother's cold denial of the truth, and the final, fateful night when it had all come crumbling down would disappear in the vast string of states between them.

By the time her Uncle Floyd picked her up at the bus station, the trial would be nothing more than a smudgy square in an old issue of the *Detroit Free Press*.

2

JANIE ARCHED HER BACK AS best she could and purred into Doug's ear. Whoever said you didn't want it when you were pregnant was full of it. It actually made her want him more: These days, just a whiff of his Abercrombie and Fitch aftershave (which, when she was being completely honest with herself, he maybe usually wore a little too much of) was enough to get her ready to create a whole new Miracle of Life.

"Ungh," Doug grunted, quickly undoing his belt. He tried to wedge an arm under her back to unhook her bra, but between the frilly pillows, back issues of *Seventeen* magazine, and religious pamphlets from the Carbon County First Church of God strewn all over her bed, there was no room. "Sit up so I can get this."

"Okay, babe!" Janie agreed. She struggled to get her shoulders off the mattress, but the weight in her belly flattened her right back down again.

"C'mon!" Doug urged, kicking off his boxers. He looked so funny with just his T-shirt on, no bottoms, that she couldn't help giggling.

"You gotta help me up." She giggled harder. Bella, her Pomeranian, jumped up on the bed and, thinking it was playtime, joined in with a series of high-pitched yips.

"Not now!" Doug snapped, sweeping Bella off the bed and into a pile of clean laundry that Janie kept meaning to fold and put away.

"Aw, don't be mean!" Janie said as Bella started to whine. The dog was tiny, and her bed was way up high—her dad had put it up on risers to make room for the plastic bins underneath stuffed with her clothes, shoes, and accessories. It made her room look bigger when it was clean, but to be honest that wasn't all that often. Between the usual mess on the floor and the ripped-out magazine pages of her favorite bands and actresses taped to the wall, her room looked busy, cozy, and fun—three words that Janie would also use to describe herself.

"Just help me up and undo my bra and then take off my pants and panties and we can totally do it. I really want to," she added, trying for a sexy pout.

But Doug had already lost interest. "Forget it," he sighed, rummaging on the floor for his boxers and jeans. "It's too much work with that gut of yours."

"This *gut* of mine?" Janie turned on her side and gingerly pushed herself up to sitting. "This just happens to be our son. I will not have you disrespecting him before he's even out of the womb!"

Doug looked like he was gearing up for an argument—she could almost see the words tumbling around under his close-cropped brown hair. He was a meaty guy, with big shoulders and arms and, between her and God, kind of a big head, too, and he tended to wear his thoughts on his face. She could see in the way his thick brown eyebrows settled back into his forehead that he'd decided to skip the fight . . . which was good, because she didn't think she could handle yet another one that day. If they were going to be parents together, they needed to stop getting into it so much!

"Okay, sorry, babe," he said instead, lying down next to her and marveling at her boobs. "Man, those are big."

"I know, right?" She'd always been busty, but now she was filling a DD cup.

"So your cousin's gonna come stay here, huh?"

"Yup! Cousin Daphne. I haven't seen her since we were little kids, but we used to have the best time playing together. I was always the princess and she was my lady-in-waiting, and we'd put on, like, these nasty old lace curtains my mom had and parade around, and then she'd talk Dad into driving us into town to get ice cream. I think he always had a soft spot for her, which I guess is why we're taking her in now that her stepdad's dead and her mom's, like, practically a vegetable over it. Poor thing, the Lord hasn't always shone his blessings down on her like He has with me. He took her father when she was still just a kid, and now this. But we'll put her right again, or at least we'll do our best. That's what family's for, right?"

"I guess," Doug shrugged. "Where's she even gonna sleep in this dump?"

"Can you please not call it that?" Janie knew her home wasn't as nice as Doug's house in town, with its fluffy wall-to-wall carpeting and shelves of ceramic frogs that his mom dusted, like, every other minute, but it wasn't a *dump*. "The couch in the living room folds out, and she can keep her stuff here in my room."

"Sounds cramped."

Janie rolled her eyes. "Pastor Ted says that if we can make room in our hearts, we can make room in our homes. So that's what we're doing—darn it, Bella, stop that barking already!"

The little dog had begun yipping, really stirring up a racket. "Bella, just c'mere, it's gonna be fine."

She reached over to take her into her arms, but midway down she froze. A pair of beady black eyes stared back at her as the biggest snake she'd ever seen taunted her with a forked and darting tongue.

The serpent was enormous: as wide as Bella and who knew how long, the thick muscle of its body flexing under a sheen of scales that glistened in an ominous black-and-red pattern, like the spades on a playing card. It flicked its tongue at her almost seductively from inside a head as red and lustrous as fresh blood.

She opened her mouth, but even the scream wouldn't come right away—not until the viper brought itself up tall and hissed, flaying the scales on its neck. Then she let loose a shriek so loud that even the ceramic Jesus on her bedside lamp looked like he wanted to take cover.

"What the—?" Doug jerked back on the bed.

"Doug, get it!" she shrieked. "Kill it, quick, it's going to eat Bella!"

"Aw, I don't know." Doug's face had gone pale under his stubble. "That thing's seriously big."

Bella whimpered from the corner. Fear had puffed the poor sweet dog up to twice her size, so her brown eyes and button nose were nearly invisible under her trembling fur.

"Doug, please!" Janie started to cry. "He's going to eat Bella and bite me and maybe hurt our baby! You have to do something—now!"

The snake swayed back and forth, beady eyes darting from Janie to Bella and back again, as if trying to decide which of them to attack first. It filled Janie with a cold dread that ran deeper than fear, as if the devil himself had sent a dark and bloodthirsty messenger to her room. Its head was at least two feet off the floor, and there was who-all-knew how much of it still coiled under the pile of laundry.

Doug steeled himself the way he did before a big motocross race, shaking his head and throwing back his shoulders.

"Fine." He grabbed one of his Nike high-tops and shoved a foot inside, not bothering to tie the laces. He quivered with adrenalin, his burly arms puckered with goose bumps even as sweat ran down his forehead. Janie shrank back on the bed, and a snarl started deep and low in Doug's chest. It burst from his throat with a loud roar as he leapt onto the snake, bringing a heavy sneaker down behind its head and crushing its neck onto the floor.

The snake hissed hideously, lashing its tail from side to side like a fresh-caught fish flopping on the pier at Hatchett Lake. Pink maternity tops and balled-up socks and long-forgotten homework assignments scattered.

"Die, dammit, die!" Doug screamed, stomping on the snake again and again. Its tail flailed, jerking back and forth in a spray of glittering scales. As Doug brought his foot down one last time, the jerking stopped and the snake stiffened. For a second, it looked like it was levitating off the ground, all of its coiled muscular energy propelling itself into one final moment of life. And then it lay still.

"Gross-ass snake," Doug spat, shaking his foot. The viper lay half-flattened, glistening muscle and guts spilling from its neck.

"My goodness, what happened in here?" Janie's parents looked blurry in the doorway, and she realized there were still tears in her eyes. Now that the shock was over, she could let them fall freely.

"Oh, Mom, it was awful!" she sobbed. Bella leapt onto her lap and began licking her tears, and Janie held the dog tight, weeping into her soft fur. "This snake just popped out of nowhere, and Bella started barking, and I was so scared it was going to get the baby!"

"Whatever, it was no biggie." Doug had fully regained his composure. "I took care of it."

Janie's dad, Floyd Peyton, knelt to examine the carcass. His eyes weren't so good after forty years sorting nuts and washers at the hardware store, but he'd never gone to get a prescription—too much money—and only wore cheap reading glasses from the local pharmacy.

"My Lord." He leaned in for an even closer look. "Don't go placing money on it, but this looks to me like a Djinn viper. I thought they were extinct around here—the last one I ever heard of was when my father was a boy."

"A what viper?" Doug asked.

"Djinn. D-J-I-N-N. It's related to the western rattlesnake, which I've sure seen plenty of in my time. But never this."

He reached down and ran a finger over the snake's lifeless tail. "See these black markings—almost like spades. That's how it got its name. 'Djinn' means 'devil.'"

Even in the warm trailer, Janie felt her skin go cold.

"What does it mean?" she asked. "Is it a sign?"

"Whatever, no," Doug laughed. "Stop being so superstitious. It's just a big-ass stupid snake."

Doug was no help in situations like these. The Good Lord Jesus Christ himself could probably show up on his doorstep requesting an invitation for dinner, bloody palms and all, and Doug would call him a dirty hippie and turn him away. He was a believer in his own way, of course, but he didn't always see the meaning in things like Janie did.

She turned to her parents instead. "Mom, what do you think?"

"I think it can mean whatever you want it to mean." Karen Peyton's voice was warm and comforting. "But maybe we should all pray a little extra hard tonight and try our best to shun temptation when it comes knockin' on our door."

She smiled that smile that made everyone in Carbon County trust her with their gossip and fears and secrets, but her eyes were on Janie's belly. As if Janie needed reminding that her mother didn't exactly 100 percent approve of her going and getting herself pregnant while she was still just seventeen. Temptation come knockin', indeed.

"Whatever it means, I want it out of my room." Janie pulled Bella closer. "Doug, will you take it outside?"

Doug wrinkled his nose. "No way am I touching that thing. It's all oozing guts and stuff."

"C'mon, baby!" Janie tried her sexy pout again, but Doug wouldn't budge. That's what she got for dating a spoiled mama's boy never made to do a chore in his life: Sometimes Doug could be an even bigger princess than she was.

Her dad sighed. "I got it," he said. "Guts or not, I may stick 'im in the freezer for a bit, 'til I can get over to the ranger station down at Medicine Bow and see if someone there can identify it for real."

"Ew!" Janie squealed.

That seemed to break the tension, and all of them had a good, long laugh before Floyd went to get a stiff piece of cardboard and a plastic bag.

OWEN LEANED HARD INTO THE curve. His elbow nearly brushed the earth as he slammed through the bend, straightening just long enough to dip deep and low in the other direction, riding the natural twists in the track.

He was ahead by a good six lengths as the motor on his bike, a vintage Husqvarna that he'd been souping up since he was fifteen, screamed into the dying evening. He knew it without looking back—and he didn't plan on slowing down until he crossed the finish line, taking home the top prize in Olympia, Washington, that day. The rest of the motocross riders swarmed in his wake like a pack of angry bees, engines whining in collective frustration. It was like this at every race: He'd start out slow, letting them think they had a chance for a lap or two before pulling out his throttle and blowing past them in a cloud of churned earth and curses.

Those first few laps, where he sized up his competition while riding with the pack, were like a tease for him, the hot promise of speed tickling his nerve endings until the desire grew like a cloud of pressurized gas and he finally ignited, shooting out ahead. More and more often lately, that moment when he overtook everyone was the only peace he knew. In the roar of triumph and flurry of dust, the searing jolt of adrenalin that propelled him forward, he was able to forget the nightmares that had begun to taunt him the night of his eighteenth birthday, the fiery visions of destruction that woke him each night to soaked sheets and fear still surging in his blood. Owning the track was the only way to calm the visions of dark specters dancing around a bonfire piled high with bodies, the only way to quiet the gravelly voice whispering in his ear to *find the vein.*

He gunned into a long jump, clearing three high mounds of earth in one go, the astonished shouts from the bleachers a dim roar through his helmet. The bike was an animal below him, one he knew better than any human, one he'd tamed well. He'd always loved to ride, had picked it up just shy of his seventh birthday and been hooked ever since, giving up friends and parties to spend days and nights at the local track back in his Kansas hometown, driving himself and his metal beast past spills and breakdowns and exhaustion until the two of them became a single steel bullet zinging through the air. But ever since he'd left home a few months before, it felt like something more than skill propelled him through each race. When he rode he was more than Owen, a lone wolf from Kansas with grease under his fingernails. Now when he rode he was all fire tornadoes and dust devils, he was pure speed and molten light.

He couldn't help gooning a little on the last jump before the finish line, showing off with the kind of stunt usually reserved for freestyle competitions. He sailed over the jump and, at the height of his trajectory when the bike was weightless beneath him, he stood up straight and hooked his toes under the handlebars, arms stretched over his head. A cliffhanger, the move was called— not that there was any suspense over who was going to win this particular race.

He felt the wild awe of the crowd as he slid back into the saddle and whizzed across the finish line, cutting at a hard angle to send up a cloud of dust and clotted earth. There he waited a moment, letting his heartbeat cool as the tingling thrill of competition drained from his fingers. By the time the rest of the riders puttered across the line, their faces set in that stony scowl of envy he'd come to know so well, the rush was already starting to wear off. It was just another race, just another trophy he'd toss in the dumpster on his way to the next town. Sure, he could use the prize money— it was what got him from track to track, what paid for repairs and cheap diner meals and gasoline—but it wouldn't quiet that horrible, gravelly voice in his head, telling him to *find the vein* until he wondered if he was crazy or suicidal or both.

It wouldn't stop his dreams.

↔

"That was some race you ran there, son." The race organizer—Tyler, according to the name stitched across the front of his American Motocross Association jacket—handed Owen a check for three hundred dollars, his first-place winnings. The sun had started to set over the cragged pine tree line in the distance, and the last of the contestants had already packed up their bikes and families and were driving away under an eggplant-colored sky. "You were like a bat outta hell on that track—I swear, in all my days, I never saw anyone take corners so tight."

"I just got lucky." Owen folded the check into his back pocket.

"That was more than luck, son." Tyler gathered a sheaf of papers from the folding table with hands as thick and dirt-streaked as hot dogs left too long on the grill. His metal folding chair screeched as he pushed it back against the pavement. "I guess I'll be seeing you on the pro circuit before too long."

He stood to leave.

"Hey," Owen said quickly. "Got a sec to answer some questions?"

Tyler paused. He was a bulky man in his midfifties, squat and square as a fireplug, his hair gray and more than a little greasy. He had the leathered face of someone who had spent his life in the Pacific Northwest, tacitly accepting sharp winds and saltwater and endless rain as a matter of course.

"I doubt there's anything I can tell *you*. But try me."

"It's not about motocross." Owen knew that everything he needed to know about *that* was coiled in his muscles, racing to leap to life on the track. "It's about this area. Have you lived here long?"

Tyler furrowed an eyebrow. "Only since I was half your size and twice as stupid. Why d'you ask?"

"I'm looking for some info on a place that used to be around here."

"Try me."

Owen kept his voice cool. "It's an old commune, called Children of the Earth."

The name, and the fact that it was somewhere near Olympia, were all Owen knew about the place he was born. As a child, his questions about it had deepened the lines around his mother's normally lively eyes until he learned, reluctantly, not to ask anymore. He guessed, but never knew for sure, that her time at Children of the Earth was the reason she sometimes trailed off in the middle of sentences, her eyes misting and growing faraway before he or his sister or stepdad could wave their hands in front of her face to draw her back. He wondered, sometimes, if the snippets of old tunes she sang, songs he'd never heard on the radio or found through online searches, came from there. Most of all, he wondered if the Children of the Earth had something to do with his dreams.

Tyler's wrinkles arranged themselves into a quizzical roadmap. "I remember it, sure. Hasn't been around for years, though. Must have shut down when you were barely old enough to piss standing up."

Owen's pulse quickened, struggling toward answers. "Any idea what happened?"

"Gosh, let's see." Tyler rubbed a hand over the stubble on his face. "It's been well over a decade since it got shut down. Nobody really knew why, but it wasn't pretty. Lot of rumors about that place. They say the Feds came and picked up their leader—what was his name? Murphy? Murdock? Something like that." He paused, staring off into the foggy peaks in the distance. "Anyway, most of 'em skipped town. A few stayed, though, ladies with kids, mostly. Got jobs around town."

"Are any of them still here?" Need pulsed at Owen's temples. He suspected, sometimes, that the Children of the Earth were the dusky figures dancing by the bonfire in his dreams. Sometimes, he drew close enough to glimpse a wild grin of dark ecstasy or the glint of an emerald eye; but their faces always receded into the darkness of his memory before he awoke, leaving him grasping at shadows.

"Well, there's one, Pam, who was around until just this past year. Worked at the laundromat. Nice lady, kinda quiet. But she finally went back to her folks in—oh, I dunno, one a' them Eastern states. Connecticut or something. Guess she got sick of trying to keep a lid on that daughter of hers."

"Daughter?" Owen felt his ears perk up.

"Oh, Luna." Tyler chuckled softly. "She's still around—hard to miss, that one. Though if you want to know about that commune, she may be your best bet."

Luna. The name roared through Owen's head, a distant siren song from his dreams.

"Any idea where I can find her?"

"Let's see." Tyler scratched his head. "I think she still performs with Ariel Crow's band—the Fine Feathered Family, they're called. You can check and see if they're still in town; they usually put posters up outside the food co-op when they have a gig."

"Thanks." Owen stuck out his hand. "I appreciate your time, Tyler. You've been a real big help."

Tyler pumped his hand up and down. "What'cha want with that Children of the Earth place, anyway?" he asked as Owen turned to go.

Owen froze. "No real reason," he said, not meeting the older man's eyes. "I read an article once, and I was curious."

"If you want my two cents, son, you'd do better to steer clear of any commune business and keep your eyes on the prize." Tyler nodded down at the motocross track, which was silent and dusky in the gathering night. "I know pro when I see it—and, son, mark my words, within a year you'll be pro."

"Thanks for the vote of confidence," Owen said. But he suspected, as he turned and made his way toward the parking lot, to his truck and Luna and the future, that in a year it wouldn't matter anymore. In a year, everything would be different.

DAPHNE JERKED AWAKE. A BRASSY blast filled the Greyhound bus, the note long and sustained. A moment later it was followed by another, lower note, sounding a deep brass fanfare.

She craned her neck, sore from sleeping kinked and curled against the cold plexiglass window, and looked around at the handful of other passengers, wondering if someone had turned on a radio or taken the opportunity to practice the trumpet. But everyone else was silent, peering up and down the length of the bus as they tried to find the source of the sound.

"Is that your radio?" a rumpled woman who'd been eating coconut flakes from the bag since they left Cheyenne asked the driver. He shook his head, eyes confused in the rearview mirror. He even turned it on to check, shuffling through country stations and classic rock and static.

"I think it's coming from outside," he surmised.

Daphne pressed her ear to the window and the notes grew louder, their tones simultaneously bright and muted, exciting and monotonous. It sounded like they were trying to introduce something, like a line of sentries sounding the arrival of a king.

They made her want to keep listening even as she pressed her hands against her ears, wishing they would stop.

"Is it trumpets?" a guy in an army uniform asked.

"Might be a sax," suggested a grandmother with a big bag of knitting in her lap.

The bus driver shook his head. "The sax has more groove," he insisted.

"And it ain't no tuba, either," the woman who'd been eating coconut flakes said firmly. "Not low enough."

"It's trumpets," the army guy said firmly. "Sounds just like 'em— and I'd know. I used to be in a marching band."

The bus sputtered through a turnaround, past a sign welcoming them to Carbon County (pop.: 3,901; elev.: 6,394 ft.), and into the dusty parking lot of Elmer's Gas 'n' Grocery. A recent rain had washed through town, and a single, golden ray of sunlight peered through the still-steely sky.

"You got a bag under here?" the driver asked as Daphne climbed off the bus, the trumpet blasts growing shriller with the first cool breath of fresh mountain air.

She nodded.

"Well, hurry up and get it out—those horns are starting to give me the creeps."

Daphne grabbed her duffel from beneath the bus and stretched her legs. A sudden high note sounded as she glanced around at the parking lot's cracked pavement and the tree growing through the window of the abandoned Sleep-EZ Motel across the street.

"There she is!" Uncle Floyd called from across the parking lot. He lumbered toward her, his face open in a wide, affable grin, and wrapped her in a bear hug. His hair had gone gray around the temples, and he walked with a bit of a limp, but he still had the same broad shoulders and mile-wide smile she remembered from her childhood. The same as her dad. "Just in time to witness this miracle from God. Good to see you again, niece!"

Burying her face in the wood-smoky smell of his plaid flannel shirt, Daphne felt her shoulders relax for the first time in months. To Uncle Floyd, she wasn't a burden or a victim or a murderer. To him, she was still just Daphne.

He held her at arm's length. "Lookit you: a grown woman. Little skinny, but a couple weeks of Aunt Karen's cooking will fix that." He laughed good and deep.

"Do you know where that noise is coming from?" she asked as the bus pulled away, kicking up a cloud of dust as it turned onto Buzzard Road.

Floyd grinned. "Isn't it amazing? It just started, practically the moment I got in the truck to come pick you up. It's like a sign from God, coming from the heavens."

Daphne frowned as she followed him to his ancient, rust-spattered pickup. "But there has to be an explanation," she said. "What about the high school band? Maybe they're practicing?"

"Doubt it," Floyd said amiably, hoisting himself into the driver's seat. "Music got cut from the school budget years ago."

Daphne rolled down her window, letting the long metallic notes sweep in on a brisk, clean breeze. "Maybe it's a trick of the wind?" she suggested. The air felt so fresh and pure on her face, it seemed almost possible that it could manufacture a sound exactly like a trumpet fanfare.

Floyd's laugh rolled deep and rich from his chest. "Could be," he surmised. "But I've lived here my whole life, and I've never heard anything even remotely like it."

He swung the pickup onto Main Street, passing the movie theater where Daphne remembered going to see cartoons with the Peytons as a child. It was boarded up, a lone *P* hanging haphazardly from the marquee. Beyond it, more stores were shuttered permanently, with dusty *For Rent* signs in the windows and tattered awnings flapping in the wind. She noticed with a pang that the ice cream parlor where she'd always ordered a chocolate cone with double rainbow sprinkles had been converted to a pawnshop—and even that looked like it hadn't been open in months. The village that she remembered as a candy-colored vacation mecca seemed more like a sleepy town ravaged by the recession, a drive-by on Highway 80 somewhere between Cheyenne and Salt Lake City.

"Hey, Hal!" Floyd called to a man sitting on a bench outside the hardware store. Daphne vividly remembered visiting her uncle there, the way he'd held her up to see the wall of flashlights and brightly colored electrical tape and helped her open the gleaming drawers full of every size and type of screw, proudly explaining to her how he'd organized them all himself.

"Floyd!" Hal, whose big, round ears stuck out of the side of his head like a pair of bolts and washers, creaked to his feet. He wore a faded flannel shirt and overalls, and the grin under his baseball cap was enormous. "Can you believe this?" He gestured at the sky. "Like it's coming straight from heaven!"

Floyd slowed to a stop, his engine idling. "Like a sign from God," he agreed.

"Straight out of the Book of Revelations!" Hal peered into the truck. "Say, is this your little niece? She ain't so little anymore!" He grinned at Daphne. "Last time I saw you, you had a bullfrog in your hands that you refused to let go. Did you bring this miracle in with you on the bus, or what?"

Daphne shook her head. She dimly remembered Hal as her uncle's boss, the owner of the hardware store. "I'm clueless," she said. "Maybe there's a band or orchestra visiting from out of town?"

"Visiting Carbon County?" Hal whooped, underscoring a series of low, brassy notes that seemed to boom straight from the sky. "That's a good one. Wherever they're from, I can guarantee there's even less to see here."

"Well, I should get Daphne home to unpack—and see what the missus has to say about all this." Floyd pointed at the sky. "Ten bucks says she's already called Pastor Ted."

"That's one bet I'm not willing to take," Hal chuckled. "See you around, Floyd."

They chugged on down the street, the trumpets waxing and waning like a fire alarm all around them. Daphne was starting to feel like the music was following her—no matter how far they drove, it always seemed to be coming from just over the next bend.

"It's good the hardware store's still open," she said. "You must be glad to be working."

Uncle Floyd's grin disappeared, and the lines in his face grew heavier. "Well, Daphne, I guess that's something I should tell you. Times are a little tough around here, and business hasn't been so good lately."

Foreboding tickled the back of her throat. "Are you only part-time now?" she guessed.

"Not exactly, no." He concentrated heavily on the road, not meeting her eyes. "Hal kept me on for as long as he could, but it's all he can do to keep the lights on. I've been out of work since December."

The tickle in her throat turned to a full-fledged ache. Why hadn't Floyd mentioned that when she called? If she'd known the family was struggling, she would have found somewhere else to go. But before she could ask, Floyd pulled the pickup past a stand of scrubby pines and up to a narrow trailer home propped up on cinder blocks. Auto parts, old metal lawn chairs, and a long-forgotten birdbath rusted on patches of dry brown grass out front.

"Here we are." His tone, behind a jovial grin, was almost apologetic. "Home sweet home, trumpet fanfare and all."

Daphne gaped. "You're still living in the trailer?" she asked before she could stop herself. The last summer she'd visited, when she was eight, the kitchen table had been spread with blueprints for the house Floyd planned to build. He'd been so proud when he pointed to the guest room where her parents would sleep, then to the square that would be Janie's room, big enough for two twin beds and all the sleepovers the girls could dream of.

Again, Floyd avoided her eyes. "I never could quite scrape together the money," he said as the mysterious trumpets sounded a mournful note. "Tax rates went up, and the bank's been pretty stingy with loans. But you should see what Karen's done with the place—we got a new living room set a few years back, and everyone swears the foldout's as comfy as a real bed. You'll be snug as a bug in a rug."

He grabbed her bag, and Daphne followed him up the scrubby path to the trailer, her head still spinning. Nothing was the way she'd imagined it back in Detroit, where the glimmer of Carbon County and her uncle's welcoming smile had gotten her through so many of the long, uncertain nights since Jim's stabbing. It hadn't even occurred to her that the Peytons might not be doing well themselves.

"There you are!" Karen Peyton threw open the trailer's door and wrapped Daphne in a cinnamon-scented hug. The trumpet blasts disappeared momentarily into the folds of her aunt's fleshy shoulders as Karen squeezed her tight.

"Welcome back, dear." Aunt Karen pulled away, still grasping Daphne's wrist in one of her pudgy hands. Wispy blond hair flew around her face, and a basket of cartoon kittens grinned from her sweatshirt. "Can you believe this . . . this . . . ?" she waved her hand in the air, at a loss for words.

"This miracle?" Floyd supplied.

"Miracle, racket, whatever you want to call it!" Karen hustled them inside, letting the screen door slam behind them. "Me an' Janie've been on the phone with everyone, and of course the first person I called was Pastor Ted."

Uncle Floyd caught Daphne's eye and winked.

"Does he agree?" Floyd asked. "This could be that sign from God he's been talking about all these years?"

"Well, he doesn't know for sure, of course. Some folks say it's gotta be a busload of trumpet players or something, some trick of the wind. But as far as I'm concerned, there's really only one explanation: The good Lord is trying to send us a message, and He found the absolute loudest possible way to do it." She raised her head to the trailer's low, curved ceiling. "We hear you up there, okay, Lord?" she said. "And we're ready and willing to do your bidding, always have been and always will be—so you can stop driving us nuts with that noise already!"

"For real!"

Over her aunt's shoulder, Daphne saw her cousin Janie coming toward them from the hall. The tow-headed girl who had once made Daphne call her Princess Janie was still blond, but now her color came with hairspray and dark roots. Her eyes were ringed in thick blue liner and accentuated with layers of mascara, and peachy gloss coated her lips. She'd filled out, too, with big breasts and pudgy shoulders and . . .

"Oh my God." Daphne set down her bag and stared at the bulge under her cousin's top. "You guys didn't tell me Janie was pregnant!"

"We don't take the Lord's name in vain in this house," Janie said sunnily. "And—yep, surprise! I'm gonna have a baby boy."

Daphne'd been wrong. This was all wrong. She'd be an imposition on the Peytons, taking up space they didn't have in a trailer that could barely accommodate them in the first place, stealing food from a baby that needed it way more than she did. She never should have come. The trailer felt like it was closing in on her, even more claustrophobic than her mother's apartment. A claw of panic seized at her throat as she realized she'd have to leave, to find a whole new place for herself in the world, one without any friends or family at all. Maybe it was what she deserved.

"I'm sorry—I didn't realize," she babbled. "You should have told me. I could have gone somewhere else . . ."

"Don't be ridiculous!" Janie swooped in to give Daphne a hug.

"We wanted it to be a surprise! There's plenty of room for all of us here—like Pastor Ted says, if there's room in your heart, there's room in your home. Now, come on, I'll show you where I cleaned off a shelf in my room for your stuff." She eyed Daphne's duffel. "Although if that's all you brought, I guess that's a good thing, 'cause I'm a bit of a slob. So can you get a load of these trumpets or what? It's all anyone in town can talk about . . ."

The claw eased its grip on Daphne's throat as Janie led her down the hall, chattering the entire way: about clothes, the ordeals of pregnancy, and the kooky trumpet sounds that still filled the air. If the Peytons minded having her there, they sure did a good job of hiding it. *I'll help out however I can*, Daphne promised herself. *I'll do the dishes, try to get a job—maybe even start a garden out back.*

Daphne reminded herself that even if the situation wasn't ideal, she was safe with the Peytons. It was time to forget about what had happened back in Detroit, to forget the nightmare of the past nine years. It was time to be a Peyton again.

THE TRUMPETS CONTINUED AS JANIE showed Daphne around the trailer, serenading them as her cousin pointed out the holder for her toothbrush in the closet-sized bathroom and how to kick the stubborn leg on the foldout couch where she'd be sleeping in the living room. As cramped as the trailer was, she could tell that the Peytons had tried hard to make it feel like a home. The pint-sized kitchen was painted a cheery yellow, and clean lace curtains hung over the windows above the sink and built-in banquette.

Two steps away, the living room was stuffed with plush, rose-colored furniture. Daphne saw her own seven-year-old face grinning from a photo on the wall, clutching an ice cream cone in one hand and her father's swim trunks in the other, the entire family wet and sunburned and smiling. The photo was surrounded by Janie's school pictures, framed certificates, and inspirational posters, and a big wooden cross decorated in hand-painted vines and flowers dominated the wall.

The trumpets blared through dinner, interrupting with blast after triumphant blast as Janie tried to lead the family in a lengthy grace blessing the Lord, the food, the baby, the baby's daddy, Cousin Daphne's poor dead stepdad, Pastor Ted and the entire congregation of the Carbon County First Church of God, and also Wal-Mart for having such cheap maternity clothes. Daphne had just finished doing the dishes when a bright green pickup truck decorated with shiny black lightning careened into the driveway, a dirt bike strapped to the back. An oversized guy in an Abercrombie T-shirt and Carhart jacket, with hulking shoulders and a thick, pink neck, came lumbering out.

"Doug!" Janie called. She threw open the door and kissed him loudly while Aunt Karen averted her eyes. "Can you believe this noise? It's, like, the craziest thing that's ever happened to Carbon County since—well, ever!"

"Sure, babe." Doug regarded Daphne over his girlfriend's head. His eyes were narrow and piggish under puffy lids, and a purple pimple throbbed ripely by his lip. "This your cousin?"

Janie bobbed between them, making introductions. "It's real nice to meet you," Doug said, a slow grin spreading across his face. Daphne forced herself to smile back, reminding herself that not all guys were giant scumbags like Jim. "You ready to watch me ride?"

"I guess," Daphne replied. During dinner, Janie had told her all about the motocross track in town, how ever since it had been built it was the main thing—and pretty much the only thing—to do on Friday nights.

"So you really never seen any motocross?" Doug asked as they headed toward his truck.

She shook her head.

"I guess not a lot of dirt bike tracks in Detroit. Just dirtbags, ha ha ha!" He guffawed at his own joke, and Janie joined in. After a moment, Daphne choked out a laugh of her own. She was liking Doug less and less by the minute—but if there was one thing Jim had taught her, it was that the bigger a guy talked, the less he liked to be contradicted.

"You're gonna love it!" Janie did her best to twist around and smile at Daphne from the passenger seat. "Some of the guys around here are real good. Especially my man here—right, baby?"

Doug puffed up at the compliment. "I guess I'm all right," he said. It was clear that he thought he was more than all right.

They passed a hand-painted sign that read *Carbon County Motocross Track: Ride at Your Own Risk!* and the road dead-ended in a parking area bordered by pines. A narrow dirt road at one end bisected into two trails, one leading to a small stand of metal bleachers and the other down to the track itself, which was a long series of packed-dirt jumps and S-curves, all arranged in a shape like a sloppy figure eight.

Doug pulled into a prime parking spot right up by the track, tooting his horn. A half dozen guys paused from untying their own dirt bikes to greet them. Strutting around like the biggest turkey on the farm, Doug dispensed high fives while Janie gingerly let herself down from the passengers' seat.

"Hey, everyone, I want you to meet my baby cousin Daphne, bringer of bizarro trumpet sounds from God!" Janie crowed to the crowd. Conversations hushed, and a couple dozen heads swiveled toward them as Daphne stood awkwardly by the truck, her hands shoved deep in the pockets of her worn black hoodie.

"You really responsible for this?" a guy with a crew cut asked, just as a brassy A-minor scale thundered from the sky.

"Uh, no." Daphne felt her cheeks grow hot from the attention. She wished she could melt back into the shadows. "It's just a coincidence."

"You sure?" a girl with brown corkscrew curls and an acne scar on her cheek asked. "'Cause, dollars to donuts, nobody from around here's special enough to kick up this kind of fuss."

The crowd laughed, and Daphne tried to laugh with them. But it came out sounding like she was being choked. She wasn't used to being in the spotlight; back in Detroit she'd been a ghost, drifting silently from class to class, ducking her head whenever someone met her eyes. Once she was past the metal detectors, it was easy to blend into the riot of color and noise—much easier than trying to make friends in the chaos of clashing cliques and shifting alliances. She was more comfortable working long shifts at the 7-Eleven or roaming Detroit's crumbling downtown on her own, hands in her pockets and the wind a bitter relief on her face.

"Where'd you come from?" someone else asked.

"Definitely heaven," the girl with the corkscrew curls said authoritatively. "Y'know—where they keep the trumpets and stuff." She broke into raucous laughter, and the rest of the crowd joined in.

"Actually, it's kind of the opposite," Daphne said. "I'm from Detroit."

"Hah—nice one." The girl extended her hand. "I'm Hilary. Welcome to Carbon County, where the most exciting thing ever to happen to us is you."

"Thanks." Daphne smiled.

"Who wants a refreshing beverage?" Doug butted between them, dispensing cans from a sweaty twelve-pack of Coors. It was becoming obvious that he was the leader of the pack—and equally obvious that he'd bought more than his fair share of beers to get there.

"Aren't they going to be racing and stuff?" Daphne whispered to Hilary as the crowd popped their tabs and began guzzling.

"Oh, it's fine." Hilary took a deep swig. "When it comes to drinking, we're all professionals. Have I mentioned this isn't exactly a happening town?"

"Daphne?" Doug smirked as he held out a can. "Brewski for you-ski?"

"No thanks." She pointed a thumb at Janie's belly. "Solidarity."

"Aw, you are too sweet!" Janie planted a pink-frosted kiss on Daphne's cheek. "Isn't she the best, everyone? Foregoing beer just to keep her preggo cousin company!"

"You want a soda?" The voice at her elbow was so quiet, it took Daphne a moment to realize he was speaking to her. She turned slowly and saw a guy with blond hair and a dimple in his right cheek. "I've got Coke and Sprite. And, uh, maybe a Dr. Pepper. I'd have to check."

"Coke sounds great," she said.

"Oh, uh, awesome. I've got a cooler in my truck, if you want to, uh . . ." he gulped, sending his Adam's apple bobbing up and down.

"Sure." She followed him to an ancient Toyota rusting at the edge of the parking lot. Scanning her brain for his name, she found herself drawing a blank. He had one of those pleasant but easily forgettable faces, like the guy in an action movie whose car the hero steals to go save the day.

"So, uh, you just got into town?" He rummaged in a cooler that was held together with bungee cords and handed her a Coke.

"Yeah. Just this afternoon. With the trumpets."

"That's crazy. You're, like, an angel or something."

She was about to protest when one of the bungees sprung loose with a loud thwap.

"Ow!" Trey jumped back, grasping his hand.

"Are you okay?"

He rubbed the flesh next to his thumb, where a red welt had already begun to rise. "Oh yeah. I'm fine. It's nothing. Just, uh, clumsy, I guess." He grimaced.

"Let me get that." Daphne leaned in to fix the cord, but he practically leapt in front of her.

"Hey, it's cool! I got it. I know what I'm doing." He fumbled for several agonizing moments, eventually snapping it back into place.

"So, uh, yeah. Detroit, huh?" He leaned back against his truck, one elbow on the cooler. "What was that like?"

"It was . . . okay," she said cagily, not wanting to talk about it. Thinking about her past still filled her with anger and regret. "Shouldn't we get back to your friends?" she asked instead.

"Oh." He looked disappointed. "Uh, sure. I guess. Yeah, let's go."

As they made their way back to the group, Doug upended the remains of his beer into his mouth, then crushed the can on his tailgate. "All right!" He straddled his bike, kicking it to life. "Trumpets or not, I'm ready to ride. Who's in?"

The boys made their way to their bikes, and soon they were swarming the track, the roar of their motors drowning out the metallic ringing in the sky. Someone switched on the floodlights, bathing the trails and ridges in a glow like phosphorescent milk, and the tinny sounds of a driving hard rock song blared through an old pair of mounted speakers, competing with the bikes' coughs and belches.

"C'mon." Janie was already waddling toward the bleachers. "Let's go get a good seat."

"Yeah—better beat this massive crowd," Hilary added, gesturing at the handful of girls drifting idly away from the parking lot. "Don't want to miss a second of nail-biting action, that's for sure."

"Darn it, Hil, if you don't like it, why do you even come?" Janie asked.

"You think my man is any less into this crap than yours?" Hilary rolled her eyes. "If I want my stocking stuffed, I better show up."

They settled into a small stand of metal bleachers overlooking the track, and Janie leaned forward eagerly. "Go, Doug!" she cried. "Show 'em what you got!"

"How do you even know which one is Doug?" Daphne asked. From up there they all looked like Lego people driving matchbox bikes, glossy round helmets completely obscuring their faces.

"Silver helmet, green bike." Janie pointed as one of the figures gathered speed and flew over a jump, his bike flashing in the glow of the floodlights.

"And rims," Hilary interjected. "Don't forget his precious rims."

"Oh yeah." Janie giggled. "He just had them special-ordered from Cheyenne. See how they spin even when his wheels aren't moving? I think he may be even more in love with them than me." She laughed like the thought of Doug loving something more than her was the most far-fetched idea in the world. Hilary snorted.

Daphne settled into a kind of cozy fog as the bikes zoomed up and down the track, occasionally disappearing behind a rise and returning moments later in a cloud of dust and bravado. It felt good to be far away from Detroit and her mother's accusing eyes. For the first time in months, the angry pangs in her stomach were gone, and she no longer felt a clawing need to escape. Maybe it was the miles of dark, empty sky above her head or the comforting chatter of girls around her who had no idea what she'd done.

"Look!" Janie poked her in the ribs. "They're trying to see who can get the most air."

Daphne returned to the moment in time to see Doug soar into the sky. One after another, the bikes followed his lead, competing to see who could take the jump highest and longest. At the end of the track, they turned in a circle and came back the other way, Doug always in the lead.

The second time Doug executed the jump with a half spin, torqueing his bike a quarter turn in the air and landing in a triumphant puddle of cheers before zooming off again.

"Go, baby, go!" Janie cheered, watching Doug's back lovingly as a rider in a teal helmet approached the jump.

Teal Helmet got a little less air and wobbled as his wheels

touched the track, but still managed to right himself and ride back to the starting line in a spray of dirt and burnt rubber.

Voices floated up to the bleachers, the remaining riders daring each other to try the trick.

"Friggin' idiots," Hilary muttered. "They all act like they're God's gift—one of these days, someone's gonna get himself killed." As crude as she was, Daphne couldn't help liking her; she wore her attitude like a feather headdress, obviously not caring what anyone thought.

The third rider executed the jump with a perfect twist, even popping a wheelie after he landed. Janie sucked in her breath. "Oooh, Doug's not gonna like *that*!" she said.

"Ten bucks he'll try to one-up him next time—then maybe take off his shirt and do a victory dance," Hilary predicted.

She was almost right. Doug had already geared up and was going through a series of easy jumps, gaining more and more air until finally soaring into the sky, torqueing his bike, and then taking his hands from the handlebars and raising his arms above his head, fingers in the *V*-for-*victory* position, before he landed.

"That's my man!" Janie cried.

"I dare any of you chicken-livered mofos to try *that*!" Doug crowed.

The boys revved their bikes like a pack of peacocks fanning their feathers.

"Oh, don't even . . ." Hilary moaned. She leaned forward on the bleachers as a rider in an orange helmet emerged from the pack. "Hey, idiot, you're not as badass as you think!"

"Is that your boyfriend?" Daphne asked.

"Who, him? Nah, that's Trey—you know, the guy you were getting all cozy with earlier?"

Trey. So that was his name. "We weren't getting cozy," Daphne said. "He just gave me a coke."

Hilary smirked. "I bet he wanted to give you a whole lot more."

Daphne opened her mouth to explain that she had the wrong idea, but Hilary had already turned back to the track, her eyes glued to Trey as he swung his bike around. Then he was racing toward the jump, leaving a plume of dust in his wake so thick she had to squint to see him hit the air.

"Yessssss!" the girls cried as his body twisted in a blinding flash of metal.

Trey raised his arms above his head, imitating Doug's pose, and Daphne opened her mouth to cheer. But he'd turned his bike too far and couldn't get it facing forward again. He grabbed the handlebars and tried to scramble into the right position, but it was too late. He slammed into the ground with his wheels facing backward, bike veering wildly from side to side as he tried, and failed, to gain control. Then he crumpled to one side.

"Aw, crap!" Hilary screamed. She shot up from the bleachers

and raced down the steep incline to the track, dark dirt streaking her jeans. Daphne leapt up and followed her, half-running and half-sliding down the hill, leaving the other girls back on the bleachers, still slack-jawed with shock.

She had her phone out by the time she reached Trey, ready to call 911 if necessary. The other riders had already hopped off their bikes; two pulled the stilled Suzuki off of Trey while another helped him to his feet. He unbuckled his helmet and looked around, confused.

"I thought I landed it?" He took one wobbly step forward, then another. Daphne's shoulders unclenched, and she slid her phone back in her pocket. She realized, with a small start of surprise, that the trumpet sounds had stopped.

"Not exactly, buddy," Doug said patronizingly. Trey's brow crumpled, and for an agonizing moment Daphne wondered if he was going to cry. Then he seemed to shake it off. He squared his shoulders, brushing the dirt from his jacket.

"Well, I guess you can't land 'em all, can you?" He turned to the boys who had helped him up. "Who wants another beer? I could kind of use one after that."

He turned and carefully, almost lovingly, righted his bike as the crowd broke up and drifted back toward the parking lot.

↔

After the guys had ratcheted their bikes back into their pickups and let the night breeze cool the sweat from their foreheads, they divvied up another of Doug's twelve-packs and hung around the parking lot, speculating about the trumpets and bragging about their escapades on the track.

Exhausted from the effort of dodging questions, Daphne wandered away from the lot, taking the trail to the track on foot. They'd turned off the floodlights, but the moon was almost full, and the sky was blanketed in stars.

She stood in the middle of the track and raised her face to the heavens, taking in great deep lungfuls of air. Her feet felt planted in the ground, like they could take root right there and reach all the way to the center of the earth. So this was why she'd felt pulled to Carbon County, Wyoming: the space and silence, the feeling of finally being exactly where she belonged. She let out a long, whistling breath and stretched her arms out to the sides. "Home," she mouthed. The word felt round and full, unusual but not unwelcome on her tongue.

"'Sup, Daffy!"

Her gaze snapped forward and caught a figure lumbering toward her. She saw the glint of a Coors can, heard the whoosh of boots tamping dust, and squinted as Doug's big head came into view.

"Daphne," she corrected. She hated phony-sounding nicknames. "Is it time to get going?"

"What?" Doug looked confused. "No, I just, uh . . . happened to be comin' out here anyway."

"Really?" She'd only known Doug for a few hours, but it was hard to imagine anything important enough to tear him away from his drinking buddies.

"Want a beer?" he offered. "I got an extra in my pocket."

"No thanks." Her shoulders went tight with the same uneasiness she'd always felt when her mom went to work the night shift, leaving her alone with Jim. "Where's Janie?"

"Back up at the lot. Sure about that beer? We could hang out here and get a little buzz on away from all a'those idiots." He was standing close to her, close enough that the cloud of cologne wafting off his neck nearly choked her. It smelled like being trapped inside a mall.

"How 'bout it?" He jiggled the can invitingly. "Just you and me."

"Really, no. I should get back. Janie's probably wondering where I am." She ducked around him and started walking toward the parking lot.

"Well, hey, I'll walk you back." Doug tossed the beer can over his shoulder and hurried to catch up. He walked close, hovering like he wanted to say something, and the silence between them felt strained and uncomfortable. Daphne picked up the pace but he met it, practically trampling her heels.

When they were just short of the parking lot, he grasped her arm and spun her so she was facing him, his meaty chin and beery breath just inches away.

"Hey," he said.

Daphne's heartbeat thudded through her veins, the pressure of panic roaring in her ears. She tried to squirm away but his grip was strong, his fingers sinking deep into her flesh.

"What?" she whispered, her throat sandpaper-dry.

"You know you're really hot, right?" Doug's voice was gruff and low. He pulled her into his chest, so she could feel the heat from his body and smell the alcohol sweat on his shirt, and pressed himself against her. A bitter bubble of nausea rose from her stomach.

"You're my cousin's boyfriend!" she hissed. She raised her other arm to push him away, but he caught it easily. His nose was almost touching hers, and she could see the dark caverns between his teeth as his lips spread in a hungry smile.

"She doesn't have to know." Hands still clamped like steel around her wrists, he raised her arms so they were wrapped around his shoulders in a gross parody of an embrace. "I know you want me, too. I could tell from the moment I saw you. It's okay."

His lips puckered, zeroing in on hers, and bile surged in her stomach. The smell of beer, the unwanted touch of a body she found repulsive: It was too much like all the times Jim had pressed into her in the kitchen, trapping her against the counter while her mom stared stubbornly at the TV or slept in the other room. She twisted and squirmed against the memory and his grip until finally, just as the first flake of skin from his chapped lips brushed hers, she brought her knee up hard and fast.

"Guuuuuuh!" Doug cried, stumbling back. His hands released her wrists and flew to his crotch as he doubled over, groaning.

Daphne's heart pounded in her ears. Her arms had broken out in goose bumps so hard they hurt, and her wrists were red and tender from Doug's tugging. She was shaking, but she managed to turn to Doug, who had staggered back like a wounded animal, still clutching his groin and moaning.

"Don't. You. Ever. Touch. Me. Again." She spat each word like a bullet, clear and silver and aimed straight at his head.

He looked up at her, eyes cloudy with confusion and anger.

"You frigid bitch . . ." he began.

Daphne didn't stay to hear the rest. She turned, still trembling, and ran back to the parking lot, back to Janie and the noise and the light.

6

OWEN PUSHED HIS WAY THROUGH the throngs gathered at the gate of the Radical Roots festival, wondering how he was going to identify a girl whose face he'd never seen. In the sea of tie-dye and patchwork, his dark hair and clothes stood out like a storm cloud obscuring a rainbow.

The sun had sunk beneath the mountains and the sky was a deep lavender as he let the throngs of people pull him along, past stalls hawking hemp energy bars and devil sticks and batik sarongs. Fragments of conversation (*hitched a ride in Boise . . . Sparklegirl kind of had a freakout . . . String Cheese Incident was off the chain . . .*) drifted in and out of his ears.

It was the kind of scene his younger sister Cass would probably enjoy: the walls of her room were covered in posters of obscure bands, and she was the only one in her eighth grade class who wore plum-colored lipstick to school every day. But he'd always preferred the company of machines to the crush of humanity. It was why he spent hours alone in the garage tinkering with his bike, or practicing by himself at the track long after his friends had packed up and gone home.

The merch stalls dead-ended at the peak of a gentle hill, which sloped down to an amphitheater draped in a psychedelic backdrop glowing under a black light. Neon fairies perched in fluorescent trees, and butterflies with human faces hovered over garish pink flowers. A giant statue of a mushroom hunkered at the side of the stage, where Ariel Crow and the Fine Feathered Family were about to go on.

The lead singer took his place at the mic and picked up a guitar, flashing a smile that was half gold teeth. Behind him, a parade of musicians clad in neon patchwork and fishnet, with dreadlocks like gnarled tree branches growing from their heads, carried tambourines and banjos onto the stage. Owen craned his neck, trying to get a look at them through the sea of people, but none of their faces sparked recognition. If Luna was among them, she was good at hiding in plain sight.

"I'm Ariel Crow, and this is the Fine Feathered Family," the lead singer said in a voice like worn, scarred leather. "We're here to play a couple songs for you—"

His words drowned in a tidal wave of cheers. The shuffling zombies who had surrounded Owen at the gate sprang to life, teeth bared with delight, arms waving like tentacles in the air.

Ariel Crow struck a note on his guitar, and the crowd began to dance, keeping time with the Fine Feathered Family's raucous, squawking vocals. Owen stood still among them, focused on the one thing he'd come for: finding Luna. The rambling jam-band tune did nothing for him; he liked his music strong and fast, with a driving beat.

Midway through the band's first song, a trapdoor opened in the top of the mushroom statue and a girl appeared, brandishing a hula hoop that shimmered with LED lights, giving off a rainbow of colors. Her neon patchwork bikini glowed under the ultraviolet lights, and her hair stood out in a riot of dreadlocks, some wrapped in neon yarn so she looked like a modern-day Medusa with a nest of vipers writhing on her head. She eased the trapdoor shut with her toes and stood with her arms stretched to the sky, the hoop framing a body that was all ropy muscle and coiled feline energy, the stage lights dancing on the glitter that dusted her limbs.

The breath left Owen's lungs in a sudden, painful rush, like he had been kicked in the chest.

It was her. Luna.

Ariel Crow let out a wail, and Luna whipped the hoop over her head and spun it onto her body, twitching her hips and tossing her head and laughing into the stage lights.

It was unmistakably her, the flashes of a face from his dreams now pieced together into a whole. Even from way up on the hill, he could trace her features with his eyes: her sharp cheekbones and the arrowhead of her chin, the taut muscles in her legs and a giant tattoo of a tree that sprouted from her lower back and grew into an ancient, wizened wonder with branches snaking down her arms. But mostly, he recognized her eyes. They slanted toward her forehead and blazed with a cold, seafoam green, like the tail of a mermaid trapped and frozen under layers of ice.

He recognized those eyes from more than just his dreams. He saw them whenever he looked in the mirror, and they gleamed coldly back at him when he caught his reflection in the widow of a passing car. They were his eyes, too.

He watched her, transfixed, for the rest of the Fine Feathered Family's set. She could do a million and one things with the hoop, rotating it around her waist and shoulders and knees, snaking it across her body and tossing it nearly into the rafters before catching it with a flourish behind her back. He saw his own punished and triumphant body in the way she moved, knew that she was driven by the same relentless energy that pushed him to make something impossible look easy. They may have expressed the burning drive within them in different ways—she with a hula hoop, he with a dirt bike—but the engine powering them through life was the same. They were unlike everyone around them. They were cut from the same cloth.

Atop the mushroom, in the luminous circle of her hoop, Luna seemed barely human—more like an animal forced into a human body by a spell in a fairy tale, like at any moment she could sprout fur or fangs or feathers and go bounding away into the darkness.

And maybe it was just Owen's imagination, but it seemed like she was watching him, too.

As Ariel Crow introduced the band's encore, Owen started pushing his way through the crowd. Sweat and incense and sticky-sweet pot smoke clung to him as he pressed past bare limbs and snarls of dry hair and steamy puffs of breath mouthing the words to the Fine Feathered Family's final song.

He was right up front when the tune reached its frenetic finale, the audience practically apoplectic with appreciation, his eyes locked on Luna's. And then the Fine Feathered Family was making its exit and Luna was sliding down the side of the mushroom, landing on the stage crouched like a cat and then swinging her legs over the side and onto the ground, the glowing hoop still in her hand.

She shook off the arms that reached for her, the mouths floating close to her ear to tell her she was great, could they play with her hoop, could she teach them to do that, could she introduce them to the band? And then she was in front of him, her face mere inches from his identical eyes.

"Hi," she said.

"Hey." He felt the heat radiating off her body and sensed that relentless buzz roaring through her veins.

"Luna?" he asked, although he already knew.

"Of course."

His throat contracted like he'd eaten a mouthful of dust at the track. "I've been looking for you."

"Here I am."

The crowd rubbed up against them as he reached for his next words. "Can we go somewhere we can talk?" he asked.

She took his hand, sinewy fingers lacing through his, her hoop glowing like a beacon leading them behind the stage, down a path that ran through a scraggly forest and out into a clearing filled with tents and camper vans. Dew sparkled on the grass, and the late spring night wrapped Owen in a bear hug, the sudden space and silence a welcome relief after the crush and jam around the concert stage.

"This one's me." Luna stopped in front of a purple tent no bigger than the bed of his pickup. A dozen hula hoops, in every color of the rainbow, leaned against the side. Unzipping the opening, she shrugged into a soft moss-colored dress with a pointed hood and unfurled a faded Navajo blanket onto the ground.

"Sit." She crossed her legs and sank down across from him, pressing a hidden button on the inside of her hoop that shut off the LEDs, leaving them with only the moonlight and the muted thump of music in the distance. "We can talk now."

"You grew up on that commune," Owen said. "Children of the Earth."

"I was born there. And so were you, Earth Brother."

The glow of her eyes was barely visible in the darkness. Owen sat back, hands in the damp, spongy grass. "How did you know that?"

Her laugh was silver, hard. "From my dreams. I've seen you there."

The blood rushed to his skin in a sudden, molten burst. "You've been having them, too?"

She nodded.

"Tell me about them," he urged. "Are they the same as mine—with the bonfire, and the dancers, and . . ."

"The voice," she finished, her green eyes flashing. "Yes. It's the same. It's all the same."

"That voice." Just mentioning it sent cold prickles down his spine. "Do you know who it is?" He leaned toward her, so close he could smell the dew of sweat and patchouli on her skin, and something pungent and earthy underneath.

"I have some ideas." She stretched her legs as he waited for her to say more, tilting her head to admire the curve of her feet, the shadowy caverns between her toes. But she didn't elaborate.

"Like . . . ?" he finally prompted.

She fixed him with a long, sideways look. "You mean you really don't know?"

"No." He hated the edge of urgency that crept into his voice, but he couldn't help it. He had to know. "If this is about the Children of the Earth, the only thing my mom ever told me was the name. She refused to talk about it. Everything else I know, even where it was, I found by searching online—and trust me, the Wikipedia page isn't that great."

Luna's teeth flashed sharp and white as she laughed into the night. "I'm sorry," she said. "It's just always been such a part of my life. I forget that the rest of you don't know."

"The rest of who? Know what?"

Luna brought her hands above her head, arching her back as she stretched. "Know how beautiful it was," she sighed. "We loved each other, and we loved the earth. Nobody owned anything or anyone: Possessions were meaningless. And every night we built a huge bonfire and worshipped the God of the Earth."

"But how did it all *work*?" Owen pressed. "Who paid the bills?"

They weren't the questions he really wanted to ask—questions about why his mom refused to speak of those days, about what was fueling his dreams—but he had to start somewhere. And Luna obviously enjoyed holding her knowledge just out of his reach, like a gypsy fortune-teller deliberately keeping her crystal ball opaque. He would have to work on her slowly, tease the information out piece by piece.

Luna waved a dismissive hand. "None of that mattered," she said. "When you're in tune with the earth, there's always enough of everything. It's only when people get greedy and start wanting more, when they start raping the planet to get it—that's when there isn't enough to go around. We didn't do that. We were pure."

"Then why did the commune get shut down?" Owen couldn't help asking.

Glitter sparkled on the ends of Luna's lashes as she lowered her eyes, hugging her knees to her chest. "People didn't understand," she sighed. "They were jealous of the way we lived. So they took the earth away from us." She sat up straighter. "But we'll get it back. That's why you're here now—it's what brought you to me. You want the same things I do, Earth Brother, whether you know it or not. It's why we're having the same dreams."

Before Owen could answer, she stood, brushed the dew from her robe, and unsnapped the rainfly from her tent. "You've got wheels, right? If we leave now, we should be in Spokane by morning."

"What's in Spokane?" Owen stared up at her, a million questions still swirling in his head.

"Nothing." She folded a tent pole impatiently. "But it's on the way. We have to follow the voice in our dreams. It's telling us to *find the vein.*"

"Do you know what that means?" It was the question that had plagued him since the night of his eighteenth birthday, the one that had forced him out of Kansas and into his desperate roamings around the American West.

Luna crouched in front of him, her eyes level with his. "I think it's a place: somewhere sacred. Veins are where you find the blood, the source of life."

"But where is it?"

Owen felt in his own veins that Luna was right: that when they reached this place, the vein, wherever it was, the madness in his dreams would cease. They were sending him somewhere, to do something. If only he knew what.

"We'll just know," she said, stuffing her tent into its sack. "So are you ready to go, or what?"

Owen nodded dumbly. *Yes,* his blood seemed to whisper, *this is right.*

It was shortly after midnight when they crossed the Olympia town line going east, the Radical Roots festival still dancing raucously behind them, Luna riding shotgun and a clown-bright bundle of hula hoops sparkling next to Owen's bike in the back of his truck.

7

"TREY TOLD DOUG TO TELL me he thinks you're cute." Janie grinned and flipped her ponytail over her shoulder. Late spring warmth suffused the afternoon as the girls walked Bella around the Peytons' front yard, the tiny dog nipping at the treats stashed in Janie's pocket.

"Cute?"

Daphne shot her a skeptical look. It was the last word in the world she would have used to describe herself: When she looked in the mirror, she saw only sharp angles and cautious eyes, a narrow nose and ruler-straight hair and hands that were too big for her body. Janie had gotten all the curves in the Peyton family.

Janie smiled impishly, showing off her dimples. "It's why he kept trying to show off at the track last night—he wanted to impress you."

Daphne remembered Trey's bike fishtailing to its side in the dust. She followed Janie through a stand of scrubby pines, their needles a soft brown carpet under their feet.

"So what do you think?" Janie nudged her. "Do you like him?"

Daphne chewed the inside of her cheek. "He's—nice," she said finally. Trey had, after all, offered her a soda when everyone else was drinking beer, and had jumped in front of her to re-secure the bungee cords on his cooler.

"Yay!" Janie's cheeks glowed. "So how'd you feel about a double date? You, me, Doug, and Trey?"

"I don't know . . ." Daphne trailed off, not sure how to tell Janie no. She'd never been on a date before, and the thought of having Doug along on her first made her queasy. The sleeves of her hoodie hid the imprints he'd left on her wrists, but she still felt sick whenever she thought about his chapped lips too close to hers and his boozy breath in her face.

"Oh?" Janie's eyes dripped with curiosity. "Why?"

Daphne looked off toward the wispy clouds forming a halo around Elk Mountain in the distance, willing them to give her an answer. "I just—don't really feel ready," she said finally, feeling lame. It wasn't that she'd never noticed guys; she'd had hints of something soft and fleeting before, brushing past the silent skateboarder from her Spanish class in the hallway or spying on a group of graffiti guys tagging up the side of a building, but she had always tamped them down. Guys, and everything that went with them, were for other girls—girls like Janie who wore bright colors and flirted, girls who didn't spend their nights armed for battle against a stepfather's heavy footsteps coming toward their room.

"What do you mean?" Janie looked at her quizzically. "You're almost eighteen. Me and Doug have been together since sophomore year!"

"Yeah, well." Daphne stabbed at a pile of dirt with her boot, wishing Janie would change the subject. "That's you. I'm me."

"You probably just haven't met the right guy yet," Janie surmised dreamily.

"Maybe." Daphne kept her voice noncommittal. She was pretty sure no guy could ever erase the years of damage Jim had done.

They passed through the pine grove and into a scrubby field beyond. The mountain range loomed like a procession of dinosaurs in the distance, purple and imposing.

"Can I ask you something?" Janie raised her big, blue-rimmed eyes to Daphne's.

"Sure." Daphne hoped it wouldn't be more questions about her love life. She didn't want to lie to her cousin, but the truth—that she could never forgive any guy for sharing the same anatomy and needs as Jim, that being close to males who weren't family sent panic rising like a flock of crows in her throat—was too ugly to say out loud to her sweet, bubbly cousin, whose world seemed to be all Jesus and puppies.

Janie turned and took her arm. "How did it happen?" she asked gently.

"What?"

"The accident." Janie tucked the words in around her like a soft, blue blanket. "That brought your stepdad home to God and made your mom so she can't take care of you anymore. How did it happen?"

Panic snapped at Daphne's tongue. She'd thought of a million stories to tell during the long bus ride out to Wyoming—car accidents, house fires, a burglary gone wrong—a million ways to avoid retelling the story that made dark bile churn in her stomach and her head feel stuffed with thorns. She couldn't bear to tell the Peytons the truth: that she was both a victim and a killer, that her past was a long, musty tunnel of shame and abuse. She didn't want them to see her as anything but the Daphne they'd known and loved when she was a child. She'd come to Carbon County to get away from the curiosity that followed her story like a cloud, to escape the prying reporters with their perpetually personal questions. All she wanted was to start fresh.

She opened her mouth, willing words to come, but all she could do was let the air rush over her tongue, parching it dry.

"It . . ." she started. "I . . ."

Then Janie's arms were around her shoulders, a pudgy hand patting the small of her back consolingly.

"It's okay," her cousin crooned in her ear, in the same voice she used for her unborn child. "You don't have to talk about it if you're not ready. I'm sorry I asked."

Daphne accepted the hug, knowing that she wasn't worthy. She'd killed a man and was covering up the truth about it. She had no right to let herself be consoled.

"God has better things in store for you," Janie whispered into her ear. "I can feel it in my heart. Those trumpets when you showed up yesterday were no coincidence. They were a sign."

Daphne's only response was to hug Janie tighter. She still couldn't make sense of the strange sounds that had heralded her arrival, but she was sure there had to be a logical explanation, something simple and obvious that the rest of the town had somehow overlooked.

Bella burst into a series of high-pitched yips, straining at her leash, and Janie released Daphne from the embrace.

"What is it, Bella?" she asked. "Do you hear a car?"

Bella stood on her hind legs, doll-sized paws raking the air.

Daphne cocked her head. She could hear a dim rumbling from down the road, growing louder as it approached.

"Maybe it's Doug!" Janie smiled wide. "Nobody else ever comes here. Let's go see!"

Bella frisked at their heels as they retraced their steps through the pine grove, emerging into the sunshine just in time to see Floyd race out of the trailer. He quickly tucked a fresh shirt into his Carharts as a tan truck decorated with the green US Forest Service shield pulled into the driveway.

"He's here!" Floyd called, practically dancing a jig on the gravel. Daphne noticed that he'd tamed his normally wild hair into submission with pomade, so it looked glued to his scalp.

"Who's here?" Janie asked.

Aunt Karen hurried out of the trailer behind her husband, the flesh on her arms jiggling under her appliqued T-shirt. "The geologist from the ranger station," she whispered to the girls. "Your father's asked him to check for oil on the land. It's another one of his get-rich-quick schemes."

"Seriously?" Janie scooped up Bella and stroked her head as she leaned in close to Daphne. "He's been doing this since he lost his job. First it was selling vitamins, then entering online sweepstakes. Who knows what this is all about?"

Karen opened her mouth to explain, but Uncle Floyd had already bounded up to the truck, an optimistic grin on his face and his hand poised to shake.

"Rick Bodey, it sure is good to see you!" he said as the passenger door opened and a steel-haired man tanned like a baseball glove stepped out, his regulation green trousers and brown belt barely containing a stomach that ballooned out almost further than Janie's.

"Hey there, Floyd." Rick gripped his hand with a strong, single pump, but Daphne noticed that his smile looked strained, like he'd rather be somewhere else—probably somewhere with just rocks and no people at all.

"And these are the lovely ladies in my life." Floyd gestured toward them. "My wife Karen, daughter Janie, and last but not least, Daphne, my niece."

"Pleased t'meetcha," Rick said to their shoes.

"Can I get you something to drink?" Karen hurried to his side. "A cup of coffee, maybe, or some iced tea? We have Crystal Light, too, and—"

"You wanted me to look at something on your land?" Rick interrupted, turning to Floyd. Karen's mouth gaped open, and Daphne felt her left eye start to twitch like it always did when she was mad.

"Well, ah, yes." Floyd twisted his hands in front of his belt buckle, face suddenly pink. "If you follow me, I think you'll see what I mean."

He started toward the dry creek bed behind the trailer, and, after a longing look back at his truck, Rick Bodey fell into step.

"I do appreciate you stopping by," Floyd said as they passed the rusting engine block. "I know you must have a lot to do."

"Yeah, well, the wildlife guys insisted." Rick's voice was flat. "They still won't shut up about that dead snake you brought in. Said I had to come see what else you had up your sleeve."

They passed the trailer and descended into a small ravine. It looked like it may have been a creek once, long ago—small, smooth pebbles lined the bottom, and it cut through the land in a lazy, meandering arc—but it had been dry even when Daphne was a kid, and stubborn bushes clung to the inclines on either side. At one point someone had decided to use it as a makeshift dump, and it still contained a smattering of old plastic bags, glass bottles, and the rusted shell of an '80s-era washing machine.

"Well, I think you'll be pretty pleased." Floyd pointed to the rocks at the base of the washing machine. "You see these guys right here?"

"Sure." Rick put a big, tan fist on each hip. "What about 'em?"

"See, well," Floyd kicked at the rocks at his feet, suddenly embarrassed. "I took a look at some of your charts down at the ranger station, and, well, see, the rock type here—it's the same as at a few other sites around the Northwest where folks found oil."

Rick Bodey's eyebrows curled up like a pair of angry caterpillars. "Just what are you trying to say?" he asked.

"Well." Floyd smiled his most affable smile. "I was wondering if you couldn't take a look and tell me if you think there might be oil down there."

Rick Bodey looked at Uncle Floyd like he'd suggested taking one of the rocks and swallowing it.

"You want me to *look* at some *rocks* and tell you if there's oil on your land?"

Floyd's face went from pink to deep crimson. "Well, ah—I mean, it's just an educated guess, and I'm no geologist," he stammered.

"But I've had this hunch for a while now, and I figured you may have some instruments and such that could help me figure it out once and for all."

A mean little laugh escaped Rick Bodey's leathery lips. "Those instruments you're talking about cost thousands of dollars. I'd need to run soil samples, test for gravitational field variations, run checks for electromagnetic and radioactive properties and sound wave velocities, commission a full report and compare it to other prospecting reports in the county, probably even dig a test well . . ."

He laughed again, shaking his big, tanned head.

"So you can't tell me if there's oil here?" The lines around Floyd's mouth sagged.

"Just by looking at some rocks? Nosirree, no way. You want to know for sure, you'd need to come up with a few grand. It takes money to make money and, no offense, but judging from that trailer there it looks like you folks barely have a pot to piss in."

Daphne watched Floyd kick at a rock, sending it skittering across the ravine. "I just thought it was worth a try," he murmured.

"Listen—you go to work and make an honest living, come up with that money, and I'll put you in touch with a guy who can run some real tests," Rick Bodey said. "Until then, you stick with your snakes and whatnot."

He turned his back and ambled away from them, hooking his thumbs into his belt loops. Daphne could swear that his walk had gained more swagger since he'd put down her uncle—since he'd put down all of them, really.

"I guess it was a long shot. Dumb of me to think otherwise," Floyd said quietly. The color had drained from his face, and he looked old suddenly, tired and defeated.

"It wasn't dumb." Karen scrambled into the ravine and put her arms around him. "You did your research—that man was just a little too big for his britches."

"Figuratively *and* literally," Janie agreed. She joined her parents, and the three of them stood with their arms around each other, strong and solid in the trash-littered ravine. Sticking together even when things weren't great. Protecting each other. Giving each other strength.

"It's just with all these miracles happening—those trumpet sounds, the Djinn viper—I thought maybe . . ." Uncle Floyd trailed off, shaking his head sadly.

Daphne's heart ached even as anger flashed behind her eyes. It wasn't fair for Rick Bodey to treat the Peytons that way—they were good people, better to each other and to her than anyone she'd ever met, and probably better than anyone Rick Bodey had ever met, either. Just because they didn't have much money was no reason to make them feel like dirt.

A familiar shot of adrenalin surged through her, the same one that had kept Jim from getting what he'd wanted from her night after horrible night—the same one she'd felt when she plunged the knife deep into his gut.

It propelled her past the startled Peytons and up the ravine, her legs springing over the dry earth and toward Rick Bodey's ample back.

"Hey!" she called. His pudgy ham-hand was on the truck's door handle, ready to escape.

"Yes, miss?" he seethed.

"You can't do that," she jogged to a stop in front of him. "You can't just treat my uncle like an idiot for asking you a simple question. He deserves better than that."

"Miss." Rick Bodey let out a sigh like a dump truck releasing a load of earth. "It's not a simple question. Your uncle was wasting my time."

"But—" The image of Floyd tapping the spot near the washing machine taunted her, so full of hope. "You can't just leave him hanging like that. It can't be as complicated as you say. Either there's oil in the ground or there isn't. Why can't you just do a simple test?"

Rick laughed his mean little bark again. "You want a simple way to test for oil? 'Cause there's only one that I know of." He threw open the hood of his truck and pulled the dipstick from his oil tank. "This right here—*this* is an easy way to test for oil. Stick it in the ground and you just see if anything comes up." He spat laughter at his own joke, showing pointed yellow teeth.

"Fine." Daphne ripped the dipstick from his hand. "Then we'll use this."

She dimly registered his catcher's-mitt face opening wide in disbelief as she turned and marched back toward the ravine, clutching the dipstick's orange handle and brandishing it in front of her like a fencer's foil.

"Hey, wait just a minute!" he called, but she was past the engine block and then the trailer, her face stinging from wind and indignation as her feet skimmed the ground.

"Come back here with that!" She could hear his huffing footsteps behind her, the change jingling in his pockets. She scaled the slope and landed in front of the Peytons.

They stared at her in disbelief, their mouths open in shock.

Finding Floyd's spot, Daphne kicked aside pebbles and found the dirt beneath, jamming the dipstick deep into the earth.

It slid in easily and felt eerily like the knife tearing through Jim's shirt and skin and sinking fatally into his flesh. The memory sent a wave of nausea spinning through her, and as Rick Bodey jangled to a stop above her, she thought for a moment that she might puke right there on the ground.

Then the feeling was gone, and she pulled the dipstick from the earth.

The air filled with gasps—from Uncle Floyd, Aunt Karen, Janie, and even from Rick. Because coating the dipstick nearly to Daphne's hand and falling in fat, glistening drops to the rocks below was thick, black oil.

↔

It must be a mirage. Or maybe there had already been oil on the dipstick before, from Rick's truck. But there couldn't have been that much. She would have noticed it. Or Rick would have. Or any of them.

Her hand began to tremble, shaking the oil off onto her forehead. It smelled mysterious and pungent, like power and death and giant decomposed lizards that had ruled the earth millions of years before. Like something dark and ancient thrusting itself upon her, christening her.

The dipstick felt hot and heavy in her hand, like a poker left too long in the fire. She dropped it and it bounced twice before coming to rest on the ground. Oil was already bubbling out of the hole where she'd jammed it in, puddling in onyx-colored slicks around her shoes.

"My God." Floyd bent and picked it up, running a hand over it in disbelief.

"Oh Lord!" Karen cried.

"Holy hell," Rick said.

And then all three Peytons were jumping in the air and shrieking, grabbing Daphne and hugging her and dancing in the growing pool of oil spreading across the ravine.

Daphne felt her jaw go from slack to smiling, heard her own unfamiliar laugh echoing in the breeze. She had done it—unbelievably, magically, she had found a way to repay the Peytons for taking her in.

She felt a strong, sure hand on her shoulder and looked up into Uncle Floyd's face. His eyes sparkled, but his tone was serious, almost somber. Even Janie stopped whooping and hollering long enough to listen.

"Daphne, you brought us this gift," Uncle Floyd said, his kind brown eyes firmly on hers. "I truly believe that the good Lord sent you here to lead us to this oil. I knew as soon as I heard those trumpets that you were going to bring good things to this town."

"But I didn't do anything," Daphne started to say. "I just . . . he just made me so mad . . ."

"You did everything," Uncle Floyd assured her. "You believed. Thanks to you, this town can finally get back on its feet again—and we can put up the money for a real church, too. And as for you," he turned to Rick Bodey, whose mouth was hanging practically to his belt buckle. "Thank you very much for stopping by. We appreciate all your help, but you can go now."

He tapped the dipstick, still slick with oil, against his foot. "We'll be hanging on to this, but don't worry—something tells me we'll be able to scrape up the funds to buy you a new one real soon."

AFTER THE PEYTONS STRUCK OIL, Daphne started to feel like someone had lit a flame beneath Carbon County and the molecules of their lives were racing away from one another in the heat, bounding in haphazard orbits that eventually bubbled over and turned to steam.

Within a week, Uncle Floyd had made a deal with Global Oil to set up a rig and extract the oil, in exchange for a percentage of the proceeds. He even agreed to defer his own share of the money until profits started rolling in, preferring to put all the immediate funds toward Carbon County's growth. The table of the banquette in the Peytons' trailer was littered with blueprints for the rig and contracts for a new school building, and Karen was constantly on the phone with Pastor Ted and the director of the local senior center, making plans for how to spend the community's newfound wealth.

"I've lived in this trailer for more years than you've been alive," Floyd told Daphne when she asked about the arrangement. "I reckon we can stay cozy for another few months while this town gets back on its feet."

As soon as the ink was dry on the agreement, a team of Global Oil contractors set up camp down the road from the Peytons, their identical tan trailers packed with complicated calibration instruments, giant white satellite dishes sprouting like mushrooms from their roofs. Black-and-yellow machines trawled the land like mythic beasts, braying at changes in the ground's chemical composition and electromagnetic force that only they could sense, their cries sending men in sports jackets and hard hats into a frenzy of pecking on their tablets and making calls on their satellite phones.

And they weren't the only ones with an eye on Carbon County. As soon as news of the oil got out, prospectors started arriving in droves, parking their trucks and vans in every available lot and racing across the once-barren valley with everything from complex calibration equipment to homemade detection devices that looked like little more than tinfoil affixed to a stick. Their hopeful days were followed by doleful evenings at Pat's, the only bar in town, where they commiserated over lukewarm bottles of Bud Light. Even though they hadn't had any success, it seemed like they wouldn't stop trying. Their greed spread like a disease, luring other get-rich-quick hopefuls to the area until the Carbon County locals had to chase them off their driveways with hunting rifles and brooms.

None of it was what Daphne had imagined when she boarded

the Greyhound for Wyoming, yet something about it was thrilling. Uncle Floyd's enthusiasm about the rig was infectious enough to send her to the library for a big stack of books on geology and oil production, and as the days stretched into weeks, and *Help Wanted* ads began to appear in the town papers and the rig reached up toward the sky, Daphne found one more reason to stay in Carbon County.

"You know you don't have to do this," Uncle Floyd said as she slid her résumé into a manila folder. Early morning sunlight filtered into the trailer, the lace curtains leaving a dappled pattern on the kitchen table where he was eating breakfast. "You don't owe us anything—we're happy to have you here. You're family."

"I know I don't have to." She sat down on the couch and began lacing up her work boots. "I *want* to."

Floyd shook his head. "Being a roustabout is darn hard work," he said. "You'd be at the very bottom of the rig crew food chain, basically doing all the manual labor the floorhands don't have time for. And I don't even know if Dale—that's the foreman, he'd be your boss—would want a woman around. Especially a young lady like you."

"Then that's discrimination." Daphne stood and pulled her hair into a ponytail. "Which happened to be illegal, last I checked."

Floyd paused, a spoonful of cereal midway to his mouth. "You're really bent on doing this, huh?"

She nodded, making his eyebrows knit

"I don't like it," he said. "It's dangerous work—I'd never be able to forgive myself if something happened to you."

"I'll wear a hard hat." She snuck a glance at the clock, wanting to catch the foreman first thing when he came in, before he got busy. She knew she was taking a chance going to him for a job, but her meager savings from the 7-Eleven were nearly depleted, and she was starting to worry about Myra being able to make rent. Besides, something about the thought of the rig pumping away without her filled her with an inexplicable emptiness. She felt as drawn to the work as she'd been to Carbon County. Weeks of sitting around the trailer with Janie, watching TV and reading parenting books, had begun to feel stale, and she wanted the satisfaction of going out and earning a paycheck, one of the few small joys in her life back in Detroit.

"You sure are determined." Floyd chuckled, but his eyebrows stayed furrowed. "You want me to go down there and talk to him with you? We've gotten pretty friendly since they moved in down the block."

"No thanks." Daphne picked up the manila folder and headed toward the door. "I want to do this on my own."

"You really are your father's daughter," Floyd mused as she bounded down the steps.

Outside the day was just beginning to warm up, the midmorning sun chasing the chill from the air. Daphne jogged across the road to the contractors' trailers, jumping the potholes that their vehicles had left in the road. She told herself that the thin sheen of sweat on her forehead was from the fresh heat of the early summer sun, but her pounding heart told her otherwise. She knew from Uncle Floyd's stories that Dale Reimer was a tough, no-nonsense kind of guy—one of the best foremen in the business, he said—and she was about to waltz onto his turf and ask for a job doing manual labor in one of the least forgiving industries in the world. All five feet, six inches, and 127 pounds of her.

She slowed down and gave herself a moment to breathe before rapping on the trailer's door, right below a hand-lettered sign that read: *Help Wanted—Inquire Within.*

"C'min!" A gruff male voice hollered from inside.

The trailer was large and spare; a bank of computers sat against one wall, some file cabinets along another. A large folding table hunkered in the center, covered in blueprints and papers and manila folders just like the one she was carrying. A half pot of coffee brewing on a counter filled the small space with a slightly burnt scent, and Dale himself was sitting at one of the computers, sipping from a steaming Global Oil mug and squinting at the screen.

He was a tall, broad man who'd spent enough of his life around oil rigs to give his skin a glossy sheen that looked dirty even straight out of the shower. A perpetual rust-colored stubble dotted his cheeks, and he wore a Baltimore Ravens baseball cap pulled low over eyes that had faded to a pale blue from years spent outdoors, supervising rigs from North Dakota to Texas.

"Hello." Daphne gently shut the door behind her.

Dale looked her over and grunted. "Can I help you?"

She took a deep breath. "I wanted to ask about getting work on the rig."

"You?" Dale nearly spat out his coffee. He managed to swallow it and coughed loudly, not bothering to cover his mouth. One massive Caterpillar work boot pounded the floor, making the whole trailer shake.

Daphne handed him the folder. "I don't have any rig experience, but I spent three years at the 7-Eleven in Detroit and was promoted to manager. I learn fast, and I'm a hard worker, plus I've been studying up on how the rig works. My résumé's in there."

Dale snorted. "Listen, young lady, once the rig is up there'll be plenty of work for you in town: hotels, restaurants, massage parlors, you name it. There's no reason for you to waste your time here."

She dug her fingernails into her palm, forcing herself to keep calm. She'd known this might happen—she just hadn't realized it would be so *quick*.

"I *want* to work here," she said.

"Sure you do—you probably heard the money's real good. But

do the math, sweetheart. As a roustabout you'd make thirty an hour, tops. Once the grifters take over this town, you'll make at least that in tips at the bar and grill of your choice—and you won't have to worry about losing a limb in an accident or getting a face full of flaming oil. I run the safest rigs in the business, but accidents still happen more often than you'd think. Just hold off another month or two, get a job where you can put that pretty face of yours to work, and you'll be rolling in it."

Daphne's eye twitched violently. "It's not about the money," she said quietly, trying to control the anger in her voice. "And I'm not afraid of danger. I want to work on the rig."

"Listen." Dale tossed her résumé on the table without opening the folder. "I'd like to be able to hire you, but I need big, strong guys for this work. Guys who can be out all day in the sun lugging a hundred pounds of pipe, who don't mind getting a face full of oil when I ask 'em to clean out a valve."

Daphne's heart pounded right along with her eye, the blood pumping through her veins in adrenalin-fueled spurts. "I see." She reached into her back pocket and pulled on her old leather work gloves, the ones she'd used to haul heavy crates of dry goods into the 7-Eleven's storage room whenever a shipment arrived. "Are any of those filing cabinets full?"

"Sure." Dale rolled his eyes. "But what does that have to do with anything?"

It took two long strides to get across the trailer. She put a palm against the closest cabinet and pushed it back gently, tipping it toward the wall. The pressure against her hand was heavy—it was full.

Daphne crouched and got both arms around the filing cabinet. She took a deep breath and reminded herself of all the heavy lifting she'd done in the past: crates of beer and Slurpee syrup, the industrial meat slicer behind the 7-Eleven's deli counter, a drunk who had once passed out in the Doritos aisle. With her gloves firmly gripping the cabinet's slippery sides, she grunted and sank weight into her feet, using her knees for leverage. Beads of sweat popped out on her forehead as she lifted it one, then three, then several inches off the ground. It felt like being crushed to death by a dinosaur, but she didn't let go.

Still holding the filing cabinet, she turned to face Dale. Coffee had sloshed over the sides of his mug, which he held uselessly in the air, as if he'd forgotten its purpose.

"Is this strong enough?" she gasped. She knew her face must be scarlet with exertion, but she didn't care.

Dale gulped.

Shuffling her feet and guessing at the distance, Daphne lugged the cabinet to the other side of the trailer. She could barely see around it, but used her peripheral vision to sense when she was across.

"I'm going to put this here now." Her voice was strained, but she wasn't panting. Yet.

"Okaaaaaaaay," Dale said.

She set the cabinet down slowly, taking extra care to make sure it didn't bang on the floor. She mopped sweat from her brow and met the foreman's mild blue eyes.

"Is it okay there, or would you like me to put it back?" she asked.

Dale looked as if he'd misplaced his voice. "I guess it's good there," he finally croaked.

"Good," Daphne said. "Now, what were you saying about needing big, strong guys?"

Dale looked at her, openmouthed, for a long moment. "I stand corrected," he said finally.

"Thank you." Daphne peeled off her work gloves and shoved them in her back pocket. "So when can I start?"

Dale still looked reluctant. "You know I wasn't joking about the danger, right?" he said. "It's not just lifting and carrying. You're in the line of fire. Things go wrong."

Daphne shrugged. "Still sounds better than waiting tables."

Dale guffawed, slapping his Carharts hard with a leathery palm. "All right," he said. "You're hired. You can start tomorrow."

"Great!" Daphne smiled.

"And now for the really killer part of this job—the paperwork." He turned and rummaged in one of the filing cabinets, producing a folder bulging with papers. "I'll need you to fill out all of these—and if you're under eighteen, I can't put you on the graveyard shift."

"Sounds fair," Daphne said. She pulled up a chair, and Dale handed her a pen, looking over her shoulder as she filled in her name.

"Daphne Peyton?" he read, eyebrows creeping up his forehead.

"Mmm-hmmm." She chewed on the pen cap, trying to decide whom to put as her emergency contact—Myra or Uncle Floyd.

Dale sat back in his chair. "Floyd's niece, huh. I've heard some things about you."

"Like what?" She looked up to see him stroking the stubble on his face.

"Pretty crazy stuff—like there were trumpets coming from nowhere the day you arrived, and you found this oil by jamming a dipstick in the ground. Is that true?"

"Sort of." Daphne felt color creep into her cheeks. She wasn't used to how fast gossip spread in a small town. "I guess."

He shook his head. "Craziest thing I ever heard. Finding the oil is usually the hard part: Global's spent millions on discovery, drilled more test wells than you can shake a stick at. And you just touch the ground and it comes pouring out." He laughed softly to himself. "Heck, maybe Global Oil should send *you* to those test sites, instead of all those overpaid scientists."

He continued stroking his chin, looking at her thoughtfully as

Daphne filled out the rest of her paperwork. When she handed it back to him, he stood and smiled, extending his hand.

"Let's hope neither of us end up regretting this," he said, pumping her arm up and down. "But welcome to the Global Oil team."

9

FROM THE MOMENT THEY LEFT the Radical Roots festival, Owen and Luna's journey took on the urgency of a phantom itch, ephemeral and omnipresent, demanding yet refusing relief. They talked endlessly as they drove from town to town, hitting races when they needed the money and pushing on when they didn't, the phantom vein from their dream pulsing like a mirage, always a few miles further down the road. They regurgitated their life stories as his wheels ate mile after mile of pavement, pouring over the details of their childhoods and looking for the loose threads that would weave into an explanation behind their shared nightmares.

Besides being born on the same commune, they discovered that she was just two days older than him, that they both hated the taste of pesto, and that they would always rather move than sit still. Their restless energy filled the cab of the truck, pulsing to the jam-band tunes from Luna's iPod, relentlessly propelling them forward. They didn't know where they were going—only that they needed to get there as soon as possible, to placate the voice in their dreams.

A few nights into their journey, at a campground in a remote logging village in Montana, the bonfire in Owen's nightmares burned brighter than ever before. Luna was there, her face no longer cloaked in shadow like the rest of the figures dancing and shrieking around them. Her green eyes glowed like embers as she writhed in a hoop made of fire, the flames lapping at her skin without leaving a mark. The bonfire grew until it nearly blinded him with its white-hot hunger, robbing the air of oxygen until he awoke, choking on his own fear, with the gravelly voice still whispering *find the vein* in his ears.

He thrashed in his sleeping bag, clawing at the drawstring that had wrapped around his neck until he'd shaken himself free. The late-morning sun was high in the sky, baking the bed he'd made for himself in the back of his truck, and he shielded his eyes with his hands, glancing around at the tents and RVs until he spotted Luna. She had rolled out a yoga mat under a pine tree and was standing in downward dog, peering at him upside-down through the gap between her legs with an unmistakable smirk on her face.

"Morning, sleepyhead," she said, kicking into a handstand.

Fear still throbbed in Owen's veins. "I had it again," he told her. "Just now."

"The dream?" She arched her body into a bridge, the charms in her dreadlocks jangling as they scraped the yoga mat. "I had it, too. It was so intense! I know we're getting closer. I can feel it."

Owen wondered whether the morning yoga session had calmed her, or if Luna simply didn't find the dreams as unsettling as he did. "Where are they coming from?" he wondered aloud. "Was it like that at the commune, when you were a kid? You mentioned there were bonfires every night." He swung his legs over the truck's tailgate and fished in his backpack for a canteen, taking a long, lukewarm swig of water.

"A little." Luna pulsed up and down in her backbend, the slim muscles in her arms straining. "But it was nothing like this. That was what was. This is what will come to be."

"What do you mean?" he started to ask. But Luna had already cartwheeled her way to standing. Her back was to him as she raised her arms to the sky in a final, long stretch, so that it looked like her tree tattoo was growing.

"I'm starving," she said, turning back to him. "Let's go get breakfast."

↔

They drove up the road to a restaurant they'd passed on the way in, a log cabin with a long lunch counter and a few small tables. From the wool hats and flannel shirts of the grizzled regulars sipping coffee and polishing off stacks of pancakes, Owen could tell it was a popular spot among the local loggers.

"Mmmm . . . fluffy blueberry pancakes, golden waffles with butter and strawberries and whipped cream, sausage links, cottage cheese and cantaloupe," Luna read off the menu. "I just might get one of everything."

"Yeah, well, try and control yourself," Owen said. "I've only got fifty bucks to last me 'til the next race, and we need thirty for gas."

"You worry too much," Luna said as the waitress came by, pulling a pencil from a bun as frizzy as cotton candy. Luna waited until Owen had ordered his omelet, then asked for the Lumberjack Special with extra bacon, waffles, and hash browns, plus an extra-large orange juice and a side of fresh fruit. Owen found himself scanning the menu while she talked, trying to add up all of her extras. He realized with an unpleasant shiver that she'd just totaled close to eighteen dollars in food.

"You know we're not going to have enough leftover for gas," he hissed when the waitress was out of earshot.

Luna grinned. "I told you, don't worry. I got this covered."

"How?" Owen asked. Luna had told him that she'd worked for Ariel Crow in exchange for festival tickets and food.

"I have my ways."

The waitress set down two mugs of coffee, and Luna busied herself pouring packet after packet of sugar into hers, leaving a pile of empty white wrappers on the table.

Owen took a quick sip, grimacing at the scalding heat on his tongue. It was strong and bitter, the way he liked it, and it helped clear his head. With the final cold fingers of his dream retreating and a new day shining bright and clear ahead of them, he was ready to stop letting Luna lead him around like a puppy on a leash, evading his questions whenever it felt like he was starting to learn something about his past. He was ready to get some answers.

"Do you remember Murdock?" he asked casually, propping his chin in his palm. He was taking a chance, he knew—it was a name he'd only read online, that the race organizer back in Olympia had mentioned in passing.

"Who?" Luna stopped mid-stir.

"You know, the leader," Owen pressed. "Of the Children of the Earth."

"Oh—you mean Galen. Murdock was his last name, but none of us called him that. We didn't believe in last names. The only reason I know his was that it was in the papers later. My mom saved the clippings."

"In the papers? Owen asked. "For what?"

Luna shrugged, sending the thin strap of her tank dress slipping down one shoulder. "A couple of people who never should have been there in the first place filed a lawsuit, and he went to jail. I think the government was just trying to silence him, though. They couldn't stand how he always spoke the truth."

"What truth?" He was getting closer. He could feel it.

"That we're raping the earth. That our endless quest for possessions and enlightenment will bring about the end of the world—and when that day comes, the God of the Earth will summon us, and we'll all come together to rule a beautiful new world."

"What do you mean, *us*? Are there others?"

But even as he said it, Owen knew. They were the shadowy figures dancing around the bonfire in his dreams, the faceless ciphers with the green eyes.

"Thirteen of us." Luna raised the mug to her mouth, and steam swirled dreamily around her face. "We were all conceived on the same night, in a magical ritual on the summer solstice under the full moon. We had a festival to celebrate it every year when I was growing up on the commune."

"All conceived on the same night? How?"

Luna smiled mysteriously. "I don't know all the details. Only that it marked us forever."

A sick feeling began to brew in Owen's stomach. "Was everyone there?" he asked as the waitress staggered back to them under the weight of a tray piled high with food. "All the Children of the Earth? The night we were . . . conceived?"

Luna licked her lips as the waitress set plate after plate in front of her. She grabbed the pitcher of syrup and poured it generously over everything, even her toast.

"I think so," she said. "Galen said they summoned the God of the Earth that night, and we were created by the power of community—and the earth—and magic."

"It sounds like an orgy," Owen said flatly. He pushed his omelet away, repulsed by the mounds of cheese vibrating gelatinously on top.

Luna crunched loudly on a piece of bacon, continuing to talk around it. "It was a ritual. It was sacred. This is where we come from, Earth Brother, like it or not."

"What do you mean, 'Earth Brother?'" Owen was feeling ickier by the second. "Are we related?"

She shrugged. "We were conceived in the same ritual, on the same night, by the same group of people, and we have the same eyes. Call it whatever you want, Earth Brother, but we're here for the same reason."

He sat back and put his head in his hands. "So my real father could be anyone," he said to the rutted wooden tabletop. "Yours, too. It could be the same guy, or someone totally different. And I'll never know."

He felt an old dream from his childhood slip away, the dream of someday finding his biological father, of looking up into a face that he could finally, honestly call "Dad." It was yet another thing he'd learned to stop asking his mom about, knowing that it made the softness in her face go hard.

There was a touch like feathers on his hand, and he looked up to find Luna's fingertips on his knuckles. Her eyes were vernal pools basking under a spring sun.

"It's okay," she said, not unkindly. "It doesn't matter. Don't you see? The God of the Earth is our father. And once we carry out his plan, we'll meet him face to face, and it'll be more beautiful than any experience you can imagine."

Owen shook his head disbelievingly. He had the same sad knot in his stomach as the Christmas Eve he'd snuck downstairs to catch Santa in the act, only to find his stepdad placing presents under the tree. The more Luna talked, the more it sounded like the Children of the Earth were just a bunch of dirty hippies making up excuses to do perverted things in the woods.

No wonder his mom had always refused to talk to him about the place he was born. She'd been young, and stupid, and probably on drugs. He suddenly regretted all the times he'd pestered her for answers: She was just trying to keep him from turning out like Luna. The strange, troubled girl across from him—his Earth Sister, or whatever—had grown up on the commune his mom had escaped, believing that their orgies were beautiful rituals and Galen Murdock's hackneyed hippie dogma was the truth. She'd been duped.

Stop it! a gravelly voice thundered.

Owen sat up straight, his heart pounding as his eyes darted around the restaurant. Everyone else was oblivious, the waitress trading gripes with the line cook while the lone lumberjack at the end of the bar quietly drank his coffee and Luna drowned a forkful of hash browns in ketchup.

"Did you hear that?" he asked.

"Hear what?" Luna cocked her head.

Blood slammed through his veins. There was no question that the voice had spoken to him—or that it was the same deep and terrible voice from his dreams. But he was the only one who had heard it; it had almost sounded like it was coming from inside his head. He gulped down the dregs of his coffee, not caring that it was still hot enough to scald his throat, and wondered if he was going crazy for real.

"Nothing." He looked down at his plate, trying to shake away the echo of the voice still vibrating in his mind. "So, any idea how we're going to pay for this feast?"

"Leave it to me." Luna winked, then slipped out of her seat and onto a stool at the end of the bar, next to the lumberjack. Owen watched as she tapped him on the shoulder and he turned to look at her, his gaze registering surprise and then something more opaque, a cross between curiosity and desire. Luna's skimpy dress hung low on her chest as she said a few words in his ear, casting her eyes downward as scarlet blooms of embarrassment rose in her cheeks.

Owen stared, shaking his head. He'd only known Luna for a few days, but she'd told him the most bald-faced, shocking truths about herself—like how she'd lost her virginity at thirteen, about the older man she'd met at a show who sent her a hundred dollars each month in exchange for mailing him a pair of her used panties—without even the slightest hint of shame. But as she talked to the lumberjack, her whole face seemed to transform, from a self-possessed seductress with a banging body and a free-love vibe to a lost and innocent waif who'd gotten herself in over her head.

The lumberjack nodded, the desire in his eyes fading to pity—but not, Owen noticed, disappearing entirely. He placed a reassuring hand on Luna's bare shoulder as she looked up at him gratefully from under lashes still sparkling with glitter from the show, a single tear slipping chastely down her cheek. With his other hand, the lumberjack reached into his back pocket and extracted two twenties, folding both into Luna's palm.

Luna's face blossomed into a smile of gratitude. She planted a kiss on the lumberjack's cheek, turning his whole face scarlet with lust and pleasure before she flitted back to their table.

"See?" she said, tossing both twenties on top of the bill. "I told you I got this. Now stop doubting me, and let's hit the road."

10

TOWARD THE END OF A lazy June afternoon, Daphne borrowed Uncle Floyd's truck and made a run to Elmer's Gas 'n' Grocery, promising to return with the jalapeno Doritos Janie had been craving. Golden light radiated off the cars on Buzzard Road, and Daphne felt loose and content after spending the better part of the day down by the swimhole, relaxing away the aches and blisters of her first week as a roustabout while Janie and Hilary giggled over Janie's gossip magazines.

Elmer's parking lot was more crowded than she'd seen it since she arrived in town, all of the spaces up front packed with vehicles that had out-of-state tags, prospectors come to try their luck at striking oil. She pulled into a spot near the road and started toward the entrance, shielding her eyes from the sun's low, late-afternoon glare.

As she passed the gas pumps, the sun caught a flash of silver that seemed to leap up and blind her, so that she had to stop for a moment and rub her eyes.

"Blinded by the light?" an unfamiliar voice asked.

She stepped forward, and the sun disappeared behind the gas pump, revealing a stranger with a shock of thick, oil-black hair gassing up a silver pickup. A smile played over his lips as he regarded her with eyes so clear and green she almost expected them to ripple. He was slim but well built, his shoulder muscles straining against a plain black T-shirt. Dizziness rushed to her head as his strange green eyes bored into hers, and she wondered if she'd taken in too much sun down at the swimhole.

"It must have been those." She pointed to the bundle of brightly colored hula hoops in the back of his truck, some covered in holographic tape that reflected the sunlight.

"Oh, those." He laughed lightly. "They aren't mine. The bike is, though—that's my baby."

"You and everyone else around here," she said.

"Really?" He scrutinized her so closely she felt her face go hot. "Is there a track in town?"

She nodded. "They have meets every Friday. It's like a religion around here."

He crossed his arms. "And you don't buy into it."

"Oh, I don't buy into anything." She took in a big gulp of Wyoming air, hoping it would help clear her mind. She felt suddenly hot and tingly, like she'd sat too close to a roaring campfire for way too long.

"So, you live around here?" he asked. The gas pump clicked,

and he removed the nozzle and replaced it with one fluid motion, his eyes not leaving hers.

"Yeah. And, let me guess, you came here to find oil and get rich quick?"

He tilted his head, one hand on his hip. "Is that an option?"

"Are you kidding me?"

He shrugged. "Listen, I don't know anything about anything. I just rolled into town and—well, you can say a little voice told me to get off the highway here."

He sounded genuine, though it was hard to believe that anything but oil or family would draw a guy like him to Carbon County. Still, she could play along.

"Believe it or not," she told him, "you're looking at America's next oil boomtown. The rig's a few miles down that way."

"Really?" His look of blatant surprise was enough to convince her that he really didn't know. "Is there work there?"

"Are you looking for work? Around here?"

"I might be." The corner of his mouth twitched into a smile.

"Well then, yeah. If I can get a job there, you should be fine— just tell the foreman you have two hands and you're not afraid to get dirty. It helps if you can lift a hundred pounds without dying, too," she added.

"You work there?" He looked impressed.

"I do." She allowed herself a small, proud smile.

"Well, hey." He reached over and tapped her forearm, leaving a small, tingly spot on her flesh where his fingers had been. "Thanks for the tip . . . I'm sorry, what's your name?"

"Daphne." She tore her eyes away from the place he'd touched her, back into the magnetic green of his gaze.

"Owen." He held out his hand, and she took it, her pulse beating against her wrist like the last burst of rain during an afternoon squall.

Then the bell over the convenience store door tinkled, and cool air brushed her hand where his had been. A girl with wild, colorful dreadlocks and a backless batik shirt came oozing through it, her legs golden and endless in cutoffs so short the pockets stuck out below the hem. She was chewing lazily on a Twizzler, her lips and tongue a lurid red from the dye.

"Want one?" she asked, planting herself next to Owen. Together they looked like a pair of panthers that had escaped the zoo, all sleek muscle and hungry green eyes.

"No thanks." Owen was still staring at Daphne—and as hard as she tried to focus on the newcomer, Daphne couldn't help gazing back.

"Suit yourself." The girl dug in the pack for another, then turned to Daphne. "Who's this?"

"I'm Daphne," she said quickly. She didn't like the possessive way the girl talked to Owen: like she owned him. Daphne already had the sense that Owen wasn't the kind of guy who let himself be owned. "I was just telling Owen about the oil rig in town."

"There's an oil rig in town?" A lazy smile spread across the girl's face. "That's brilliant. It's . . . really kind of poetic."

"This is Luna," Owen explained, when it became clear the girl wasn't going to introduce herself. "She's my . . . well, we . . ."

"He's my Earth Brother," Luna jumped in, taking Owen's arm. "See how we have the same eyes?"

Daphne nodded. It wasn't just their eyes: They almost had the same body, slim yet packed with powerful muscles, and the same energy buzzed around them like a force field. It was strange that even though they looked so similar, Daphne found herself liking Owen so much more.

"Daphne works on the rig," Owen explained to Luna admiringly.

"Beautiful." Luna grinned like a cat. "I knew this was the place. I could feel it as soon as we pulled off the highway. *Finally*." She turned to Daphne. "We've been driving around forever, looking for the right spot. You think a hippie hooper could find work around here, too?"

"Probably." Daphne recalled her first conversation with Dale, when he'd told her about the bars and massage parlors that would inevitably follow the oil boom. "Maybe not right away, but soon. As long as you don't mind waiting tables or whatever."

"I'll make it work," Luna said, winking at her. She turned to

Owen. "You want to go hit a campground, or should we bite the bullet and try to find an apartment or whatever?"

"Let's stick with camping for now," Owen suggested. "Until I can nail down some work."

"Sure, whatever." Luna was already bounding toward the cab of the truck. "See you around, Daphne."

Owen stayed planted a moment longer, his eyes lingering on hers. "So I guess I'll see you soon?" he asked. "At the rig or whatever?"

Daphne nodded. Her skin was still tingling, and her throat felt tight. She hoped she wasn't getting sick—a cold would make working on the rig torturous, but skipping work for something so trivial was unthinkable.

"Wish me luck." Owen smiled, and it was like a break in a thunderstorm. She couldn't help smiling back. "I'll see you around."

"See you," she whispered.

She turned and started back to Uncle Floyd's truck, her feet landing mechanically on the cracked pavement, willing herself not to turn around as the roar of Owen's truck disappeared down Buzzard Road. She got in and started the engine, taking a deep breath to try and still her racing pulse before pulling away.

She was halfway home before she realized she'd forgotten all about Janie's Doritos.

11

THE CARBON COUNTY FIRST CHURCH of God was in a former Pizza Hut just a ways past the mostly deserted All Good Things Shopping Plaza on Route 16. Volunteers from the congregation had painted the roof white and affixed a narrow steeple to the top, but the shape was unmistakable, and the faint scent of pepperoni still lurked beneath the fresh coats of varnish on the pews. Heavy curtains obscured the windows, giving the light inside a murky, underwater quality, and a brigade of volunteers led by Aunt Karen had covered the walls in needlepoint Bible verses and hand-painted wooden crosses.

Daphne fiddled with her dress, a gray castoff dotted with pink flowers that had once hugged Janie in all the right places, but hung slackly from her own bony shoulders. She wasn't used to wearing dresses, and the feeling of her legs touching under the loose cotton made her almost as uncomfortable as the gaze of the life-sized wooden Jesus hanging from a cross above the pulpit.

"It's getting crowded," Daphne marveled. The church was almost full, but Carbon County residents kept filing in, packing the rows of seats. The family in front of Daphne scooted down to make room for two elderly ladies in stiff pastel hats who cooed and preened like pigeons as they settled in.

"It didn't used to be like this," Aunt Karen leaned across Janie's lap to whisper. "Back when Ted Senior was pastor, Madge and Eunice were practically the whole congregation."

The two old ladies, hearing their names, turned and offered doddering smiles.

"You'll love Pastor Ted, dear." The one in the purple hat patted Daphne's arm. "We all do."

Her friend shushed her as the church filled with recorded organ music and a young man in a gray suit emerged from behind the purple velvet curtain that separated the chapel from what had once been the Pizza Hut's kitchen.

"Hello, friends!" he called over the organ's swell.

The congregation was on its feet in seconds, clapping and cheering. "Praise be!" someone called, and the chant was taken up throughout the church. "Praise be!" "God bless!" "I believe!"

Daphne clapped mechanically. Pastor Ted had the kind of clean, unlined face that reminded her of people in commercials for Disney World, always standing next to Mickey Mouse under some fireworks display with their eyes open wide in wonder.

"What a glorious day for Carbon County!" Pastor Ted leapt onto the stage and was behind the pulpit in two easy bounds, adjusting the microphone as the applause reluctantly died down. "Who's feeling God's blessings today more than ever before?"

A murmur rippled through the chapel. Daphne felt it bubbling out of the Peytons like oil from the dry ravine on their land, the simmering excitement of an unexpected discovery. Floyd's insistence that they thank the Lord for their good fortune *in person*, as he'd put it, was the only reason she'd agreed to join them at church that day. Since she'd arrived in Carbon County, she'd concocted a different excuse each Sunday— staying home to keep an eye on the stew bubbling in Aunt Karen's crockpot, waiting for a package to be delivered, faking a cold—but the thought of Floyd's disappointment if she bailed yet again was even harder to bear than the uncomfortable sense of judgment she felt whenever she set foot inside a place of worship.

"Today, I want to address some unequivocal signs from above." The church fell silent as Pastor Ted trained his gaze slowly around the room. For a moment, Daphne felt like his summer-blue eyes were staring directly into hers.

There had been a period in her life, shortly after her father died, when her mother insisted on church every Sunday, zipping Daphne into a stiff dress and forcing her to sit, silent and fidgeting, on a hard wooden bench. Those days had ended when Myra met Jim, but the miserable feeling of sitting fatherless in a chapel full of families had remained, and Myra still trotted out the Lord's name when she wanted to make Daphne feel especially guilty about something.

"We've been seeing some pretty amazing things here in Carbon County lately," the pastor continued, "some true signs from God. I'm talking angels. I'm talking miracles. I'm talking End Times. Do you believe?"

"I believe!" the congregation thundered, startling Daphne half out of her seat. When she'd attended church as a kid, she was expected to sit quietly through the sermon. Here, talking back was obviously encouraged.

"In Corinthians," Pastor Ted continued, his cheeks pink with fervor, "it says that when the trumpet sounds, the dead in Christ will rise and the living will become immortal. That time is coming—that time is almost here! We all heard the trumpets—how could we miss 'em? And they have marked the beginning of the End Times, when Christ will come back to claim us, the Children of God. Are you ready, Carbon County? Do you believe?"

"I believe!" The response around her was automatic, galvanic. Elderly Madge and Eunice trembled in front of her with conviction, their faces upturned to Pastor Ted like tulips drinking in the sun.

"And the wonders didn't stop there," Pastor Ted continued. "First there were the trumpets, and then another holy miracle—the discovery of oil, right here in Carbon County. Because God, in His greatness, has chosen to dole out His blessings in small doses. He's given us this oil as a reward for our piety and worship. But mark my words, this isn't the last miracle Carbon County will see. There will be many more. Do you believe?"

"I believe!" The chant was a blast of sound, almost loud enough to blow the peaked red roof off the former Pizza Hut.

On either side of Daphne, the Peytons leaned forward, waving their hands in the air and crying out to the heavens. She felt out of place sitting silently among them, her hands folded on her lap like her mom had taught her. But she couldn't bring herself to start screaming along. It would have felt fake, like she was lying not just in front of her family and their friends, but to the huge wooden Jesus hanging above Pastor Ted's head.

"Finally, I want to welcome a newcomer to our fold," Pastor Ted said. His kindly blue eyes met Daphne's as the congregation quieted, turning to stare at her. Suddenly, it was like all the air in the church had been sucked out through a vacuum. She fidgeted miserably, looking down at her lap and praying that Pastor Ted would move on.

"Folks, we are so blessed to have Daphne Peyton in our midst," the pastor went on. "Daphne arrived on the same day as the trumpets, like an angel coming down to us from heaven, and she also happens to be the one who discovered the oil. It could be a coincidence—but I say it's a sign. I think God has big plans for Daphne Peyton, and I for one can't wait to see what they are."

Daphne's face went scarlet, and she dug her fingernails hard into her palm. She knew Pastor Ted meant well, but being in the spotlight felt more than just humiliating. It felt dangerous. She'd come to Carbon County to lay low and try to forget what had happened with Jim in Detroit. With her name on everyone's mind, how long would it be before her secret came out?

"Now, let us pray," Pastor Ted concluded. He bent his head, and the congregation followed, murmuring words about shepherds and pastures. Daphne lowered her eyes, but her lips stayed in a single straight line. She couldn't remember the words, and they would have been false coming from her lips anyway.

Why had Pastor Ted singled her out, as opposed to Floyd? It wasn't like she'd found the oil on purpose—it had been Uncle Floyd's hunch, and Uncle Floyd who had gotten that terrible Rick Bodey out there to prove it. All she'd done was get mad and jab a stick in the ground.

As the congregation finished their prayer and Pastor Ted urged everyone to join him at the picnic tables out back for a potluck lunch, she vowed to herself that she'd let Floyd take the credit—and the spotlight.

He deserved it so much more than she did.

12

THE MOMENT THE SERVICE WAS over, Janie grabbed her arm and pulled her through a crush of people to the front of the church, muttering something about getting all the good food before it was gone. The congregation had already pulled the purple curtain aside to reveal the Pizza Hut kitchen perfectly intact, its metal prep tables covered in casserole dishes and giant Tupperware containers, cakes blanketed in inches of pink icing.

"Here." Janie shoved a paper plate at her, and they dove into the fray. The congregation swarmed the dishes like a many-tentacled squid, grabbing at potato salads and bean dip, devilled eggs and lasagna and tuna noodle casserole.

It was a relief to step out the back door and into the early summer air. They sat at one of a dozen picnic tables covered in plastic gingham, and Daphne tried to pay attention to the food on her plate, wondering which lump was which: They all looked like identical masses of noodles and coagulated cheese.

"That was some sermon, wasn't it?" Karen Peyton plonked down next to Janie, carefully setting down a plate piled with coleslaw and hot dog casserole, a paper cup of pink lemonade, and a big bowl of melting ice cream.

Uncle Floyd climbed in next to her. "Daphne, what do you think of Pastor Ted?" he asked.

"He's—very charismatic," she said carefully.

She was about to dig into what looked like mac 'n' cheese when she felt Janie's pink gel mani pressing into her thigh. "The Varleys are coming over here," she hissed. "They haven't spoken to me since I got preggers!"

Daphne looked up to see a man in a blue gingham shirt striding toward them. He wore cowboy boots polished to a rich mahogany and a large, round belt buckle embossed with an elk's head. Even if Doug hadn't been slinking along behind him, it would have been obvious that the man was his father. He had the same oversized head and rolling, pigeon-toed strut, and he exuded the same cockiness. Taking up the rear was a thin, faded blond with a ski-jump nose, carrying a small baking pan.

Karen Peyton stood, sandwiched between the bench and the picnic table. "Well, Vince and Deirdre, Doug, what a nice surprise! Please join us."

"I baked you a Bundt cake." Deirdre set the pan down between them.

Next to Daphne, Janie was practically vibrating. "That is so nice!" she cried. "What a sweet gesture—baby loves cake, don't you?" She patted her tummy happily.

Deirdre's smile looked like it hurt. "We couldn't be happier for you," she began, smoothing her prim blue skirt as she sat.

"Happy for *us*," Floyd interrupted. "For all of us. This is some gift we've received from the Lord, isn't it?"

"Yes." Vince Varley nodded approvingly. "I'm glad you see it that way, Floyd. It's a gift for *us*."

Floyd's eyebrows knit. "Well, of course it is—my daughter, your son, and we all get to share the joys of being grandparents."

"Of course they're a little young," Karen added. "But what can you do? The Lord works in mysterious ways."

A cloud passed over Vince Varley's face, wiping away his good-natured smile.

"Of course He does!" Deirdre interjected quickly. "And we're just thrilled about all of it—*aren't we, Vince?*"

Her meaningful look kicked his smile back into place. "Yes, yes, right." He cleared his throat. "As Pastor Ted was saying, we're blessed in many ways. And about that oil . . ." He struggled for words, then stopped and tried a different tactic. "Floyd, you know, the Varleys and the Peytons go back quite a ways," he said.

"I do," Floyd agreed. "Our great-grandfathers settled this land together, and our grandfathers were the best of friends."

"Exactly." Vince's grin inched wider. "That's why my grandpa John just about *gave* your Grandpa Noah that land your trailer is on today."

"Don't think I don't know it," Floyd said mildly. "Selling that whole parcel for one measly dollar was just about the kindest act one man could do for another, particularly with our family hurting so hard at the time—and that's why I keep the deed framed in our living room, so I can remember that kindness every day."

"It's a code to live by," Karen nodded approvingly. "If only we could all be as good and godly as that man."

"So—you kept the deed." Vince's lips set in a tight line.

"Of course. It's as precious to me as our family photos—though maybe not as pretty." Floyd laughed heartily.

Vince's eyes narrowed. "Don't you think, given the circumstances, we deserve a cut?"

"After all, if it weren't for Vince's grandfather's generosity, your family wouldn't be sitting on that oil at all!" Deirdre cut in.

"Oh, you two don't need to go showering me with logic like that." Floyd was still chuckling. "If you thought I'd forget your great-granddad's kindness, I'm afraid you must not think very much of me at all. When that oil money starts coming in, Vince, I'd say it's only fair that half of it should go to your family. For history's sake— and for the sake of our grandchild."

Daphne started. *Half the oil money?* To a family that clearly wouldn't have shared as much as a cent if the tables were turned? She wanted to believe that Floyd was doing the right thing, but it seemed like he'd lost his mind.

Across the table, Karen's face went white. She reached for her lemonade with a shaking hand and took a long gulp. When she saw Daphne looking at her, she offered a weak smile before abruptly averting her eyes, turning her attention back to the Varleys.

"Well, that's awful big of you, Floyd," Vince boomed, beaming. "I should have known I could count on you to make the right choice."

"Don't mention it," Floyd said.

"So, I'll have you down to my office later this week, and we can have my lawyer finalize everything, then." Vince was suddenly all business. "Does tomorrow work for you—say, ten a.m.?"

"Oh, I don't know that we need to go involving lawyers and all that," Floyd chuckled. "Like your grandpa, I'm a man of my word."

"But," Vince began. "How . . . ?"

Floyd's laugh boomed across the church's lawn. "How long have we known each other, Vince? Since our mamas used to put us down on the living room floor to crawl around together so they could get down to some good old-fashioned gossip?"

Vince nodded.

"And in all that time, have you ever known me to go back on my word?"

"No," Vince admitted. But he looked troubled.

"Let's shake on it, then." Floyd stuck out his hand. After a moment, Vince met it with a vigorous pump.

"Yay!" Janie erupted, clapping her hands. "Doug, honey, we're gonna have the richest baby Carbon County's ever seen!"

"It'll be a baller," Doug agreed. "We can get it a diamond binkie and stuff."

Everyone laughed, and Karen turned to Deirdre. Doug's mom had regained her fragile smile, but her cheeks were still waxy and pale. "So I guess we'll be seeing quite a bit more of you all, then. Maybe you and I can get together and plan a nice baby shower."

"That sounds lovely," Deirdre said in a voice like cut glass. She checked her slim silver watch. "We have to be going, though. So much to do. Enjoy the Bundt cake!"

There was a rustle of goodbyes as the Varleys stood to leave. Doug kissed Janie lightly on the forehead. "I'll text you later, 'kay?"

"Yay!" Janie said by way of response. She waited until they were just out of earshot before putting her hands together in prayer and raising her face to the heavens. "Oh, thank you, Lord, for finally making the Varleys accept this child." She turned to Daphne. "That sure was a long time coming!"

"Janie." Daphne knew there was no nice way to say it. "Don't you think maybe this has more to do with the oil money than the baby?"

Janie's pink-frosted mouth fell open, and Daphne wondered if she'd gone too far.

But Janie just laughed. "Honestly, who cares? The important thing is that they accept the child. Maybe that's *why* God led us to the oil in the first place. God and you, of course."

"Not me," Daphne corrected. "I wish everyone would stop saying that. Floyd, you studied the rocks. You made an educated guess. I had nothing to do with it."

The three Peytons stared at her, and for the second time in five minutes, she wondered if she'd gone too far. She'd wanted to temper her opinion, to let them believe whatever they wanted to believe, but she couldn't handle everyone heaping praise on her, giving her credit that she'd never deserve. She was still a killer, still taking advantage of relatives who didn't know, still living in their house inside the delicate bubble of her lie.

The crease between Floyd's eyebrows deepened, but a moment later they relaxed. He smiled.

"The Lord works in mysterious ways," he repeated.

13

"EVERYONE SAY HELLO TO THE new guy." Dale addressed the rig workers clustered around the admin hut, most still wolfing down last-minute energy bars and wiping the sleep from their eyes. "This is Owen Green—the lucky guy who scored the last roustabout position on our crew."

Daphne's face flushed as she finished tightening the laces on her work boots. She stood quickly, just in time to meet Owen's eyes. He looked strong and well rested, his pale skin glowing in the early morning sunlight.

For a moment she felt dizzy, like she'd skipped breakfast or given herself a head-rush by standing too quickly. Then the corners of her mouth tugged into a smile, returning his.

"We've got a lot of work to do, so let's get to it!" Dale rubbed his hands together and rattled off a list of names and assignments for the day. Daphne, Owen, and a handful of other roustabouts were in charge of digging a ditch in the far corner of the oilfield.

"Hey, thanks for the heads-up about this," Owen said, lightly touching her arm as they headed for the maintenance shed. The same hot, tingly sensation that she'd felt talking to him in the parking lot of Elmer's Gas 'n' Grocery rushed to the surface of her skin. "Dale's a good guy—as soon as I told him I rebuilt my bike from scratch, he offered me a job."

"Don't thank me yet," Daphne said, selecting a shovel. "Life around here is pretty grueling."

"You think I can't handle it?" Owen teased. He took the shovel from her hands. "Let me carry that for you."

"I can carry my own gear!" Daphne made a grab at the shovel, but he held it above his head, out of her reach. "Now you're making it seem like *I'm* the one who can't handle things around here," she said, exasperated.

"I never said that." Owen shouldered her shovel along with his own and started across the field. "I'm just being a gentleman."

"Yeah, well, this isn't exactly a debutante ball." She fell into step, her long strides matching his.

He glanced at her sideways. "And, let me guess, you're not exactly a debutante?"

Blood rushed to her face. "Do I look like one?" she countered, gesturing to her cargo pants and steel-toed work boots.

"You look like *something*," Owen responded cryptically.

They reached the far end of the field, where the outlines of the ditch had been marked in blue construction tape.

"This is where we start digging," Daphne said. "So you better give me back that shovel, unless you want to work for both of us."

"I would if I could." Owen tossed it to her, and she caught it with one hand. He raised an eyebrow. "Good reflexes."

"I don't sleep on the job." She jabbed the blade deep into the earth and wriggled it around to loosen the dirt. She could still feel Owen's eyes on her, and for a moment she was horribly self-conscious: She had already started to sweat, and the bottoms of her cargo pants were covered in dirt.

She tunneled in, focusing on her work. There was something comforting in the physical labor: The simple act of transferring dirt from one place to another seemed solid and sensible compared to the weird stew of sensations brewing inside of her, and she soon lost herself to the repetition of the movements.

By the time Dale came by to call a break, a deep Y of perspiration had soaked the back of her shirt. The ditch was starting to take shape, a long, low trench in the ground. She looked up in time to see Owen shrug off his hard hat and wipe his brow. His thick black hair stood out in all directions, and his white T-shirt clung to his chest, outlining the taut muscles beneath.

"Want to grab a snack?" he asked.

"I'm actually not that hungry," she confessed, Something about the way Owen looked at her made her feel like her stomach was full of bubbles, and even though she was usually ravenous by the mid-morning break, at the moment a snack was the last thing on her mind.

"Cool, me either. I still haven't really gotten the lay of the land here. How 'bout giving me a tour?"

The rest of the roustabouts were heading toward the canteen, dreaming out loud of ice cream bars and sodas. "You coming?" Eric, a nineteen-year-old from Nebraska who slept in his truck and sent all his money home to his wife and baby, called to Daphne. She shook her head, and he arched an eyebrow, asking her a silent question before turning back to the rest of the crew without saying another word.

"You're pretty popular around here," Owen observed.

She shrugged. "Everyone was a little weird about having a girl on the team at first, but now they're used to it."

"Looks to me like you work as hard as anyone," he said. "Maybe harder. I don't think I even saw you stop to take a water break."

"You were watching that closely?" she challenged.

He grinned mysteriously. "Maybe. So do I get the grand tour or what? Let me guess—this is the ditch."

She laughed in spite of herself. "It will be. And over there, that's going to be another ditch. And there . . . well, guess."

"A third ditch?"

"Bingo." She started across the oilfield, pointing out landmarks along the way: the place where the derrick would go once it was trucked in, the company vehicles, the sheds where they kept the tools and calibrators and drilling mud. They crossed through the grove of pines and into the ravine behind the trailer, where Uncle Floyd had bought a small plaque to mark the spot where the oil had first been found.

"*Here God's blessing touched us,*" Owen read. "*Site of the first Carbon County oil discovery, made by Daphne Peyton on May 28. And may His blessings keep coming.*"

He turned to her. "You were the one who found the oil?"

"Not really." She brushed some dirt from her sleeve, wondering what had possessed her to bring Owen to the ravine.

"That's not what the plaque says."

"Well, it was kind of a group effort," she relented, telling him an abbreviated version of the story with Rick Bodey and the dipstick.

"And that's how all this happened?" Owen gestured to the trailers and huts and rows of construction vehicles, the crews in hard hats bustling around.

"Basically, yeah." Daphne looked down at the ground, where a faint slick of oil was still visible on the rocks. "It all started here."

"That's crazy." Owen crouched in the ravine and touched the oil slick, a bemused smile on his face. "There was oil under here all along, and it took you to come along and realize it."

He stood, examining his fingers where he'd touched the oil.

"Whoa." His voice dropped, and a trace of fear flashed across his eyes. "That's weird."

Daphne looked at his hand, and a cold shudder of dread seized her body. On the tips of his fingers, where the oil should have been, was a shimmering patch of deep red blood.

She stood gazing at it for a long moment, waves of frigid nausea crashing in her stomach. A droplet fell from his hand to the ground, cascading in slow motion until it plopped red and ominous onto the stones below.

"I must have cut my hand on a rock," Owen murmured, wiping the blood on his T-shirt so that it left a long, bright streak like a scar. His eyes had darkened to the color of moss in a rainstorm, and his playful smile was gone.

"Are you okay?" Daphne asked uncertainly. "There's a first aid kit in every hut; we can go get you a Band-Aid."

He nodded shakily. "Maybe that's a good idea," he said.

They hurried to the nearest trailer. Once inside, Daphne grabbed the first aid kit from the wall and riffled through it.

"Let me see," she commanded, opening an antiseptic wipe.

Owen held out his hand, and she took it in hers, ignoring the prickles of heat that rushed up her arm. She examined his fingers closely, turning them over in her palm and swiping at the flesh carefully with the wipe.

But she couldn't find any sign of a cut, not even the faintest scrape. His palms were rough and cool, with smooth callouses on his fingertips from the hours he put in at the track. But the skin was intact.

She glanced up at him to see if he was seeing what she was seeing, but he was looking at her. Her palms went clammy as their eyes met, and she quickly let go of his hand.

"We have to get back," she said apologetically, tossing the unused Band-Aid in the trash and returning the first aid kit. "Dale will get mad."

"It's fine." Owen was already pulling on his work gloves. His skin looked pale, but maybe it was just the trailer's fluorescent lighting. "It was probably just one of those things that bleeds all over the place and then disappears, like a paper cut."

"Probably," Daphne agreed. They hurried back to the ditch, their banter forgotten in the strangeness of the incident and their rush to get back to work. But for the rest of the afternoon and into the early evening, as the ditch grew deeper and the ache in her arms became a burn and Owen worked silently and tirelessly by her side, Daphne couldn't shake the image of the blood from her mind. There hadn't been a cut—she was sure of it.

It was almost like the oil had turned to blood at his touch.

14

JANIE LEANED CLOSE TO THE bathroom mirror, brushing sparkling shadow over her eyelids.

"You should let me do your makeup," she called.

"Why?" Daphne stared up at the trailer's ceiling, trying to muster the energy to sit up. It was Friday night and she'd just come off a grueling shift at the rig that left every muscle in her body feeling like a stage for tap-dancing fire ants. "We're just going to the track, right?"

"Oh, no reason." There was something forced about Janie's casual tone. "It's just that you're so pretty, and you never do anything about it. I could totally bring out your eyes."

"Maybe next time." Daphne felt bad turning Janie down: She knew it would make her cousin happy, and it was the least she could do while she was sleeping on the Peytons' couch, eating their food, and keeping secrets from them about her past. But she was just too tired. She finally picked herself up off the couch, telling Janie she'd wait for her outside.

The trailer's screen door banged shut as she stepped into the first golden tinge of sunset. One of the contractors waved as he hurried past, covered in dust and yelling into a walkie-talkie over the screech of static, heading toward the new oil derrick.

It had arrived that morning, trucked in on a doublewide flatbed surrounded by a phalanx of safety vehicles flashing amber lights. Now it sat in pieces about a half mile from the Peytons' trailer, huge chunks of metal scaffolding waiting to be assembled into a tower that would reach ten stories into the sky.

She turned at the sound of Doug's truck pulling into the driveway, spraying gravel as it skidded to a stop.

"Hey, Daff!" He leaned out the window, beady eyes grinning. "You ready for our hot date?" He licked his lips suggestively, and her stomach turned over. Just looking at his oversized head made her feel ill.

"I'll get Janie," she said curtly. But her cousin had already emerged on the steps, stuffed into a hot pink sundress and blinking rapidly to dry her mascara.

"Hi, boys!" she called, waddling down the steps.

"Boys?" Daphne turned just in time to see Trey climb out of the truck, holding the door open to help them in. He wore a button-down shirt over khaki shorts, and his blond hair was combed neatly against his scalp.

"Hey," he said to Daphne, ducking his head.

"Hi, Trey," Daphne said, surprised. Nobody had told her he was catching a ride.

"You girls ready to roll?" Doug asked. He put the truck in reverse and backed up abruptly, gravel skittering against the windows.

"Watch it!" Janie called. "We don't even have our seatbelts on yet!"

"Well, hurry up and buckle 'em." Doug was already barreling down the road, swerving around a slow-moving water truck and jouncing over a series of potholes. Global Oil's construction vehicles had chewed up the road to the consistency of hamburger meat, and it had developed a treacherous pattern of potholes in protest.

Daphne pressed her forehead to the glass and watched the dust clouds drift and the day fade and the low, scrappy mountains rush by. The scenery danced to a blur out the window, like a painting gone over one too many times with a brush. Her head thudded against the ceiling as they careened over another bump.

"What's with the speeding?" She turned to Doug, rubbing her head and trying to keep the irritation out of her voice.

"What speeding?" His tone dripped with false innocence.

"You're going really fast, and the roads suck now. You sure that's safe with your baby momma in the car?"

"I don't know what you're talking about." Doug stepped on the accelerator.

"You *are* going pretty fast," Janie said tentatively. "Maybe you should—"

"I know how fast I'm going!" Doug snapped. His eyes in the rearview mirror narrowed into slits, and the back of his neck glowed an angry red. Janie ducked her head and began to cough, waving away the dust pouring in through the open window.

"Doug, slow *down*," Daphne said through clenched teeth. "Janie's *pregnant*, for chrissake!"

In the rearview mirror, Doug bared his teeth. "Listen—" he began.

Trey cleared his throat. "Hey, man, she's right. Pregnant girls are more delicate."

Doug's glare turned to a silent hiss. He eased his foot off the gas, loosening his neck with a menacing crack. "Whatever," he said. Daphne's shoulders sagged in relief. "We're almost there anyway."

He turned onto a gnarled road that twisted up into the mountains. It was so narrow that the tree branches met above them, forming a dark tunnel through which only a mottled patchwork of light left sunspots on the ground.

"Where are we going?" Daphne asked. "This isn't the way to the track."

"Oh!" Janie turned to her, a slightly guilty look in her eye. "We actually, uh, thought we'd go check out the new house real quick. Just to, um, see how it's coming along."

Ever since Uncle Floyd and Vince Varley had shaken hands at the church picnic, Janie had been talking nonstop about the new house the Varleys planned to build with their share of the money. According to Janie, it was going to be modeled after a French castle, with real marble baths and a special wine refrigerator and a whole wing just for her and Doug and the new baby. Daphne didn't think all the wine refrigerators in the world would make living with the Varleys worth it, but she'd managed to keep her mouth shut so far.

"Aren't they still clear-cutting the land?" she asked. It seemed to her like the Varleys were putting the cart before the horse, starting to build before they had more than a verbal agreement in place. But maybe that was just how things worked in small towns.

"They're done," Doug smirked. "Wait'll you see the view. It'll be, y'know, romantic 'n' crap." He grinned at them in the rearview mirror, and Janie giggled.

Daphne looked from Doug to Trey to Janie and back again. Doug and Janie were repressing laughter, while Trey stared resolutely out the window.

"What's so funny?" she asked.

"Doug's family's owned this land forever," Janie said quickly, evading the question. "They've always wanted to build a house up on Elk Mountain—and now they can, thanks to you!"

"You mean, thanks to your dad," Daphne corrected. It was bad enough that everyone thought she'd manifested the oil, but it *really* hadn't been her choice to give half the money to the Varleys.

Doug eased the truck up a steep incline, past an earth-mover and logging truck crouched by the side of the road. Just when it felt like they couldn't climb anymore, the road took a hairpin turn and flattened out in a wide dirt circle on the mountaintop. Orange tape marked the massive hole that would be the house's foundation, and several bags of concrete were stacked at the edge of the tree line. Aside from that the space was clean and empty. Clear-cut.

"Here we are." Doug cut the engine, and the sudden quiet wrapped around them like a quilt. The sun sat low in the sky, the color of a ripe nectarine, and a thin crescent moon had already begun to rise over the mountains.

"Let us out so we can see the view!" Janie chirped.

Trey fumbled with the handle, got it open, then caught his foot in the seatbelt, nearly falling face-first onto the gravel. Janie stifled a giggle as he righted himself and turned to offer his arm, his face tomato-red. He helped Daphne down from the truck, his hand lingering on her elbow. She took a step forward, and then another.

Carbon County spread out below them, mountains fading to gentle rolling hills that eventually bottomed out into the flat, brown valley they called home. She could see the railroad tracks and the makeshift steeple on the Carbon County First Church of God, the flagpole in front of the high school and the pieces of the oil derrick waiting to be assembled.

Across the valley, the hills rose into jagged peaks, some still topped with the last vestiges of snow. Mountain lakes hovered in their crevices, still and shiny as pennies bouncing back the last light from the sun.

"Wow," she said. "You guys weren't kidding about the view."

"Isn't it amazing?" Janie agreed. "We all come up here for parties sometimes. It's actually the first place me and Doug ever—well, you know!" She began giggling uncontrollably.

"Wanna go relive the memories?" Doug appeared behind her and kissed her neck, a beer already sweating in his palm.

"Why, Doug, how dare you even insinuate!" Janie teased. She ducked out of reach of his lips and fixed her hair, still giggling.

"What, you're gonna get all virtuous on me *now*?" Doug helped himself to a handful of her butt, and she leapt to the side, squealing.

"You stay away from me!" she cried, already trotting toward the woods.

"I'll get you, and you'll like it," Doug retorted, chasing her into the shadows.

"Wait, where are you going?" Daphne called after them. The only answer was a frenzy of cracking twigs and giggles. As their laughter turned to slurps and sighs, she realized she was alone with Trey.

"What was *that* all about?" she asked, turning to him. "I thought we were going to the track."

Trey blushed furiously, refusing to meet her eyes.

"Wait a minute," she asked slowly, putting the pieces together: Janie's guilty looks and Trey's button-down shirt, the surprise detour up the mountain. "Are they trying to set us up?"

The silence unfurled around them, rolling away into the darkness. "Uh, yeah," Trey admitted finally. "At least, that's what they told me. Is that not what they told you?"

"No," Daphne sighed. She couldn't believe she'd let her cousin trick her.

"Wow." Trey sucked air in through his nose and ran a hand through his hair, messing up the carefully combed strands. "Well, this is awkward."

"Seriously." Daphne paced back and forth, her hands shoved deep in the pockets of her cargo pants. "I can't believe they didn't even tell me."

"Uh, yeah. That's pretty weak," Trey agreed. "Do you, uh, want a beer or something? All my soda's in my truck," he added apologetically.

"I guess I'll have a beer," Daphne grumbled.

Trey rummaged in the cooler and fished out a pair of Keystones. He opened both and handed her one. "Cheers?"

She hoisted herself onto the tailgate and settled in at one end. After a moment, Trey joined her. They sipped silently, watching the sunset turn purple over the mountains. There really was something romantic about being alone on the mountaintop, the day coming to a spectacular close all around them. For a moment, she found her thoughts turning to Owen, to the way he made her skin turn hot when he looked at her and the strange occurrence with the oil that seemed to have turned to blood on his skin. If he were up there with her, would they be sitting silently, drinking beer and wondering what to say? She shook her head quickly, trying to chase away the thought. Owen was her coworker, and maybe her friend. Anything more was more trouble than she was ready for.

"Are you okay?" Trey asked after a while.

"Huh?" she asked.

He fiddled with the tab on his beer can. "You were scowling."

"Sorry." Daphne forced herself to smile. "It's not you. Trust me."

"I really am sorry about all this," Trey said. "I mean, if I'd known you didn't know, obviously I wouldn't have agreed to it. I just, well . . ."

He trailed off and looked down at his shoes.

"What?" Daphne asked.

Trey took a long swig of beer. "I was psyched that it seemed like you liked me," he said in a rush.

Daphne twisted her fingers in her lap, searching for the right words. She felt terrible for leading Trey on, even though she'd never been anything but friendly, even though she'd *told* Janie she wasn't up for a double date. It was just more proof that dealing with guys—*any* guys—was way too complicated.

"It's totally not you," she said. "It's me." She knew the words were a cliché, but she couldn't think of any others. Someone else, someone who had experience with guys, might know what to say. But not her.

"I know what that means," Trey said darkly. "It means it's me."

"No!" She shook her head vehemently. "It's really not. You're a nice guy, and you're cute. I just—I've been through some kind of rough stuff with guys. Honestly, going on dates or being touched or even just being alone with a guy kind of freaks me out."

It was the closest she could come to explaining the panic that rose in her chest whenever someone got too close, the irrational but inescapable fear that whoever it was would turn into Jim and pin her down, not letting her go until he'd taken everything she had.

She forced herself to look at Trey. He shook his head slowly, his eyes heavy with pity. "I'm sorry," he said. "That really sucks."

"Yeah." Daphne kicked her heels angrily against the truck's mud flaps. "It really does."

"Well, uh, look." Trey's hand hovered over her knee before he brought it down heavily on his own. "You think I'm cute, and I think you're really pretty, and cool, and . . . like, interesting. I know you're not into having a boyfriend or whatever now, but if you ever change your mind . . ."

"Thanks." Daphne tried to smile, but it stuck in her throat. "I really appreciate it. But don't hold your breath."

"O-*kay.*" Trey's voice was iced over with hurt, and she realized her words had probably come out wrong.

Somewhere deep in the woods, an owl hooted. Trey hopped off the tailgate, set his empty beer can on the ground, and stomped it hard. Instead of crushing flat, it went flying from under his foot, landing several feet away with a tinny plink.

"Dammit!" he cursed, running after it and tossing it angrily into the truck.

After watching him pace back and forth across the clearing, not meeting her eyes, Daphne couldn't take it anymore. She put two fingers in her mouth and whistled, the sound splitting the air and sending what sounded like a whole colony of small, furry creatures scuttling toward the underbrush.

Trey glanced at her, startled. "What was that for?"

"I don't know about you, but I'm ready to go. Those two have a whole lifetime to fool around." She wanted it to come out light and funny, to make him crack a smile, but it was a lost cause. He was pissed at her—and she'd never been one of those girls who could smooth it all over with a joke.

The bushes rustled, and Doug and Janie emerged, adjusting their clothes and grinning sheepishly.

"You rang?" Janie asked, adjusting her flip-flop. She looked from Daphne to Trey. When she saw the expression on his face, her smile faltered.

"Yeah," Daphne agreed. "You're right, the view up here is awesome, but it's dark now." She looked Doug in the eye, daring him to contradict her. "I think we should go."

15

JUDGING FROM THE LOOK ON Daphne's face, Janie guessed she could forget her dreams of someday being a celebrity matchmaker with her own reality TV show. Her cousin and Trey were as far away from each other as possible, faces bitter as a box of Sour Patch Kids.

"Well!" she said brightly, trying to scrape the best out of the situation. "It's just about time to head over to the track anyway. You guys don't want to miss the meet, do you?"

Trey nodded slowly. He was brooding the way Doug used to when they first started dating, before she'd let him go all the way. The way he still did sometimes, even when she did.

Anxiety knotted in her gut as the truck crawled back down the mountain, headlights piercing the wooded gloom. She knew Doug wouldn't say anything in front of their friends, but later on he'd lord it over her about how he was right about Daphne: She was a cold fish who thought she was too good for everyone, even Trey. Janie had brushed him off the first time, thinking he was just being his usual better-than-everyone self. He'd met Daphne exactly once, so what did he know? But now that Daphne had obviously blown off Trey, Doug would never let Janie forget it.

As the truck bounced down the last of the mountain trail and turned onto Buzzard Road, Doug hummed along off-key with the radio, taking big gulps of the beer nestled between his knees. She could tell he was in a great mood, and she just bet it was because he was planning to let her have it later: *PS, babe, I was right and you were wrong.*

The floodlights were already on when they reached the motocross track, the parking lot bright and buzzing like a beehive. Janie loved Friday nights at the track—it always felt like a little nucleus where all the town's energy came together to race in circles, creating the sparks and friction that would power them through the rest of the week. And being there with Doug Varley was like being the queen of the hive.

Doug honked his horn and stuck a hand out the window in greeting. But when he rolled up to his parking space, he stopped short. There was already a truck there, a stranger with inky black hair bent over the ratchet straps holding an old Husqvarna in place.

"Hey!" Doug leaned his head out the window. "You're parked in my spot."

The stranger's head snapped up, meeting Doug's gaze with a pair of icy green eyes. Next to her in the backseat, Daphne froze. What was with her, anyway? She'd been acting cranky and weird ever since they left the trailer.

"I didn't realize it was your spot. Is there a sign?"

The back of Doug's neck turned an angry red. "There doesn't need to be. Everyone around here knows it. Who *are* you, man?"

The stranger shrugged. "I'm new in town."

Doug took a long swill of his beer and wiped his mouth with the back of his hand. "And if you want to stay here, you'll park somewhere else."

The stranger looked annoyed, as if it was Doug encroaching on his territory instead of the other way around. "Come on, I've already got my bike halfway off," he said. "How about you drive approximately twenty feet and park over there? If you've got a problem, we can settle it on the track."

Without giving Doug another thought, he turned and finished untying his bike, thick black hair glistening with indifference as Doug fumed in the driver's seat.

"He's asking for it," Doug muttered under his breath.

Daphne opened her mouth to say something, but Janie shot her a *look*. If anyone could handle this, it was her: She'd been dealing with Doug's moods since they'd started dating sophomore year.

"You'll show him good on the track," she said reassuringly, reaching around the seat to rub his shoulders. "And then we'll get a sign that says 'Doug's Parking Only' and put it up right there, and everyone will know what's what. Okay?"

Doug's face was still dark, but he put the truck in gear and pulled into an empty parking space a few feet away. "I hope he knows what's coming to him," he glowered. He swigged the last of his beer and tossed the can out the window.

"Hey, you gonna be a gentleman and help me out, or what?" Janie asked.

She waited for him to offer his arm, then planted a big, wet kiss on his mouth. "I love you," she reminded him. Then she whispered in his ear: "And I can't wait to finish what we started in the woods earlier. Rawr!" She made her hand into a fake kitty claw and pretended to scrape it down his chest.

He drew her close, his body big and powerful against hers in that way that always made her weak. "I'll make you see stars," he growled in her ear, his stubble scratching up her chin. Then he bit her earlobe so hard she shrieked.

"Watch it!" she cried, rubbing her ear.

But Doug had already let her go. She watched him amble off, wishing he'd stayed and held her just a few moments longer—biting and all. She knew Jesus probably wouldn't approve, but she secretly kind of liked PDAs: They showed the world that she and Doug were together and that they didn't care who knew it.

Doug joined the knot of people passing around a bottle of Jack Daniels over by Bryce's truck.

"Lemme see that," he said. Trey handed it over, wiping a small trail of whiskey off his chin. His eyes were already a little glassy, and as he talked she could see the group sneaking glances over their shoulders. She wondered if they were talking about Daphne. Had Trey decided she was a cold fish, too? She didn't understand how guys' brains worked sometimes. Sure, Daphne didn't exactly wear her heart on her sleeve, and maybe she hadn't gone for Trey the way Janie had hoped, but she was still a nice person. They just needed to learn to be more accepting—and probably pay a little more attention in church.

Where had Daphne even gone, anyway? She looked around for her cousin, hoping to get her into a corner somewhere and find out exactly what had gone down with Trey. She wasn't in the group hanging out by Bryce's tailgate—they'd all given up trying to sneak glances over their shoulders and were staring openly at something over by the track.

She followed their gazes, and her heart sank. There was Daphne, all right—standing at the front of the parking lot, twisting a strand of hair around her finger as she smiled at that jerk who had taken Doug's parking spot.

↔

"I'm sorry about Doug," Daphne said. She couldn't believe he'd already managed to make an ass of himself in front of Owen. "He can be such a jerk."

Owen shrugged. "I'm used to it. There's a lot of testosterone around motocross tracks. I don't take it personally."

"I wish I felt that way," she sighed. "If I were his size, I'd kick his ass."

Owen laughed, his teeth gleaming straight and even. "I've seen you dig a ditch—I bet you could kick his ass just as you are. Why do you put up with him?"

"He's my cousin's boyfriend," she explained. "And I'm kind of crashing with her, so . . ."

Owen winced sympathetically. "That's tough."

Daphne shrugged. "I've dealt with worse, if you can believe it."

"I can believe just about anything."

She watched him finish wiping down his bike and adjust a gauge near the handlebars. "I like your bike," she said.

He raised an eyebrow. "Do I sense a potential convert to the Church of Motocross?"

Daphne fought off a smile. "I like that it doesn't look like the others," she clarified.

He nodded. "It's vintage—I always liked the lines better on the older ones." He leaned against his truck and crossed his arms. "You know I could say the same about you. You don't seem like the others," he said, glancing at the crowd of locals clustered by Bryce's truck.

"I just moved here this summer," she explained. "I grew up in Detroit."

"Wow—city girl."

She shook her head. "It's not who I am. Just where I'm from."

"I see." Owen took a rag and began polishing the bike's chrome accents, making them shine.

"It looks so new," she commented.

"Thanks. I fixed it up myself—so you're basically looking at three years of blood, sweat, and tears."

"I guess it was worth it." She reached out and touched the gleaming metal. Even though it was cool under her hand, something about it felt restless, almost like it was alive. When she looked up, he was watching her.

"Let's go for a ride," he suggested.

She narrowed her eyes. "Both of us?"

"No, me and Doug. Of course us." He climbed on and gestured for her to get behind him.

She eyed the few spare inches of seat. "I don't think that's meant for two."

He tilted his head, the ghost of a smile on his lips. "You're not much bigger than my little sister, and I took her out tons of times."

She hesitated. Some crazy part of her wanted to, but she could feel a whole crowd of eyeballs boring into her back, just daring her to choose sides. Plus there was something strange about Owen, something a little dangerous. She couldn't shake the image of the oil turning to blood on his hand.

"C'mon." He nodded toward the group by Bryce's tailgate, as if reading her mind. "I know you secretly love the idea of getting a rise out of those guys." He reached into the truck bed and pulled out a helmet. "What do you say?"

Before she knew what she was doing, her hands were cupping the helmet like an oversized egg.

"You know how to adjust it?" Owen asked as she slipped it on. It smelled sharp and tangy, like sweat and victory and secrets. His face had been right there so many times before, she thought, right up against the foam padding that cradled her ears and chin.

"Sure." The world around her grew muffled as she tightened the strap and the foam pressed into her ears.

He reached up and pushed a stray piece of hair out of her eyes. "There," he said. "Now hop on and hold on tight."

She looked from the back of Owen's well-worn leather jacket to the tiny piece of saddle where she was supposed to sit. Then she was behind him, arms wrapped around his waist, palms hyperaware of the layers of leather and cotton and skin beneath them. She wondered if he could feel her heartbeat.

He kick-started the bike, and it sprang to life, bucking between their legs. Then he hit the gas, and they cruised out of the parking lot and onto the track, her thighs tense and shaking as they gathered speed.

"You okay back there?" Owen called over the engine and the wind.

She leaned into his ear to tell him she was fine, catching a whiff of his hair—soap and motor oil and an earthy loam that seemed to come from deep inside of him. Her throat went dry.

The track dipped and crested, Owen riding it like a wave. She felt herself moving with him, anticipating the way his body responded to each bump and curve in the track, pressing into him in the turns and relaxing against him as they flew straight and sure over the rises.

She hadn't understood motocross the few times she'd visited the track with Janie before, but riding with Owen made perfect sense. The bike was more than a machine: It was an animal that sensed confidence or fear and reacted to even the slightest touch, that could be gentle and relenting or deadly, depending on how you treated it. And she could tell from the sure, solid feeling of the bike beneath them, from the way it responded to even his tiniest movement, that Owen was a good rider.

He called something out to her, a question, but it was lost in the wind.

"Yes," she blurted.

She spent so much time saying no that the syllable felt strange and liberating on her tongue. The wind whipped against her face and Owen's scent danced around her and the bike picked up speed, and next thing she knew there was no more track under their wheels, just air and wind and the engine's wild vibrating. A scream rose in her throat (of fear or delight, she could hardly tell the difference), but she shut her mouth around it, swallowing it back.

Owen yanked the bike hard to a stop, a curtain of dirt rising around them. Daphne heard a strange, high-pitched sound and realized she was laughing. She could still feel her body vibrating as he cut the engine and she reluctantly removed her arms from around him, stepping shakily onto solid ground.

"Oh my God," she said, fumbling for the strap to undo her helmet. "That was amazing. Really. I can't believe you actually took that jump . . ."

"Let me get that." Owen reached down and unbuckled the helmet, lifting it gently from her face. The brush of his fingers on her cheek sent a jolt of adrenalin down her spine so strong it eclipsed the feeling of flying through the air. "So what do you say, Daphne?" he said, his voice husky. "Do you believe in motocross?"

She smiled. "I believe."

"'Atta girl."

A voice like sneakers screeching against a gym floor interrupted their moment. "And just what the hell do you think you're doing?"

Doug stood a few feet away, a bottle of Jack in one meaty hand and an angry scowl in his eyes. His entire crew was behind him—Trey, Bryce, Ted, Jed, Mike, and Mike, and a whole sea of others—and Janie stood nervously by his side, her eyes wide as lakes.

Owen's smile went a shade cooler as he climbed off the bike. "Just testing out your track. It's a nice one."

"With her?" Doug pointed at Daphne, his face shiny from rage and booze.

Owen shrugged. "Why not?"

"Because she's my girl's cousin, that's why not." Doug weaved slightly, jabbing his finger in the air.

"And?" Owen asked mildly. He obviously wasn't cowed by Doug's bullying—he actually looked kind of amused.

"And nobody here knows you, or trusts you."

Daphne couldn't believe what she was hearing. Anger flared hot and sharp in her belly, replacing the vibrating warmth from the ride. She stepped forward.

"*I* know him," she said.

It took the words an extra moment or two to penetrate Doug's thick skull. He reeled slightly, as if buffeted by the wind.

"You do?" he asked.

"We work together." Daphne crossed her arms. "I'm the one who told him about the meet tonight. If you guys even plan to ride."

"Oh, we're gonna ride all right." Doug contemplated the last inch of Jack sloshing in the bottle, then shoved it at Janie. He stepped forward, puffing up his chest. "You want to ride? I'll race you—and I'll beat you so hard you won't—"

His eyes bulged, and a sudden, burp blossomed from his chest like a foghorn. Daphne watched Janie struggle to suppress a giggle, covering her mouth with the back of her hand.

"You were saying?" Owen asked when he finished.

"I was saying I'm gonna race you," Doug continued, undaunted.

"No." The voice came from next to Doug's elbow, quiet but sure. "Let me."

16

TREY STEPPED FORWARD, OUT OF the shadows. He stared hard at Daphne, and she could read the hurt saturating his eyes like a stain. She glanced from him to Owen and then back again, realizing her mistake. He must have seen the way she looked at Owen, how she didn't think twice about climbing onto his bike and wrapping her arms around his chest, less than an hour after she'd told Trey she could hardly bear to be touched.

She tried to make eye contact, to tell him it was all just a mistake, but Trey deliberately avoided her eyes, staring ahead of him like she was made of stone.

"Hah." Doug laughed like an engine turning over and over, unable to start. "Good call. Show him what he gets for trying to steal your girl."

"Trey and I are just friends," Daphne insisted.

But nobody was paying attention. Doug reached into his back pocket and yanked out his wallet. "I'll even put money down." He turned to Owen. "You got a hundred bucks to spare? 'Cause I can't wait to take your money."

"Doug, no!" Janie grasped at his elbow. "A hundred bucks? Are you crazy?"

"Whatever, baby, we're about to be so rich a Benjamin's pocket change." Doug grasped a few twenties, waving them in the air. "So how about it, buddy?" he said to Owen. "You want to get your ass handed to you and pay for the privilege?"

"I'll race him, if that's what you mean." Owen's voice was calm. "And I'll meet your wager, too."

"Let's see it," Doug spat.

Owen produced a well-worn wallet and showed Doug the money. It was the last of his winnings from the last race back in Salt Lake City, the emergency money that was supposed to tide him and Luna over until he got his first paycheck, but he didn't think he'd have a hard time beating Trey. The buzz of competition pounded through his veins, the same powerful need to conquer the track that had driven him across every finish line since he'd left Kansas. He didn't think Carbon County was going to be any different.

He turned to Trey. "You ready, man? Want to go get your bike?"

Trey looked suddenly small.

"Yeah," he croaked. But he stayed rooted to the ground, worry and machismo fighting for control of his face. Daphne thought of how expertly Owen handled the track, the way he made the bike buck and hum like a well-trained beast beneath him. With Trey's uncertain, amateur style, and the spill he'd taken on her first night in town, she knew he didn't stand a chance.

She approached him cautiously, forcing herself to rest her hand on his arm, to touch him the way she couldn't earlier. Maybe she could make it better that way. "Trey," she said softly. "Are you sure you want to do this?"

He yanked his arm away like she was made of the plague. "Yes, I want to fucking do this," he spat.

Behind her, Doug cackled. "Hey, man, use my bike," he boomed, clapping his hand down on Trey's shoulder. "We all know it's better than your piece of crap anyway."

The cold from the metal bleachers seemed to seep into Daphne's blood as Trey and Owen took their places at the starting line. They had agreed to five laps around the track, to be judged on speed only—the first man to cross the finish line won.

She could sense Owen's loose confidence from where she sat. He straddled his bike easily, rolling his shoulders back to loosen up as the Carbon County regulars flitted around Trey like flies on a rotting piece of fruit, offering last-minute tips and encouragement.

Perched on Doug's massive dirt bike, Trey appeared tiny. His helmet swallowed his head, making him look like a mushroom, and Daphne could see the tension in his shoulders as he hunched forward to check the gears.

"Hey, Daphne." Hilary tapped her on the shoulder. "You rode with that new guy back there—is he any good?"

"Yeah." She bit her lip. "He's really good."

"Great." Hilary sighed theatrically, shaking her corkscrew curls. "Trey's gonna get his ass handed to him."

"I'm sure he'll do fine," Janie said primly. "He's been getting a lot better lately, and Doug's bike is the best."

Hilary waited until Janie had turned away, then pointed at her head and made the universal sign for "cuckoo," circling her finger next to her ear.

Down on the track, two engines roared to life.

"Ready?" Doug's voice floated up to them. Two helmets— Owen's black and Trey's orange—nodded.

"Get set . . ." Doug warned.

They tensed, straining forward, hands poised over the throttle.

"Go!"

The starting bell blasted, and they were off, two streaks of metal and exhaust flashing through the night.

They kept pace until the first turn, their bikes synched like two sets of wheels on a car. At the first bend, Trey kicked up a gear and pulled forward. A cheer rolled up from the boys huddled around the starting line, and it seemed to propel Trey even further. His orange helmet was a bike's length ahead of Owen, then two, and the cheer turned into a guttural roar.

Daphne's breath caught in her throat. Had she been wrong about Owen? Riding behind him, she'd been sure he was good—better than anyone Carbon County had ever seen. But it wasn't like she was the world's leading expert on motocross. Maybe she'd been so distracted by the way he made her feel that she'd missed something crucial about the way he rode.

Trey accelerated around the second bend, rims flashing. He was nearly four lengths ahead, body straining forward on the bike. Behind him, Owen seemed in no hurry to catch up. He had settled into the saddle and was taking it at a leisurely trot rather than Trey's full-tilt canter. Even his arms seemed loose and relaxed on the handlebars.

The track dipped after the second bend, then climbed sharply to a jump. Trey, all the way out of the saddle, nudged his bike into a higher gear, making it buzz like an insect trapped under a glass.

Behind him, Owen picked up speed on the bend. The acceleration propelled him down the dip and up again in one smooth swoop. The crowd's cheers turned to gasps as he overtook Trey on the jump, soaring forward with the even grace of a hawk and landing with only the slightest bounce several lengths ahead.

Seeing he'd been edged out of the lead, Trey forced his bike into a higher gear. He swerved through the engine's angry jolts but managed to straighten out before hitting the whoop, a section of track sculpted into small, even bumps like ripples on the surface of a pond. His helmet bobbed as he jangled and jittered over them, trying to make up lost ground.

But Owen had already cleared the last jump and was heading into the final stretch. He dipped through the hairpin turns, wheels turning up elegant sprays of dirt, and crossed back over the starting line into his second lap.

Daphne realized she'd been holding her breath. She let it out in a shaky rasp and pulled her knees into her chest, trying to redistribute some of the cold racing through her blood. The girls around her were silent—in her peripheral vision she could see their teeth nervously chewing frosted lower lips.

Trey swung his bike crazily through the final hairpins, wheels fishtailing in the dirt. His desperation was obvious going into the second lap. He took the straightest path possible through the first turn, veering wildly and flinging mud in the spokes of Doug's precious rims. He seemed to throb with rage at Owen, who was already sailing across the first jump, torqueing his front wheel to let the extra air carry him into the next turn.

Trey gunned the jump too soon and almost flipped on the landing, his front wheel ramming painfully into the earth. There was a collective gasp in the bleachers and the angry scream of Trey's gears as he forced his rear wheel to the ground.

He jostled over the whoop like a cowboy losing a fight with a bucking bronco, each tiny bump tossing him further forward on his seat until he was nearly over the handlebars going into the next turn.

"Sit back, fool!" Hilary hissed. Her voice was strained and frozen in the chilly evening. Down at the starting line, the guys were shouting similar encouragements, yelling for him to get it together, sit back, grab the bike with his knees.

"Beat him, you goddamn pansy!" Daphne heard Doug screech.

Trey jerked his body back as the bike surged forward, a beast determined to throw its rider. The wheels slid to the right, lilting at a forty-five-degree angle as Trey struggled to regain his balance. He was heading for the big jump, trying to ramp up speed on the incline even as he flailed back and forth on the seat. Owen had already crossed the finish line a second time and was coming up behind him, cruising comfortably. It was clear to everyone who the better rider was . . . everyone, it seemed, but Trey.

He launched into the jump, just clearing the lip and barely getting any air, and landed with a thud at the lowest point of the dip. As he yanked furiously at the gears, Owen rocketed over his head, the chrome accents on his bike twinkling like stars.

Trey sizzled with anger. He lurched over the whoop and slammed open the throttle, flinging himself into the turn.

His wheels skidded away from him, sending up a geyser of dirt. He threw himself into the skid, but it was too late—the bike went screaming off the track, tumbling over itself once and then again as Trey held desperately to the handlebars, refusing to let go and admit himself the loser once and for all. He trailed behind the bike, his body flapping in the dirt: first orange, then brown with dust, then streaked with red.

A wail went up from the starting line as Trey and the bike, by then one intricately tangled object, crashed to the side of the track. There was a silent, collective moment of horror as they thundered to a stop in a pricker bush. Trey lay still, beaten and bloody with the bike on top of him, custom rims still spinning.

Daphne had already gotten to her feet when the tangle of limbs and hot metal burst into flames.

17

THE FIRE SHOT RED AND angry into the sky. It consumed the pricker bush in moments, filling the air with thick plumes of acrid black smoke. Crouched in the bleachers, somewhere between sitting and standing, Daphne watched the outline of Trey's body flicker in the blistering heat, helmet melting into the flames as the bike glowed a molten crimson. He lay motionless—if the impact hadn't killed him, it would be only minutes until the fire did.

Up ahead on the track, Owen cut his motor abruptly. In the sudden silence, the only sounds were the dry crackling of flames engulfing the bush, the bike, and the boy. Everyone seemed frozen in disbelief, useless and immobile. A fireball rolled out from somewhere deep in the inferno and exploded into the air, obliterating the bike's gas tank with a boom that resonated deep in Daphne's stomach.

Owen leapt off his bike, knocking it to the side. He took a shaky step toward Trey, then another. Silhouetted against the flames, he looked larger than life and black as oil—his skin glowed with a dark energy that seemed to rob the night of moonlight, to soak in all the heat and noise from the flames. He walked toward the fire without flinching, beyond where it seemed possible for a human to go.

Daphne waited for him to turn or crumble, to start coughing and drop to the ground, but he stood straight and tall. Eddies of flame lapped at his boots as he reached toward the fire, his steady hand glowing with an unnatural dark light.

Janie screamed a high, haunted note. That broke the spell. Suddenly everyone was rushing and scrambling, running in all directions and yelling and swearing. Doug led the pack, barreling onto the track with the force of a dump truck, eyes squinted against the glare in angry slits. Just as Owen's hand started to pass through the flames, Doug tackled him, yowling with rage as they thudded to the ground in a cloud of dust. His fists were everywhere, oversized feet kicking at anything they could reach, massive knee pinning Owen to the ground.

"Doug, stop!" Janie cried. Daphne grabbed her hand, cold sweat prickling the backs of her knees as they rushed down the incline, slipping on dirt and patchy grass.

Doug grunted heavily as he swung at Owen, grimacing as his fists landed on leather, packed dirt, and flesh. Owen squirmed beneath him, trying to wriggle out from under his bulk, only his helmet protecting him from the force of Doug's fists. Both of his arms were pinned, his legs flailing uselessly under Doug's weight. As he struggled, he seemed to glow with an even darker luminosity, as if the heat from the nearby fire was inside his skin and trying to escape.

With what little strength he had left, he jerked his body forward, his shoulder connecting with Doug's chest. Doug's mouth opened in a cavern of surprise as the impact shuddered through him—and then he was in the air, as high as he'd ever gotten on his bike, all six feet and 240 pounds of him cartwheeling backward. Doug's arms and legs waved helplessly before he landed on his back several feet away, launching a cloud of dirt into the air.

"What the—?" he bayed, clawing at the ground as he struggled to sit up. He spat dirt and glared at Owen, eyes hateful slits. "What the hell are you, man?"

"Baby!" Janie ran to him, mud splattering the backs of her calves. She got to her knees and wrapped her arms around his shoulders. "Are you okay?"

Doug stared at her, jaw trembling, as if he'd temporarily forgotten who she was. Then he buried his head in her chest, quaking like a volcano, muffled sobs erupting from between her breasts.

"Shhhhh," Janie cooed, stroking his crew cut. "You're okay, baby. Everything's going to be okay."

"He killed Trey!" Daphne heard him sob into her chest. A crowd gathered around them, eyes darting nervously from the couple embracing on the ground to the fire still lapping at Trey's blackened body. She saw Hilary take out her phone and call 911, her voice detached and oddly formal as she explained that they'd need an ambulance at the motocross track.

The air stank of burnt rubber and singed hair, and Daphne had to sit down suddenly in the dirt, stomach churning. Earlier that evening, she and Trey had been drinking beers on Doug's tailgate. Now he was dead. The image of him rolling into the pricker bush, limbs and chrome entangled in a bloody mess, played over and over in her head. She had to will herself not to be sick.

She couldn't escape the feeling that the whole thing was her fault. If she hadn't rejected Trey . . . if she hadn't turned around and gone riding with Owen . . . if she'd insisted that Trey not race . . . maybe he'd still be alive. Her mother's words echoed in her head: *You're a murderer—you know it and I know it and the Lord knows it.* Maybe Myra was right. Now she had two deaths on her hands . . . and unlike Jim, Trey had done nothing to deserve it.

A few feet away, Owen stirred. He sat up and looked at Daphne, dazed. His skin no longer glowed in the firelight—in fact, he looked paler than ever.

"Are you okay?" he asked groggily.

"I don't know." A cold sweat had soaked through her tank top and she was shivering violently, her stomach cramping with grief. "I can't believe he's . . ." She couldn't bring herself to say the word.

Instead she watched Owen pat his arms and legs, checking for broken bones.

"What about you?" she asked. "What happened back there, anyway?"

Owen shook his head slowly. "I'm not sure," he admitted. "I passed him on the jump, and next thing I knew he wasn't behind me. I wanted to help him, but then Doug . . ." he trailed off, trying to piece together the details.

"You threw him," Daphne prompted. "You sent him flying. How did you even do that?" It still didn't seem possible that Owen could have tossed Doug off of him like that—he was smaller, he was pinned, and even if he was twice Doug's size, it didn't seem physically possible to throw a human that high and that far, with that much force.

Owen shrugged. "Adrenalin, I guess. I've heard it can make you crazy strong."

"I guess," Daphne said. She'd heard stories of mothers lifting cars off their children, of kidnapping victims clawing their way out of locked basements, but it still seemed hard to believe.

From off in the distance an ambulance wailed, the faint ululation growing louder and closer as red shadows began to chase each other over the low hills and across the sky. Then the Carbon County volunteer fire department was there, dousing the fire and carefully covering Trey's charred remains with a sheet while several police cars screeched into the parking lot. The county sheriff circulated the crowd, issuing tickets for riding drunk and reckless endangerment, warning the shell-shocked crowd that if they were caught drinking and riding one more time, the track would be closed permanently.

Up in the parking lot, engines roared to life as the crowd departed one by one. Doug sat huddled in a blanket, clutching a bottle of water and answering questions from the local sheriff, Janie still standing with a protective arm over his shoulders.

"Hey." Daphne looked up to see Owen standing beside her. "You want a ride home?"

She looked over at Janie—she and Doug were still deep in conversation with the sheriff, and between the two of them she was pretty sure they could talk all night. She knew she should stay with them. But she could feel her answer forming, hurling forward with the force of a geyser.

"Yes," she said.

She stood and brushed the dirt off her pants, and together they headed for the parking lot.

18

HER FACE, REFLECTED IN THE window of his truck as they drove silently through the dark night, looked like a ghost. It flickered in and out of focus as Owen navigated around turns and over potholes, making her feel like only half of a person, like she belonged to two worlds: the cozy daytime world of Janie and the Peytons, and a dark underworld where human life could be snuffed out as fast as a dirt bike skidding through a turn.

"It's not your fault."

Owen's voice was soft and somber in the quiet cab, but it still made her jump.

"What do you mean?" she asked, even though she knew. He'd seen her talk to Trey before the race, and he must have guessed how responsible she felt for his death.

"I've been riding motocross for most of my life," he said. "And I've seen plenty of people get hurt on the track. People get stupid or careless, they don't know their own limits. It's never anybody's fault but their own."

Daphne nodded, biting her lip. She knew, rationally, that was the case with Trey, that he'd accepted a challenge he shouldn't have and refused to back down when he was in over his head, but she couldn't pin the blame on him. He was dead, and she was still alive.

Owen sighed, his hands resting loosely on the steering wheel. "I'll just keep telling myself that," he said softly. "I never should have gone up against him. That was one time winning wasn't worth it."

In the dim glow of his headlights on the country road, Owen looked as troubled as she felt. She tore her eyes away from his profile only to catch the glow of their faces in the windshield, both pale and haunted, spectral twins in the night. Maybe it was the shared sense of guilt, their implicit roles in the evening's horrible events, that made her feel drawn to him. It was the only explanation she could accept, the only way to make sense of whatever it was that was buzzing between them in the car: The feeling of being filled to the brim, threatening to spill over, to dislodge something inside of her that had been locked away for most of her life.

He stopped opposite the Peytons' trailer, his motor humming quietly.

"Thanks for the ride," she said, unbuckling her seatbelt.

He turned to her, his lips parting to form a question, or maybe just to wish her goodnight. She paused, waiting for him to gather his thoughts. But instead of speaking, he lunged forward, piercing that pocket of stillness and bringing his lips to hers.

The hot print of his hand on her cheek, his mouth on hers, detonated something inside of her, igniting emotions she didn't even know she had and sending them spiraling through her like the last embers of a firework dying in the sky. Owen's lips were soft and warm, feathery and enticing, exactly the opposite of how she'd always expected a kiss to be. For a moment she just let it happen. The kiss set her skin aflame and plummeted through her nervous system, sparking along the way until it felt like her entire body was singing. Then reality plunged like an anvil to her stomach.

"Stop," she gasped, pushing him away.

Owen sat back, breathing heavily. Longing hung like smoke between them, choking the truck's cab.

Her heart felt like a bird smacking against a windowpane. "This is not okay. Trey just *died*."

"I'm sorry," Owen said. "I shouldn't have."

"No, you shouldn't have!" Her voice was sharp. She couldn't believe she'd come so close to giving herself up, to letting Owen take what she was never willing to give. She'd spent her whole life protecting it, against Jim and the drunks who came stumbling into the 7-Eleven and jerks like Doug—and Owen had just come and practically waltzed away with it, like the piece of herself she'd guarded so fiercely for so long was just a cheap knick-knack you could pick up at the dollar store.

He dropped a hand onto the steering wheel and laughed a soft, ironic laugh. "I'm usually pretty good with girls."

"I'm not like other girls." Her voice cut through the haze that had cluttered her head.

"So I've noticed." Owen smiled a slow half smile, making her stomach twist and leap. But she forced her eyes to stay stony.

"No, really," she said, quiet but firm. "I don't do this—not now, not ever."

He looked at her quizzically, eyes glowing softly in the dark. "Isn't that a little extreme?"

"I have to go," she said quickly, ignoring the question—and the way his lips looked forming it. Lips that had just been on hers. Kissing her. Making her insides bloom with fire. "I'll see you around."

And before he could protest, she was scrambling out of the truck and slamming the door behind her, running across the road so fast that it felt like she'd left a part of herself on the other side.

19

THE SUN BEAT DOWN ON the funeral party like a cruel joke. It was the first truly warm day of the season, the air so clear Daphne could make out the bald-cut top of Elk Mountain from the cemetery behind the church, and rivulets of sweat trickled down her back, trapped in the black polyester dress she'd bought for her trial and hoped she'd never have to wear again.

Pastor Ted stood at the foot of the open grave, his face pink and slick with perspiration. "The other day, our community suffered a serious loss." His voice cracked with emotion. "Trey Stonehouse, a young man in his prime, was called home to God."

In the chair next to Daphne's, Janie sniffled and swiped half-heartedly at her nose, her Kleenex already streaked with melted makeup. Doug reached for her hand, and she squeezed it tightly. He'd been quiet since Trey's death, almost comatose, but the way his lip kept twitching back into a snarl sent an uneasy prickle up the back of Daphne's neck. His eyes were red-rimmed and bloodshot, boiling with a quiet rage.

Pastor Ted's voice gained strength. "Trey was quiet and hardworking, always putting friends and family first. He was dedicated and loyal."

The evening of Trey's death played miserably in Daphne's mind, ending with the memory of Owen's lips on hers. The whole thing sent a wrench of guilt twisting through her stomach.

"Trey was a true child of God, a true citizen of Carbon County," Pastor Ted continued. "He represented what's best about this place—what we have to hold on to when things start to change.

"Because change is coming—it's already here. As the oil flows and our pockets bulge with riches, we may be tempted to forget the values that make us God's chosen people. Our humility. Our community. And, above all else, our commitment to God. Do you believe?"

"I believe," the congregation murmured. A sob caught in Janie's throat, and Doug squeezed her hand tighter, his face darkening.

"Let us remember that this oil is God's gift to the Children of God—our reward for doing His will and living His message. We can use it as a bargaining chip with the devil, making cheap deals with outside forces for our own personal gain, or we can use it for good, donating it to God and our community like Floyd Peyton has done with his generous gift to our church. We can let Trey's death be a message and continue living as he would have wanted: as glorious beings in the eyes of the Lord."

Pastor Trey's head snapped up, blue eyes bright as the sky. "What will it be, Carbon County? Will we let this boy die in vain, or will we hear God's message? Will we make deals with the devil, or will we follow God's plan for us? Do we still believe?"

"We still believe!" the congregation chanted.

"God rewarded us with this oil, but now He's testing us." Pastor Ted's voice sizzled like bacon frying in a pan. "If we fail and fall to sin, you know where we're going—straight to Hell, do not pass go, do not collect two hundred dollars. But even if we pass God's test this time, there will be more tests to come. I pray that we won't lose any more of our own, but I also believe in my heart and soul that this is just the beginning and that someday even this pain will pass, and we will receive the greatest reward of all. Do you believe?"

"I believe!" Daphne opened her mouth to say the words, but they still wouldn't come. Trey was dead because he'd been reckless—because she'd *driven* him to be reckless. It wasn't because of God. It was because of *her*.

Pastor Ted bent his head. "Now, let us pray."

Janie's back heaved as she mouthed the prayer along with Pastor Ted, tears dripping off the tip of her nose and splattering onto the tissue forgotten in her lap.

Doug bent his head too, but his mouth stayed shut. He trembled slightly, his massive frame shaking like an earthquake, his neck an angry red.

"Does anyone have words to share about the departed?" Pastor Ted asked gently, bringing the prayer to an end.

"I got something to say." Doug jumped to his feet, toppling his chair. His neck cracked as his head swept the room.

"Trey was a good guy," he continued. "The best. He was my best friend. And now he's gone."

He took a deep, shaky breath. Janie reached up and patted his hand encouragingly, but he yanked it away.

"And it's his fault!" Doug pointed a quivering finger at the back of the cemetery, to the knot of latecomers standing behind the last row of chairs.

Daphne followed the trajectory of his finger and saw Owen at the edge of the crowd, Luna by his side. Flames of recognition leapt in her chest at the sight of him, licking with a mixture of anger and excitement as she remembered the way he'd lunged at her in the cab of his truck. Both Owen and Luna were clad in black: he in a simple button-down shirt, and she in a diaphanous dress that floated in gauzy layers around her ankles. There were dark circles under Owen's eyes.

"That devil you were talking about, the one from the outside world—that's him, right there." Doug jabbed his finger in the air. "He's the reason Trey's dead."

Owen's gaze dropped to his shoes. He shifted from one foot to the other, letting the attack wash over him.

"Are you people just going to let him get away with it?" Doug's face darkened to the color of a bruise. "He should be in jail—or driven out of town! A guy like that doesn't belong here. He already killed Trey; who knows what else he'll do?"

He sat down abruptly, shoulders heaving. Next to him, Janie reached out a hand to pat his shoulder, but seemed to think better of it. Her frosted fingernails hovered in midair, then folded back into her lap. She shrank further away from her boyfriend, the sadness in her eyes tinged with a new uncertainty. She looked afraid.

"Young man." Pastor Ted's voice arched over the crowd, landing at Owen's feet. "Do you have anything to say?"

Owen gazed out at the sea of strangers, wilting and miserable in the relentless sunshine. They had twisted in their chairs to get a better look at him, and their faces were damp with sweat and tears. He had nothing to say, but he could feel their collective need for words to make sense of something as senseless as Trey's death. He cleared his throat.

"I'm Owen Green," he began. "I'm new in town, and I appreciate all the hospitality Carbon County has shown me."

The crowd shifted in their seats, damp and curious. It was suddenly, vitally important that they believe him.

"I was racing Trey when he died," he continued. "I was in front of him when he crashed, and I stopped my bike to try to help him. Unfortunately, I was too late."

The memory of Trey's body, twisted and blackened in the flames, blazed in his brain. He remembered approaching the burning pricker bush, reaching out his hand—but he remembered something else, too. In that moment, he'd been sure he'd seen that very image (flesh and metal enmeshed together, twisting smoke and whirling flames) before. Many times before. Since his eighteenth birthday, it had haunted his dreams, and since the terrible night of Trey's death he'd barely been able to sleep, terrified that it meant his other night visions, the piles of bodies and whirling demons and endless, flickering flames, might someday come true as well.

The congregation's sweat-slick faces stared up at him, ghostly white in the harsh sunlight. He had to continue. He owed it to them.

"I never really knew Trey, and I'm sorry I didn't get to know him. I'm sorry for any part I played in his death. To his friends and family: I know you lost someone you care about deeply, and I'm sorry for your loss. I know I can't bring him back, but if there's anything I can do to make it better, I promise you I will."

His eyes dropped back to the ground as the congregation sighed and shifted. He felt their anger dissipating, floating off into the mountains on a warm summer breeze, leaving only a stagnant sadness.

Only Doug still seethed. Owen could see it in the tight way his shoulders hunched and his elbows dug into his knees, in the snarl that never seemed to leave his lips. He imagined Doug would always hate him, and probably would have even if Trey were alive and well. He knew he posed a threat to guys like Doug, guys who wanted to be the best on the track but weren't willing to put in the time and the elbow grease, to give up parties and friends and girls. There was one at every track, and he'd learned long ago that all he could do was give them a wide berth and try not to rub it in their faces when he inevitably won.

A panting sob broke the silence. In the front row, Trey's mother rose to her feet, narrow shoulders heaving. Her nose had the same small hook as Trey's, and tears had streaked the concealer under her eyes, revealing bruise-dark circles.

"I wish you could bring my son back," she said shakily. Owen nodded, holding her gaze. "But I know you can't—and I believe that it wasn't your fault." Tears leaked from her eyes. "I forgive you," she whispered, before crumbling in a volley of sobs.

Her husband, gray as a pillar of ashes, rose beside her. Putting a protective arm around her shoulder, he trained his eyes on Owen. His voice was hoarse and raw.

"*We* forgive you," he amended. "It's what God would want. What Trey would want."

He covered his face with one hand and sank quickly into his seat, his wife's peroxided head disappearing into the crowd next to him.

"Thank you," Owen said quietly.

Pastor Ted nodded. "Let us finish with Psalm Twenty-Three," he said. Their voices rose—thin and mournful, muffled by tears and shattered by shock—into the close, sunbaked air.

↔

After the service, the mourners circled the funeral parlor's beige reception hall, nibbling on refreshments and offering muted condolences.

Daphne perched on the edge of a stiff floral sofa, picking pieces of celery out of her egg salad. With Doug and Janie comforting Trey's parents and Karen and Floyd talking to Pastor Ted, she felt alone and exposed. She sensed curious eyes on her, the outsider they believed had brought them trumpets from heaven and oil to save their hometown, but they quickly shifted their gazes whenever they caught her looking.

After a while she slipped out a side door and into the cemetery, where the sun still shone relentlessly on the headstones. The rows were straight and the grass was freshly mowed, yet the headstones stuck out at odd angles and a few trees poked their way up around the perimeter, throwing welcome shade on the hot afternoon. She picked an aisle at random and wandered down it, reading the names: Peyton, Varley, LaClaire, Johnston.

She stopped at a small gravestone, calculating the age of the deceased. *Jonah Peyton, 1923–31. Now you shall sing among the angels,* it read. Her hands went clammy: Jonah Peyton must have been one of her relatives, and he'd only been eight years old when he died.

"Hey." It was Owen, his voice apologetic. "Sorry to sneak up on you—I just saw you leave, and I wanted to . . ."

"It's okay." She felt herself blushing, remembering her harsh words before she hurried away from the truck. She could see why Owen might have thought she'd overreacted. To any other girl, a kiss was just a kiss. To her, it was an uncross-able divide.

"Can I walk with you?"

She nodded, biting her lip to keep the blaze from rising to her cheeks, and Owen fell into step beside her. As they made their slow way down the row, she became unbearably conscious of the few inches of space between their shoulders. It shimmered in the heat, galvanized like an electrical charge.

"I'm sorry about the other night," he began. "I guess I just got carried away. I heard people respond that way to death sometimes."

"What way?"

"You know." Owen ducked his head, sending a wave of black hair falling over one eye. "Physically. It's almost, like, a way to refute death."

"Is that all you were doing? Trying to refute death?"

He paused at the end of the row, meeting her eyes. "Is that all you wanted me to be doing?"

She blinked hard. If that was the only reason Owen had kissed her, then it meant he didn't have any feelings for her. He was just being a guy, doing what humans do. As long as he promised not to do it again, she was safe around him. She wouldn't have to shut him out completely, the way she had with every man who tried to take advantage of her in her past.

"Yes," she said firmly.

He shrugged. "Then that's all it was."

"Good." The word came out sounding hollow.

They reached the end of the row, and she ducked into the shade of an oak tree, leaning against the trunk and letting the spread of branches provide a welcome respite from the blaring sun. "I'm glad we can be friends."

"Me too." He joined her under the tree, their bare arms brushing casually as the heat flattened them against the trunk. The tiny hairs on her skin stood at attention, straining toward his touch. She ignored them. "I could use all the friends I can get right about now," he said with a small laugh.

She nodded. "I'm kind of surprised you want to stay here, after everything. You're not exactly the most popular guy in town right now."

"I don't really care about that." Owen tilted his head so their faces were only inches apart. "There are motocross guys all over

America who hate my guts. I'm used to it. The weird thing is, I feel like I'm *supposed* to be here. Even after what happened to Trey, I don't think I can leave."

He wondered if he should tell her about the gnawing ache that had sent him prowling the great American West, the voice in his dreams that had whispered *find the vein* until the day his truck pulled into Elmer's Gas 'n' Grocery and he saw her face for the first time.

But Daphne was nodding slowly. "I know what you mean," she said. "When I left Detroit, this was the only place I wanted to come. I didn't really feel okay until I got here."

"And then you struck oil," he teased. He slipped his hands into his pockets, making his arm rub against hers.

"How many times do I have to say it? *I* didn't strike oil," she corrected him. "It was all Uncle Floyd. I just happened to be there."

"You sure? I overheard some people in there talking about it." Owen gestured toward the funeral parlor. "They think you're pretty special—maybe even blessed." His tone was gentle, joking.

"People around here take Pastor Ted a little too seriously," she replied. "I think he's been looking for something to call a sign from God since way before I came around."

"You may be right," Owen said after a silence. She could smell the clean, minty scent of his shampoo and the hint of metal and motor oil that she guessed must live in the under-layers of his skin. "About Pastor Ted and all that. But I've got to say, when I heard people in there talking about you?" He squinted at her. "I kinda knew what they meant."

"What do you mean?"

"You are different," he said, nudging her. "Special, or whatever. Maybe it's why I got carried away the other night."

Daphne frowned, shaking her head. "You don't even know me—"

"There you are!" a voice called from the direction of the funeral home.

Daphne's head snapped up. A dark, diaphanous shape was floating down the funeral parlor stairs.

"I can't get over the food here," Luna laughed, coming closer. She carried a plate of the green Jell-O salad that elderly Eunice made for every church gathering; maraschino cherries and chunks of canned peaches clung to the inside as the mound jiggled violently. "It's total art."

Luna glided through the graveyard like a circus act, impervious to the shadowy presence of the dead. The wilting heat made her glitter even brighter, her body flowing and languid in the sultry afternoon.

"Ready to go?" She placed a slender hand on Owen's shoulder. "If we split now, we can see if there's an air conditioner for sale anywhere in this town."

Owen looked at Daphne almost apologetically. "We're going crazy in this heat," he explained.

"Crazy," Luna repeated emphatically, steering Owen toward the parking lot.

He locked eyes with Daphne as Luna carted him off. "See you at work tomorrow?"

Daphne shrugged. "Okay," she murmured.

He looked back at her as Luna led him away.

"Wish us luck!" Luna called.

Daphne felt suddenly exhausted as she watched them leave, two dark panthers loping away through the afternoon. Loose ends of thoughts tangled in her brain, unwilling to tie themselves into neat little knots—Trey's death, Owen's kiss, Luna's strut, the oil that turned to blood on Owen's hand, Doug's anger, Owen's feeling that he was meant to be here and the eerie way it echoed her own. Everything kept coming back to Owen, no matter how hard she tried to push him out of her mind. And it seemed like instead of escaping the trouble she'd found in Detroit, she was finding even more in sleepy Carbon County.

She let her thoughts pull her down until she was sitting with her back against the oak tree's solid trunk, sweat cooling on her forehead in the shade. Soon she'd get up and go back to the funeral parlor, ready to comfort Janie and make small talk with Karen's friends, ready to face a town that had somehow made her into something she wasn't. But for now, for just a few minutes longer, she was happy to stay quiet and unseen, a shadow among the dead.

20

AFTER THE FUNERAL, SUMMER SWEPT through Carbon County like a traveling carnival, turning the dry brown grass in front of the Peyton's trailer a garish green. Cotton candy–colored blooms sprouted on the cherry trees in the town square, where birds cawed like midway barkers hawking plastic jewelry and overstuffed toys, and the townspeople hung out brightly striped awnings to shade their front doors.

A week into the heat wave, it was steamy even inside the Peytons' trailer, and the strawberry ice pops that Janie craved constantly melted faster than she could eat them, leaving her fingers sticky and unnaturally red:

"You look like you stabbed a clown," Daphne joked, coming across her cousin slurping the last viscous dregs off the bottom of the wrapper.

"Seriously, if a clown messed with me right now, I might." Janie waddled to the sink, running cool water over her hands. "You try being seven months pregnant in a heat wave."

A strong and insistent knock sounded at the front door, rattling the trailer on its cinderblock risers.

"Ugh, what now?" Janie groaned. "Can you grab it? It's probably someone from the rig looking for Dad."

Daphne opened the door, expecting to find Dale or one of her coworkers. Instead, she came face to face with the Varleys.

"Is Floyd around?" Vince asked. A man with thin-rimmed glasses and oatmeal-colored hair stood between him and Deirdre, wearing a camel-colored suit and carrying a briefcase.

"He's down at the rig." Something about the man in suit made Daphne uneasy—he reminded her of the colorless, humorless drones carrying briefcases through the courthouse halls during her trial, his suit too clean and pressed for Carbon County's casual, backcountry ways. "I can go get him if you want."

"Great," Vince Varley said coolly. "In the meantime, how about letting us in? It's hot as a bull's nuts out here."

Daphne called for Janie and Karen as they filed past her, Deirdre sniffing with distaste at the trailer's décor.

"Oh!" Karen came running from the bedroom, where she'd been folding laundry. "Vince and Deirdre, what a pleasant surprise! I wish you'd called, the place is a mess, but come on in. Can I make you some lemonade?"

As they settled into the living room, Daphne ran down to the rig to fetch Uncle Floyd. By the time they returned, the Varleys had arranged themselves around the coffee table and were sipping Crystal Light from gas station glasses, the man in the suit still clutching his briefcase and Deirdre fanning herself with a copy of Karen's *Good Housekeeping* magazine.

"Vince, Deirdre, a pleasure to see you!" Floyd Peyton's T-shirt was streaked with dust and sweat, his hair standing out in all directions. He turned to the man in the camel-colored suit. "And you are—?"

"Elbert Benton, attorney at law." He rose and offered his hand.

"Hope you don't mind if I wash up before I shake—I've been going over the drill procedures all morning." Floyd poured dish soap over his hands and splashed them under the faucet, drying them on a dishtowel before pumping the lawyer's hand.

"I have some papers for you to sign regarding the oil." Elbert Benton snapped open his briefcase. "All boilerplate, of course—just to make your agreement with my client official."

"Vince always did stick by his paperwork," Floyd said with a laugh. He thumbed through the thick pile of papers. "There sure is a lot in here."

Elbert Benton cleared his throat. "Let me paraphrase," he said.

Vince and Deirdre leaned forward hungrily. From the kitchen, where she'd fixed herself a glass of Crystal Light, Daphne could sense how eager they were for Floyd to sign.

"It basically just says that you relinquish half the profits of the rig to the Varleys here—everything else is just a bunch of legalese."

"Just like you said after church the other week," Vince interjected quickly. "Just like we shook on."

"Right." Floyd reached for the pen Elbert Benton proffered. "Vince, I know you care about Carbon County as much as I do, so I'm sure you'll be putting a pretty penny back into our community. It wouldn't be right to keep all that for yourself while the town flounders."

"Sure," Vince nodded. "Of course. So you'll sign?"

"Well," Floyd grinned. "I am a man of my word." He poised the pen over the paper, ready to sign.

The sickly-sweet lemonade seared Daphne's throat as she flashed back to the tense days before her trial. If there was one thing her court-appointed lawyer had taught her, it was to be careful what you signed. *If you want to win this thing,* he'd said, zipping into her cell with a cup of lukewarm tomato soup in one hand and an overflowing case file in the other, *you won't sign, say, or even* think *anything without asking me first. Someone puts a paper in front of you, don't even pick up a pen until I give you the okay.*

"I need you to sign a few places," Elbert Benton said. "First, here . . ."

He pointed at a large black *X.* Floyd's pen hovered over it.

Daphne knew it wasn't her place to tell Uncle Floyd what to do, but he'd never been through the legal system the way she had. She couldn't just let him sign something he hadn't even read himself, let alone shared with an attorney of his own—especially something from people as slimy as the Varleys. The Peytons had done so much for her, even as she was covering up the seamy details of her past. The least she could do was make sure they weren't taken advantage of.

She scanned the room. Vince and Deirdre were on the edges of their seats, excitement and greed dancing in their eyes. Janie simply looked hot and bored, disappointed that the Varleys had shown up without Doug. Only Aunt Karen was frowning, her mouth puckered with concern.

Daphne looked around for a distraction—anything she could say or do to prolong the moment, to keep Floyd from signing the papers. Her eyes landed on the pitcher of Crystal Light sweating on the counter. "Would anyone like some more lemonade?" she practically yelped.

Floyd paused, the pen a millimeter above the page. "I believe I would," he said. "It sure is hot out there, isn't it?" He turned to the Varleys for confirmation, but all they could do was nod icily, eyes glittering with frustration.

Daphne's hand trembled as she rushed to Floyd's side. She bent to pour him the lemonade and whispered the only words she could think of in his ear: "Can we talk before you sign that?"

Floyd drew back, surprised. "Why, sure," he said out loud. "Now?"

Daphne flushed. She wished the exchange could have been subtler, but it was the best she could do with the Varleys and their lawyer sitting two feet away. She nodded.

Floyd got to his feet, looking befuddled. "Excuse me," he said. "I need to have a quick word with my family."

Deirdre's smile crumbled, and Vince let out a long exhalation that sounded like the hiss of air escaping a leaky tire. Daphne ignored them as she led the way to the master bedroom at the back of the trailer, Floyd and Karen behind her and a grunting Janie taking up the rear.

"What's this all about?" Floyd asked when they'd closed the door, one bushy eyebrow cocked.

Daphne looked at Karen, hoping she'd take the lead, but her aunt simply sank onto the bed and sighed.

"Daphne?" Floyd turned to her.

"I think you should have a lawyer look that over before you sign." The words tumbled out of her in a harsh whisper—the walls in the trailer were thin, and the Varleys had already heard enough. "You have no idea what's really in that contract, and it's not like they're going to give you the whole story."

"Oh, I don't know about all that." Floyd's eyebrows drew together in a fluffy V. "I made them a fair offer, and you know how Vince is—he just likes to dot all his i's."

"And *you* should, too," Daphne urged. "Get a lawyer of your own."

Floyd looked troubled. "Vince and I go way back," he said. "I know he wouldn't try to cheat me. He's owed this, really—if it weren't for his grandfather's gift, none of this would have happened."

Daphne couldn't shake the feeling that the Varleys had something up their sleeve—the looks in their eyes were too eager, too hungry, too calculating. But Floyd seemed determined to think only the best of everyone. An old proverb tugged at her memory, something about the world being the mirror to the soul. What if Floyd was right, and she only saw the evil in the Varleys because she was a bad person herself?

"I'm not saying you shouldn't sign it," she said. "I just think you should have a lawyer look at it first. He can actually tell you what all those pages really mean, and negotiate to make sure everything is fair on your end."

She noticed them looking at her strangely, probably wondering how she knew so much. "I used to watch a lot of *Law and Order*," she added quickly.

"Oh, Floyd, why don't you at least sleep on it?" Karen broke in. She'd twisted the hem of her sweatshirt between her fingers like a balloon animal, and the worry lines in her face were deep. She'd known the Varleys as long as Floyd had, and Daphne wondered if she knew something about them that Floyd didn't, or saw something he simply didn't want to see.

Floyd seemed to notice his wife's concern for the first time. "Is this really troubling you?" he asked.

"Yes." Karen gave her sweatshirt another twist. "I don't know what it is, but something about this just gives me a funny feeling. I wish you wouldn't go rushing into things."

"Then I'll sleep on it." Floyd kissed the top of her head, and Karen's fingers relaxed.

."You'll have to work on me to hire a lawyer of my own, though," he continued. "I like to think I can make my own deals."

He opened the door and started back toward the living room, Janie behind him. In the narrow hallway, Karen squeezed Daphne's hand.

"Thank you," she whispered in her ear. "At least it's a start."

"Happy to help," she whispered back. The Peytons were good people—better than she deserved.

↔

The Varleys had been having a hushed conversation of their own. They quieted as soon as Floyd entered the room, staring up at him expectantly.

"Get everything cleared up?" Elbert Benton's voice was mild, but there was a steel rod running through its center.

"Yes, well, y'see . . ." Floyd scratched his chin, where salt-and-pepper stubble had sprouted since his last shave. "If you don't mind, I'd like to sit with this a spell." He tapped the contract, which sat open on the coffee table, the pen resting on top of the dotted line. "I'll read it over tonight and have an answer for you tomorrow."

"Now, Floyd," Vince began.

His lawyer shushed him with a look. "Of course," he said, standing abruptly. "Take all the time you need."

Daphne noticed Deirdre shoot the lawyer daggers beneath her pencil-thin eyebrows, but Elbert Benton ignored her. "Here's my card." He produced a silver box from his breast pocket and offered Floyd a cream-colored square of paper. "Don't hesitate to call me if you have any questions."

"Well, thanks." Floyd turned it over in his hands as the Varleys stood and gathered their things. "Thanks for stopping by. Vince and Deirdre, it was good to see you, as always."

"The pleasure was ours," Deirdre said tightly. They were nearly out the door when Vince turned, one hand on the knob. Heat shimmered around him like a nest of translucent snakes.

"Don't forget, Floyd: You're a man of your word."

He turned and shut the door forcefully behind him, and they were gone.

↔

The air outside the Peyton's trailer had gotten hotter; the Buick's door felt like a frying pan left too long on a hot stovetop.

"He was about to sign," Vince muttered, buckling his seatbelt with a vicious click.

"Well, what do you expect from the Peytons?" Deirdre sniffed. "They're being selfish, like the trash they are."

"It's that girl." Vince backed out quickly, honking long and loud at a slow-moving water truck. All that money under their feet, and he'd be lucky if he got to see a pretty penny of it. "He was about to sign, and she put a bug in his ear. I saw her do it."

"If I may," Elbert interjected. He was the best idea Vince had ever had, a real city lawyer from Laramie who specialized in partnerships and contracts. "From here on out, we need to be strategic. Let's assume that Mr. Peyton reads that contract—"

"Big assumption," Vince snorted. In all the time he'd known him, Floyd had hardly been one to crack a book.

"Or, worst case scenario, he hires a lawyer." Elbert's eyes sparked behind his thin-rimmed glasses. He actually seemed to like this stuff, this endless speculating game of cat-and-mouse. Vince didn't care one way or the other, as long as he was always the cat.

"Any lawyer worth his salt would kill that contract on the spot," Elbert continued. "It's full of traps and skews grossly in your favor. Then I'll have to negotiate, which will take months, possibly years. If that's the case, you'll be lucky to end up with ten percent, let alone fifty."

"*Years?*" Deirdre shrieked from the backseat. "To only get ten percent? We can't afford that—we've already borrowed over a million to build our chateau!"

Elbert ignored her. "Our other option is to put together a lawsuit."

Vince nodded. He liked the sound of that. "Tell me more."

Elbert's face took on the sheen of a freshly minted penny. "It's risky, of course, but with a good lawyer, anything is possible. If I do my job correctly—and, Mr. Varley, I always do—you may get the lion's share of this oil fortune."

"That's the first good news I've heard all day," Vince grunted.

"Of course, we'll need to be vigilant," Elbert continued. "You say the bun in that young lady's oven is a Varley?"

"It's my son's," Vince confirmed bitterly. He'd warned Doug time and again to be careful with the girls—he'd wanted more for him than a life like his own, stuck in Carbon County as a young dad while big, exciting things happened out there in the rest of the world. That it had been dumb, busty Janie Peyton who ensnared his only son, with her cubic zirconium crucifix and pious belief that God Himself wanted her to have the child, had been the bitter icing on the cake. Until now.

"I'd recommend making that relationship official as soon as possible," Elbert said. "The closer your family is to the Peytons, the easier this will be."

"And by official, you mean . . . ?" Deirdre let the question float free in the Buick's chilled air. Vince knew that she knew what Elbert meant, and he wasn't sure he liked it any more than she did. Carbon County wasn't a wealthy town, but some folks did a little better than others. The Peytons had always been poor as dirt, and that trailer of theirs with the rotting auto parts and rusted lawn chairs scattered around their sorry excuse for a yard was the eyesore of the town.

But things had changed. White trash had struck black gold, and now they were Carbon County royalty. Whatever happened in the past, all the Varleys could do now was try to accept it—and, more importantly, cash in.

He met his wife's eyes in the rearview mirror. They were saucer-wide, her lashes trembling with shock.

"Deirdre," he said, striving to keep his voice firm. "It's time for you to take Doug ring shopping."

21

ON THE PULLOUT SOFA IN the Peytons' living room, Daphne's eyes snapped open. The trailer was still shrouded in milky darkness, the furniture quiet black shapes. But someone was there, tiptoeing around, making the floor vibrate almost imperceptibly.

She shot upright, instinctively curling her hands into fists, ready to fight off the intruder. The cold fear of memory gripped her throat, reminding her of the times Jim had managed to jimmy the cheap lock on her bedroom door and creep in while she was sleeping.

"Who's there?" she whispered.

"Shhh." The voice came from the kitchen. She whipped her head around.

"It's me—Uncle Floyd."

Her shoulders un-tensed as her eyes slowly adjusted to the darkness. She made out his outline, sitting over a bowl of cereal at the kitchen's banquette, hair still damp from his shower.

"What time is it?" she asked.

"It's early. Go back to sleep. I can go eat outside."

"It's okay." The adrenalin hadn't stopped surging through her veins, and sleep was a distant dream. She padded over to him, helping herself to a bowl of Froot Loops.

"Why are you up so early?" She pushed the cereal down with her spoon, soaking it in milk before bringing it to her mouth. The sudden sugar rush erased the last of slumber's dryness from her tongue.

He shrugged sheepishly. "I've got a lot on my mind."

"Is it the contract?" She tried to make out his eyes in the dimness.

He sighed. "That's part of it. Vince has that lawyer calling me up just about every day—and, to be honest, I can't make head or tails of all that legalese. It's like a whole other language."

"That's why you need a lawyer of your own," Daphne insisted. "To tell you if it's fair."

"Oh, I'm sure it's fair." Floyd looked uncomfortable. "I'm being plenty generous—why would Vince want to cheat me? But that's not the main reason I'm up." He seemed eager to change the subject. "Mostly, I was just too excited about the day ahead of us to sleep."

Of course. It was marked on the calendar in the admin shed with a big red *X*, the day they were to start extracting oil. "I guess it's a pretty big deal, huh?" she said.

"The biggest day of my life, since Janie was born." He leaned forward, elbows digging into the linoleum tabletop. "Daphne,

I know things've been busy around here lately, and we haven't really had a chance to sit down and have a proper talk, just you and me."

"It's all right." Her cereal was dissolving, leaving swirls of pink and green in the milk. "We've both been busy with the rig."

"Well, see, that's the thing." Uncle Floyd ran his hand self-consciously through his hair. "I feel like I haven't thanked you properly. There wouldn't even *be* a rig if it weren't for you."

"That's not true . . ." Daphne began. But Floyd hurried over her words, anxious to let his thoughts spill onto the table.

"There's something special about you, Daphne, something . . . *chosen*. Everything changed the day you came to stay—first there were those trumpets, and then you led us to this blessed gift, this oil. It's not just me whose life this is going to change: It's everyone in this town. You don't know how much we needed this."

His eyes were intense in the weak blue light from the kitchen window. Daphne shook her head. He had it all wrong. She'd killed a man and covered it up so the Peytons would take her in. She wasn't a blessing. If anything, she was a curse.

"Let me tell you something about Carbon County." Floyd sat back on the banquette and crossed his arms. "Before you showed up, our town budget was half a million dollars in the red. We were going to have to close the school, lay off those poor hardworking teachers, and bus all the kids to Rawlins. Our septic system wasn't up to code, but there was no money to fix it. Carbon County needed this oil like a dying man needs water, and we found it because of you."

Daphne sat back, stunned, as Floyd placed an urgent hand on hers. "We needed you here, Daphne. And you came to us just when we needed you the most."

Conflicting emotions struggled for purchase in her mind. She didn't believe that stabbing a dipstick into the earth in a fit of anger made her blessed, and she still couldn't understand why Uncle Floyd thought it did. He'd always been so rational, so down-to-earth, that it was hard to understand how he saw divine intervention in a fact as physical as the oil.

But the urgency in his eyes and the weight of his hand made her reconsider. For the first time in her life, she wasn't a burden: Instead of enduring her mother's hateful looks and Jim's sneers, she was being thanked. She was needed. Floyd had said so himself. And as odd as it felt, it also filled her with warmth.

"I guess you're welcome," she whispered.

Floyd patted her hand. Sunrise had begun to streak the sky outside the window, striping the horizon with shades of peach marmalade.

"I hope you remember that when we start pumping today—and not just today, but always. This is all here because of you, Daphne. You're more special than you realize."

The rest of the morning was a flurry of activity as they prepared to start extracting. By the time Daphne joined the rig crew in front of the derrick, her T-shirt was caked in grease and her hair was a damp and tangled mess under her hard hat.

All their hard work over the past few weeks had paid off. The derrick was up, a webbed steel monolith rising ten stories into the sky, with thick pipes running up its center and a flare stack to burn off the excess gasses at the very top. It sat atop a squat concrete building that housed the bulk of the machinery, the engines that powered the drilling mechanism and the pumps and flow lines that pushed drilling mud down and brought oil to the surface. Around the rig, a flat square of earth had been stripped of grass and trees, so that the area looked like a baking patch of death against the towering green of the mountain range.

Uncle Floyd stood before the crew, looking solemn. He'd changed out of his usual flannel shirt and Carharts and donned a suit and bowtie for the occasion, and the Northwestern VP of Global Oil stood mopping his brow next to him.

"I just wanted to say a few words to you all before we start her up," Uncle Floyd said to the assembled crew. "This is like a dream come true. I'm"—he paused and fumbled in his breast pocket, producing a well-creased sheet of notebook paper—"I'm humbled to help bring such blessings to Carbon County," he read. "And I wanted to thank all of you so much for busting your tails to make this happen. I want to thank Global Oil and all the good people who work for them, particularly Dale for hiring such a wonderful crew. And I want to thank my niece Daphne for not only being one of the hardest-working members of our team, but for having faith in my crazy notion that there might be oil in this here ground— and for leading our community to this gift like Moses leading the people out of Egypt."

Daphne felt her coworkers' eyes on her, and her face went hot.

"But most of all, I want to thank the Lord," Floyd said. "When we first saw that oil bubbling out of the ground, I knew He had a plan for us. It made me believe—well, even harder than I've ever believed before.

"We're gonna start extracting in just a few minutes, and it's going to change this town forever. I believe it's going to make our lives a whole lot better. But I hope one thing about this town never changes: our faith. I know this ain't common in situations like this, but I hope you'll pray with me for just a moment here. Let's all thank God for his blessings, okay?"

He closed his eyes and bent his head, and Daphne followed suit. She listened to the rare silence around the rig, wondering what it felt like to really pray. It seemed to bring the Peytons so much comfort, but to her it seemed as useless as screaming into the sky.

"Thank you," Uncle Floyd said finally, quietly. The crew shifted and breathed. "And now let's fire this baby up!"

Dale barked a quick series of orders, and the crew scattered like ants, scurrying around the base of the derrick and positioning themselves to start turning the huge metal wheel that would activate the drilling. Daphne stood with Owen and the rest of the roustabouts near the equipment sheds, ready to grab whatever the floorhands and engineers needed. Excitement swelled in her chest. She'd gotten to know the rig intimately while they were building it, to understand the vast network of pipes and valves and gears that would keep it pumping day and night, but she had still never seen it in action. The rig would usher in a whole new era of prosperity for a town that had desperately needed it—and maybe, in some small way, she was responsible.

"Ready?" Floyd asked Dale.

"Ready!" he shouted.

"Okay." Floyd addressed the roustabouts. "I want you all to count down from three with me. Are you ready?"

"Ready!" They called. Daphne looked around at their faces, hungry with an emotion she couldn't quite name. It seemed to swallow the air and charge it with desire, to send waves of commingled hopes and dreams and lusts and needs radiating out into the sky, where they coalesced on a single, massive object: the rig.

Floyd held up three fingers. "Three!" he chanted along with them.

He raised his hand high into the heavens, so it was silhouetted against the brilliant blue sky. He dropped one finger, making a momentary peace sign.

"Two!"

The crew roiled with energy, and Daphne felt their frenzy. This was it—Carbon County was about to change forever.

"One!" They all screamed together.

For a moment, there was absolute silence. A bird chirped, and then there was a great mechanical clanging and a rush of motors starting up loud as jet engines.

The floorhands scrambled over and around the rig, pulling levers and hoisting pipes and frantically screwing and unscrewing gaskets, and deep in the pit of the rig the machinery began to pump rhythmically, dipping into the ground and emerging with a brief shuddering eruption before plunging back in again.

The roustabouts cheered, and Daphne joined them. The rig was working: drilling deep into the earth and bringing up barrels and barrels worth of rich, black oil. She felt her own face stretch into a smile, her hands come together in applause.

She looked over at Uncle Floyd, but he was staring up at the flare stack, the worry lines between his bushy eyebrows deep as tire tracks on a muddy road. Why wasn't he smiling like everyone else?

As she followed his gaze, a sound like a stampede of wild horses ripped through the flare stack, exploding from the top in a fireball of sudden, blistering heat and blinding light.

Plumes of flame erupted from the flare tower, shooting molten fire into the sky and sending a deluge of red-burning natural gas plummeting toward the rig. Uncle Floyd's face was frozen in horror as thick black smoke swirled through the rain of flames and Daphne realized with a sick shock what was happening: The pressure of the excess gas was too great for the narrow pipes in the flare stack. All of the gas was trying to shoot up from underground at once, turning what was supposed to be a controlled burn into an unbridled blaze.

Floorhands dropped to the ground at their feet like bombs, racing from the rig one after another, the skin on their faces and arms already blistering from the heat. They crawled away, choking on smoke and gasping for air.

Daphne turned and saw Owen standing open-mouthed and enraptured, his eyes glazed over as if the billowing flames had him in a trance. "Come on!" she screamed, taking his hand and dragging him back. He shook his head quickly, seeming to register her for the first time.

"Fire . . ." he said slowly.

"We need to put it out!" she rushed through the knot of roustabouts, grabbing whomever she could. "Purple K's in the safety shed—let's go."

The safety shed was the closest to the derrick, a fire hose thick and heavy as an anaconda coiled on its wall. She grabbed the end, grunting under its weight, and began lugging it toward the blaze. A moment later, she felt the pressure on her shoulders slacken as

Owen and the other roustabouts fell into line behind her, grabbing sections of the hose.

Pointing its tip at the roiling spumes of flame still tumbling from the stack, Daphne released a blast of Purple K, a chemical fire suppressant that filled the air with what looked like a massive cloud of violet cotton candy.

The flames met the Purple K with a hiss and sizzle like a dragon dying. Violet smoke choked the air, and Daphne had to close her eyes against the sudden sting. When she opened them, Owen was dousing the last of the mutant fireball with a final blast of chemicals. Floorhands raced into the rig's guts, struggling three at a time to turn the huge wheel that would lock the valve into place, choking off the extra output of gas until the flame atop the flare stack burned even and controlled.

Her heart pattered erratically as they began coiling the hose.

"Thanks for saving my ass back there," Owen murmured, his breath feathering against Daphne's ear. "I don't know what came over me, looking into those flames."

Daphne opened her mouth to respond, to say that he'd looked like he was in a trance, but before the words were out of her mouth Dale was upon them like a hurricane, his hard hat pulled low over his trademark scowl.

"That never should have happened," he muttered, head close to Floyd's. "We calculated everything—the velocity, the pressure. There must be way more oil under there than we realized."

He turned quickly to Daphne, clapping a hand on her shoulder. "Way to save the day, though, kid," he said. "Today I'm thinking you're just about the best hire I ever made."

"Thanks," she murmured, still not quite processing what had happened. There had been fire, and she'd known what to do, had remembered from their safety training and been the first to act. She'd been able to stop chaos in its tracks.

Floyd joined them, draping an arm over her shoulders. "Well, that was some way to get 'er going, wasn't it?" His voice was hearty, though the back of his suit was drenched with sweat.

"You can darn well say that again." Dale shook his head, squinting up at the flickering flame. "I'm just glad nobody was hurt."

"Well, if you ask me, it's a good sign—maybe even an omen from God." Floyd stared wonderingly into the rig's machinery, a slow smile spreading across his face. "Judging from that little blast, there's enough oil in this ground to make that flame up there burn for all eternity."

A gleeful hoot came from the back of the crowd. Someone else took it up, and soon the entire crew was cheering, waving their hands in the air and giving shrill, two-fingered whistles.

Her face black with soot and eyes still stinging from smoke, Daphne joined them.

22

"WILL THAT BE ALL, MISS?"

Janie looked down at her shopping cart, which was piled high with infant clothes and stuffed animals, soft toys and the most adorable little terrycloth bath hoods shaped like monkeys and frogs.

"I guess so." She smiled her sunniest smile as the Babies "R" Us cashier began to swipe her items, the numbers on the register going up and up. It was okay for her to keep smiling, she told herself as the numbers went past a hundred, then 130. She had her dad's credit card, the new gold one that had come in the mail just the other day, and her mom had said to put as much on there as she wanted. Things were different now. They were rich.

The cashier lifted an infant car seat out of the shopping cart, and the number on the register soared to 225. Janie's smile faltered, then dropped entirely. She loved shopping almost as much as she loved Jesus, but she could swear on His cross she'd never spent that much in one go in her life. It felt wrong to just waltz into the mall and pick up whatever her heart desired, without going around to every dollar store and looking online for a deal first.

But things were changing, just like Pastor Ted said, and her son wouldn't have to grow up wearing off-brand labels. She put her hand on her belly and felt the warmth of the tiny life growing inside of her, the miniature person she already loved more than anyone else in the world.

"When are you due?" the cashier asked.

"September sixth." Janie reluctantly looked up from her belly. "Gosh, it's so soon!"

The cashier smiled sympathetically. "Don't worry—you'll be ready." She nodded at the overflowing bags in Janie's cart. "And if not, you can always come back."

"I guess so—it's a trip, though!"

"You're not from Cheyenne?" The cashier gently arranged a diaper pail and baby monitor in one of the bags.

"Nope," Janie shook her head. "I'm, like, three hours away, in Carbon County."

The cashier froze. "Where they found the oil?"

"Uh-huh—right in our backyard!"

"Oh." Something cooled in the cashier's smile, which had been wide as a summer sky just moments before. "That must be nice." She dropped her eyes and busied herself bagging the final items. "That'll be four hundred seventy-three forty-nine, please," she said briskly, not meeting Janie's eyes.

For a second, Janie thought she'd have to pick her jaw up from the floor. It was more money than she'd ever spent on anything in her life, almost more than she'd even thought it was possible to spend. Her fingers trembled as she reached for the new gold credit card, and she suddenly felt like one of those spoiled, snobby girls on the reality shows, the ones who went throwing daddy's money around like it grew on trees and then had tantrums when they didn't get the car they wanted for their sixteenth birthday.

Was that why the cashier had gone so cold all of a sudden— because she thought Janie was a rich snot like those girls? She felt like explaining that her family still lived in a trailer, and that she'd take a strong hug and a prayer over all the fancy baby clothes in the world any day of the week. But she shouldn't have to explain herself to this girl! What right did she have to go judging Janie just because her family had gotten lucky?

She signed the receipt, thanked the girl in the most clipped and formal voice she could muster, and hustled her shopping cart on out of there, struggling to keep the wheels from fishtailing on the floor.

In the shade of a fake palm tree near the mall's food court, she lowered herself onto a bench and texted Doug. He'd gone into Cheyenne to find a new dirt bike and asked her to come with him, suggesting she could pick up a few things for the baby—and since it was the first time he'd really asked her to do anything since Trey's accident, she'd jumped at the chance.

There in 30, Doug texted back. *Wut r u wearing?*

She giggled into her palm, then looked around to see if anyone had seen. Doug was being cute and funny again—and it felt so good to see him getting his sense of humor back!

U know wut—same thing i wore here! she replied.

A second later, her phone buzzed.

Go buy urself a nice dress, the screen said. *Im takin u somewhere fancy 4 dinner.*

"Yay!" Janie squealed out loud, this time not caring if anyone heard. She couldn't believe Doug was turning the excursion into a real date. He'd never really been the romantic type—it just wasn't his thing, he was too much of a *guy*—and lately he'd barely even acted like a boyfriend. He'd been drinking more since Trey's death, his neck constantly red and his eyes puffy and bloodshot, and he'd been moodier than ever before. A couple of times, he'd flown off the handle for no reason, screaming at her and calling her a fat cow when all she wanted was to satisfy a perfectly normal pregnant-lady ice cream craving—and once he'd even raised his fist in anger, making her cower away from him in terror before he lowered it quickly and resumed his normal sneer of disgust. She figured it was just the way he grieved, that if she showed him enough patience and turned the other cheek he'd eventually come around. Now it looked like she'd been right.

Her ankles were swollen and beginning to ache, but she struggled to her feet and waddled through the mall to Mimi

Maternity, where she told the salesgirl she was going to a *really* fancy dinner and let herself be sold a floor-length black gown with a slit halfway up one side and silver sequins glittering on the neckline. It cost five times what she'd spent on her prom dress, but when she handed over the credit card, she only felt a tiny pang of guilt—much less than the tidal wave that had flattened her back at Babies "R" Us, although she still made a promise to herself that she'd make a big fat donation to the church when she got home.

She wore the dress out, stopping at Sephora to freshen her makeup with the free samples they left lying around everywhere, and even splurged on a pair of dangly black chandelier earrings that the guy at Kay Jewelers assured her looked *very* elegant. Waiting for Doug in the sheltered area outside the mall, watching the sunset turn the sky over Cheyenne into a big bowl of strawberry-peach yogurt, she felt like the star in one of those rom-coms about people in cities with really perfect hair. The air had cooled, sending a refreshing breeze skipping across the parking lot, and just before Doug's pickup pulled up she felt the baby kick, reminding her of the sacred bond that would keep her and Doug and their brand-new little family together for always.

Doug rolled down the window and let out a long, low wolf whistle when he saw her. "Hey, sexy," he called. "When I told you to buy something nice, I didn't think you'd come out looking *this* good!"

She glowed at the compliment. She always did her best to look hot for her man, but it wasn't every day that he noticed.

"Why, thank you, handsome." She fluttered her eyelashes. "You want to help me with these bags?"

Doug put the truck in park and hopped out. His hair was slicked back, and instead of his jeans he had on the dark blue suit he'd worn to their senior semiformal. He'd put on some weight since, and the seams cut in a little at his shoulders, but with his white shirt and dark tie he was still as great-looking as Janie had ever remembered him, the big, muscular hunk she'd fallen in love with her sophomore year.

"You buy the whole store?" he joked, loading bag after bag with the Babies "R" Us logo (and, okay, a few that said Mimi Maternity, too) into the truck.

"Just the good stuff." She leaned in and kissed him, breathing in Abercrombie cologne and that musky Doug smell that always got her kind of hot. "It's for our baby."

"I know it is," he said, helping her into the passenger's seat. "That kid's gonna be mad rich—first-generation oil money, like a boss."

Janie sat back happily as Doug maneuvered out of the parking lot and onto Prairie Avenue. It felt so good to have the old Doug back: the Doug who joked and laughed and noticed when she looked pretty, instead of the moody creature who had taken over her boyfriend's body practically the moment she'd announced she was pregnant. Sometimes it seemed like the more their child grew, the surlier Doug got, as if he was the one with hormones rushing all over the place instead of her.

She glanced over at him, stopped at a red light. He was nodding along to the hard rock song on the radio, his face scrunched up against the sun's low, orange glare. He had that look on his face—the tense one that meant that something was bothering him—but she shook it off. He was probably just squinting at the road.

"Where are you taking me, anyway?" she asked, fiddling with one of her new earrings.

"Somewhere special." His eyes didn't leave the road. "Like you."

He turned at a maroon sign that read *Luigi's Ristorante* in curly gold script, and stopped in front of a building with a fancy circular entrance supported by white columns. A man in a uniform with gold buttons rushed to open Janie's door, and she had to swallow a squeal of delight as he took her arm and helped her alight on the pavement. It was like a fairy tale: the red carpet, the potted shrubberies that twinkled with fairy lights, the glass doors beyond which she could hear muffled jazz music and laughter and the clink of glasses. People on TV went to places like Luigi's Ristorante all the time, but the closest Janie had ever been was the banquet hall of the Rawlins Holiday Inn for prom.

Maybe that would change, too, she thought as Doug came around the side of the truck and took her arm. Maybe being rich would be even better than she thought.

"I told you this place was nice," he said low in her ear.

The man in the coat with the gold buttons held the door open as Doug escorted her into the restaurant. Inside it smelled like garlic and roses, and a woman with milky skin and dark hair took their names and led them through a maze of tables where couples older than Janie's parents sipped wine and gazed at each other over flickering candlelight.

"It's like an American Express commercial!" she whispered in Doug's ear. He smiled tensely, obviously feeling out of his element: His shoulders were all hunched up, and he walked awkwardly in front of her, trying not to bump any of the tables.

"You like it here?" he asked once they were seated. Their table was at the back of the restaurant, under a trellis hung with imitation ivy and more twinkling fairy lights that made it feel like they were in an enchanted garden.

"It's beautiful," Janie breathed. A rush of gratitude caught in her throat, so strong that for a moment she thought she'd cry. Even in his grief over Trey, Doug was doing his best to make her happy. Even if he'd been tough to be around (and, okay, maybe a little scary sometimes), his moodiness hadn't been his fault. He'd just been upset about Trey. Soon he'd be over it and they'd be back to normal . . . maybe even *better* than normal.

A waiter in a white shirt with a long, black apron came by and introduced himself as Lorenzo. "May I start you off with some wine?" he asked, handing Doug a leather-bound book the size of the Peyton's photo album. Janie started to say no and gesture to her belly, but Doug cut her off.

"Yeah, uh, we'll have a bottle of red," he said.

"Of course, sir. May I ask which variety? We have one of the most extensive wine lists in the state." Lorenzo leaned over and flipped open the book, revealing what looked like an entire page written in Italian.

Panic flickered across Doug's face. Janie knew he was more of a beer kind of guy—the only time she'd ever seen him drink wine was when Bryce's parents had gone out of town for the weekend and they'd all chugged pink zinfandel until the ceiling spun and Janie had practically wet her pants laughing.

"Perhaps you'd like a Chianti," the waiter prompted, turning the page and pointing at a random set of words. "This bottle is very popular with our patrons—it's robust and flavorful but easy to drink, delicious with steak and meat-based pasta dishes."

"Sure, we'll take it." Doug was still squinting at the wine list, and Janie didn't blame him. An entire book, just for bottles of wine? It seemed insane.

"Are you going to drink the whole thing?" she teased after the waiter had floated away.

Doug colored. "Maybe." He cracked his neck from side to side. "It's, like, what you're supposed to do in places like this."

"I guess I can drive home if I have to," Janie offered. It was nearly three hours back to Carbon County, and working the clutch on Doug's truck made her ankles hurt, but she'd been extra sensitive about driving under the influence since Trey's accident.

A flash of anger darkened Doug's face, and she instinctively cowered away from him. Lately, it was like she never knew what he might do next—and she wasn't sure anymore of how to make it right. She was still fumbling for something cute to say, something that would scoop the magic of the evening right back up and into their laps where it belonged, when Lorenzo returned with a bottle in one hand and a corkscrew in the other. He made a big show of uncorking the wine at their table, flapping and flourishing like a flamingo, and then poured the tiniest little amount of wine Janie had ever seen into Doug's glass.

"Uh, okay, thanks." Doug eyed the magenta liquid distrustfully while the waiter hovered over them, still holding the bottle.

"Would you care to try it, sir?" he asked.

"Oh, uh, sure." Doug downed the wine in one gulp. "It's good?"

"Excellent." The waiter filled his glass halfway and then took their orders, assuring Doug that his steak would arrive as rare as was legally possible in the state of Wyoming.

"I can't wait to try that fettuccine Alfredo!" Janie reached across the table for Doug's hand. "It looks so amazing. I still can't believe we're really here—this place is like a dream!"

"Yeah." The wine had eased some of the tension from Doug's shoulders. He poured himself another glass, this time filling it almost to the rim—way higher than the waiter had, Janie noticed. She reminded herself not to say anything. At least he was drinking with her and not his buddies or who-knows-who-else.

"Did you find a bike you liked today?" she asked.

"You bet I did." Doug reached under the table and massaged her leg, sending a shiver running up it, straight to *there*. "This new baby's gonna be all custom—one hundred percent. I sat with the guy for a couple hours and we went over everything: It's gonna have a KTM one twenty-five cc two-stroke, titanium frame, all-leather seat and handlebar covers. Oh, and get this—he knows a detailer who can give me a custom paint job with Trey's initials. Like, in memory and stuff."

"That's so sweet of you." A ball of emotion rose in Janie's throat, thinking about the friend they'd both lost. Doug was so brave to want to remember him every single time he rode. Sometimes all she wanted to do was forget.

"Whatever." Doug downed the rest of his wine and reached for the bottle again. "What about you? Find good stuff for the baby?"

"So much cute stuff! I got a car seat and some onesies and this adorable stuffed giraffe and some chew toys and—is that what they're called for babies? Chew toys? Or is that for dogs?"

Doug snorted. "Heck if I know."

"Do infants even need chew toys? Or is that for older babies?" Janie thought of the colorful silicone rings sitting in their Babies "R" Us bag in Doug's truck. She hadn't actually checked the age on the box, and to tell the truth she'd barely skimmed the baby books Daphne checked out of the library for her. She'd just kind of assumed they'd figure it out as they went along. People had babies all the time: How hard could it be?

"I have no clue," Doug said. "I thought you knew all that stuff. You're the one who wanted to keep it so bad."

"Doug!" Janie felt her face go scarlet and her lips start to tremble. She was about to remind him which one of them had begged to try it without condoms when the food arrived, with silver domes over their plates that Lorenzo pulled aside like he was doing a magic trick.

"Now that's a steak," Doug said approvingly, watching the juices trickle out and darken his mashed potatoes.

Janie could barely wait for the waiter to finish sprinkling grated cheese and pepper from a mill the size of a grain silo onto her pasta before diving in. It was ten thousand times better than the Stouffers fettuccine Alfredo she liked to heat up in the microwave, with enough cheesy, creamy goodness to satisfy an entire week's worth of pregnancy cravings.

"Doug?" she looked up mid-bite, thick green noodles falling off her fork.

"Yeah?" he said around a mouthful of meat.

"You don't think we're too young to have a kid, do you?" she asked.

"Aw, babe." He swallowed his steak and went to work sawing off another hunk. "I don't know. And it's too late now, anyway. Why are you even asking?"

Janie let the rest of the noodles slide off her fork and back onto her plate. "I just want to make sure we're doing the right thing." She took a deep breath. If she and Doug were going to be parents together, she had to tell him everything—even stuff that made her feel icky inside.

"Me and Daphne saw this commercial about adoption the other day, and she asked if I'd ever consider it. I said no, of course— because, like, if God didn't want me to have this baby, why would He have let me get pregnant in the first place? But every once in a while, I realize that I don't even know if you're supposed to give an infant a chew toy or if they're even called chew toys or whatever, and I wonder if we really know what we're getting ourselves into."

Doug had stopped chewing. His mouth hung open, a slick of steak sauce visible on his tongue. "Daphne wanted you to give up the baby for adoption?"

"No!" Janie rushed to defend her cousin. "She totally didn't say that. She just asked. She told me it's always an option. But it's not, right? I mean, we *want* this baby. *God* wants us to have this baby!"

The words tumbled out of her mouth and tangled like the fettuccine on her plate.

Doug closed his mouth. She could almost see the thoughts somersaulting through his head, chasing each other and stumbling to abrupt halts like kids playing a game of freeze tag. She hadn't meant to turn their date into a big, deep philosophical conversation— sometimes she felt cursed by her own stupid tendency to always say what was on her mind.

When Doug opened his mouth again, the glossy sauce slick had disappeared. He poured himself the rest of the wine and took a long gulp.

"Babe." He put his hand over hers, making her feel tiny and protected. "Why are you even asking these questions now? We're having this baby, and we're keeping it. End of story."

She let herself melt under his touch, and tears teased at her throat. She hadn't realized how much it meant to her to hear him say those words: that he wanted the baby, too. That the three of them were going to be okay.

He leaned in and kissed her, a strong, sloppy kiss that tasted like wine and meat and something sour and nervous underneath. "Be right back," he said.

She watched his wide back disappear, weaving slightly in the maze of tables. At the front of the restaurant, he paused and said something to the hostess with the milky white skin. His face was close to hers, and his arm disappeared momentarily around her waist. Was he touching her? Jealousy snaked a burning path through Janie's gut—she knew Doug could be a flirt, and she accepted it as best she could, knowing he was devoted to her in his heart. But did he really have to flirt right in front of her, on the most romantic date they'd ever been on?

She sat quietly as the waiter cleared away their dishes, scraped the crumbs off their tablecloth with a device that looked like a silver straight razor, and handed her a smaller menu bound in rich brown leather.

"Whatcha want for dessert?" The chair opposite her scraped the floor as Doug sank back into it. There were beads of sweat on his forehead, and he hunched forward awkwardly, drumming his fingers on the table.

"Oh, I don't know." She rubbed her belly absently. "I'm so full from dinner, there's barely any room for the baby in there!"

His fingers paused above the tabletop, frozen like claws. "But you always get dessert."

"Yeah, and then you always make fun of how much weight I'm gonna have to lose!" she teased.

But Doug didn't smile. A bead of sweat trickled down the side of his cheek. "What about the chocolate lava cake?" he asked. "I heard it's the best here—better than anything in, like, Denver, even."

"Yeah?" Janie snuck another glance at the menu. As stuffed as she was from her meal, she did have a soft spot for chocolate . . .

"Just get it," Doug pressured. "You don't even have to eat the whole thing. Just take a bite or two."

"Fine," Janie laughed as the waiter appeared at their table. "He really wants me to get the chocolate cake, for some reason," she explained, gesturing at her boyfriend. "And who am I to say no?"

"An excellent choice, miss. And for you?"

"The banana split." Doug's face was slick with sweat—and maybe it was just a trick of the candlelight, but his skin looked almost green. Janie wondered if the bottle of wine had maybe been too much for him, and hoped he wouldn't get sick on the way home.

"Are you okay, babe?" She reached out and touched his forehead, but it was impossible to tell if he was feverish under the clammy feel of his skin.

"I'm fine." Doug's voice was strained. "Just, uh . . . it's hot in here, right?"

Janie shook her head. "I wonder if you're getting sick. We can skip dessert and just get out of here," she offered.

"No!" The word boomed through the restaurant, and several other diners turned to look at them. "Uh, our dessert is here anyway," he croaked.

The waiter set Doug's banana split down in front of him.

"Oh, that looks good!" Janie said. Her own dessert was coming, the waiter smiling like he had some huge secret as he placed it in front of her. It really did look scrumptious: thick, glistening chocolate surrounded by drizzled raspberry sauce, with a dollop of whipped cream and . . .

"Oh!" Janie cried. Another sound, something between a squeal and a deep, guttural sob, rose in her throat, and she was powerless to hold it back. Doug stood from his chair and came around to her side of the table, sinking to one knee beside her and taking her hand in his.

Time slowed down, and the world grew fuzzy around the edges.

The garnish on top of her chocolate lava cake was a diamond engagement ring.

The rock was the size of a maraschino cherry, bigger than any Janie had ever seen in person. It refracted the candlelight into a million dancing rainbows that flitted across the white expanse of their tabletop.

"Janie," Doug's voice sounded thick and faraway. "Will you marry me?"

Her back heaved, and tears streamed down her face. Everything was a blur: Doug's hand in hers, the expectant faces at the other tables, all turned to her, the candlelight and the music and the smell of roses.

"Yes!" she said. And then she was on her feet, squealing and crying and jumping up and down, her arms around Doug's shoulders and her feet kicking in the air as he lifted her off his feet, the sweat from his forehead licking at her face and the entire restaurant clapping and cheering.

"Doug Varley," she said when he finally put her down and they'd slipped the ring onto her finger and decided it fit. "You just made me the happiest girl in the world. That was the best dinner ever, and I can't wait to be your wife!"

23

THE SACK OF DRILLING MUD weighed seventy pounds, but it may as well have been seven hundred. Daphne struggled to keep it aloft, arms shaking, as she carried it from the forklift to the rig.

"Need a hand?"

Owen was waiting for her by the derrick, smiling devilishly.

She set the bag down with a thud. "A little late to ask now, isn't it?" Owen had been at her side all day, cracking jokes and making her laugh in spite of herself. She turned back to the forklift, Owen falling into step beside her.

"Allow me to escort you." He took her arm playfully, the rough leather of his work glove tickling the skin inside her elbow. His scent was strong in the hot, close day, that unexplainable combination of grease and metal and leathery earth overpowering the primordial smell of oil all around them.

"I can stroll unaccompanied, thank you very much." Daphne elbowed him lightly in the ribs, suppressing a smile as she tried to shake off his hand. But it remained on her arm until they reached the forklift, and she didn't try that hard to remove it.

"Are you two gonna work, or just stand there flirting all day?" Dale called, rushing by on his way to the admin shed.

Daphne leapt away from Owen, brushing his hand away like it was made of fire. "We weren't flirting!" she called after him. But Dale was already gone.

"You're going to get me in trouble," she complained to Owen, grabbing another bag of drilling mud.

Owen hefted a sack onto his shoulders. "If anyone gets you into trouble, Daphne, it'll be you."

She smiled. Work on the rig was still back-breaking, but she was secretly happy to be lugging mud next to Owen and away from the wedding madness that had taken over the Peytons' trailer. The Varleys wanted to rush the big day so the baby would be born to legally married parents, and had hired a wedding coordinator to plan the affair. Daphne came home each evening to find the trailer's tiny living room packed with caterers, decorators, or florists, and she couldn't sit down on the couch without Janie shoving a bridal magazine in her lap and asking for her opinion on page after page of bubblegum-pink wedding dresses. As far as Daphne was concerned, sweltering days on the rig were easier to tolerate than dress shopping.

A bead of sweat trickled into her eye, and she blinked reflexively, small explosions dancing behind her lids. In the scarlet darkness her toe hit something hard, pitching her forward and slamming her into Owen's back. Her eyes flew open as she teetered on the edge between standing and falling, the weight from the sack pulling her backward.

"What the—?" She righted herself and looked around, heaving the bag higher on her shoulders.

Owen had stopped in his tracks. His sack lay forgotten at his feet, and he gazed upward, one hand shading his eyes, mouth open in wonder.

"What, are you too good to work now?" she teased.

But Owen merely raised a finger, pointing at the sky. "Look," he said.

Daphne reluctantly followed his gaze. Her arms went limp and the bag of drilling mud fell to the ground with a hollow thud.

The sky was a mass of teal and fuchsia. At first it looked like a kite-flying contest, the clouds over Carbon County obscured by swooping streaks of color that danced on the air currents, trailing multi-hued streamers behind them. But then she heard the chirping. It nearly drowned out the jet-engine roar and clang from the rig, a cacophonous twittering like an orchestra of xylophones. As she looked closer, she realized that the kites' long tails were really feathers, and they weren't tethered to the ground by strings. A flock of birds, what seemed like hundreds of them, painted the air with wings the color of Froot Loops, dipping and soaring on air currents visible only to them.

Daphne felt the normal hustle and bustle of the rig chug to a halt, even as the drilling continued. One by one, the workers stopped to stare.

"What's going on?" Floyd called, dashing out of the admin trailer with Dale, a sheaf of papers forgotten in his hand. "What's everyone looking at . . . oh my Lord. Look at that."

The birds seemed to sense that they had an audience. Their sweeping tail feathers cut elegant curlicues in the air as they huddled into a tight tornado of color, chirping a cheerful call-and-response and beating their wings with enough force to send a stiff breeze blowing around the rig.

"Do you know what they are?" Daphne asked.

Floyd shook his head slowly, shading his face with one hand, his eyes never leaving the sky. "They look just like . . . but how?" he wondered aloud.

"Like what?" Dale asked. Even he seemed softened by the birds, a sight unlike any he'd seen in twenty years of working on rigs.

"Well, I watched a documentary once, on Animal Planet," Floyd said. "And God strike me dead if I'm wrong, but those look just like 'em. Birds of paradise, they're called. But they sure are a long way from home."

"Where's that at?" Dale scratched at the silver steel wool of his hair.

"New Guinea." Floyd's voice was gruff with astonishment. "In the South Pacific. It's a miracle that they got all the way up here."

Daphne could barely take her eyes off the flock. She wished the birds would stay forever: They were like an elaborately painted scene on a china teacup, and their chirping filled her with the kind of inexplicable joy that she'd felt as a child, climbing onto her mother's lap and smelling the faint scent of her jasmine perfume after a long day of play.

The birds, as if acting on an invisible signal from above, formed two loose lines and soared higher, heading toward Buzzard Road and downtown Carbon County.

"They're leaving!" one of the floorhands cried.

A sense of loss tugged at Daphne as she watched them go. She wished she could fly with them, borne along on whatever invisible breeze they'd ridden in on.

"Okay, all right everyone, birds 'r' gone, back to work!" Dale barked. "You think I pay you all to loaf around playing amateur ornithologist all day?"

Uncle Floyd stayed as the rest of the crew scattered, staring into the sky where the birds had been.

"This is another sign, I'm sure of it," he said to himself. He turned and saw Daphne looking up at him. "Don't you think?" he asked.

She gulped. The birds had stirred something powerful in her, a strange cocktail of joy and emotion. They made her want to believe in *something*. But she wasn't ready to accept God the way Uncle Floyd did. The concept was still too alien, too far from the misery she'd known for most of her life. How could she approach the purity of her uncle's belief with her stepfather's blood on her hands and the truth she'd concealed from the Peytons still stuck in her throat?

"I don't know," she said quietly. She didn't want to disappoint her uncle, but she didn't want to lie, either.

"You will," Uncle Floyd said. He gave her a quick kiss on the forehead before turning and walking away from her, back to the admin shed.

24

A LOUD BLAST OF A terrible country song smacked Owen in the face as he walked through the smoked-glass door of Pat's Bar. He'd been hauling gravel all day, and his shoulders felt like they were being branded with hot irons. He was exhausted, ready to fall into bed. If only he had his keys.

The air in Pat's was blue and stale, lit only by the neon signs that buzzed on every wall, advertising brands of beer that not only were no longer served but probably no longer existed. It smelled strongly of old beer and industrial-grade floor cleaner, and water stains spread ominously across the white office-style ceiling tiles.

Despite the lack of atmosphere, the bar was packed with prospectors. They tossed darts at a dingy board and played half-hearted rounds of pool, clutching sweaty bottles of Bud as they sat heavily around feeble card tables, commiserating over the day's failures. So far, Luna had confided in him, not one of them had even come close to striking oil. But that hadn't stopped anyone from trying.

Owen pulled up a barstool and waited to get Luna's attention. She was down at the other end of the bar, pouring shots for a grizzled pair of men in grease-stained jumpsuits. They pointed at the bottle and then at her, insisting she join them. Luna slid her eyes slyly left and then right, checking to make sure the coast was clear and the eponymous Pat wasn't around. Then she winked at the men and grabbed another shot glass, filling it to the brim with amber liquid. A naughty smile slid across her face as the men clinked their glasses against hers. But when they upended the whiskey into their mouths, Luna quickly tossed hers into the trash behind her. A moment later she was eye-to-eye with them again, laughing and wiping her mouth with the back of her hand, saying something that made them roar and slap each other on the back. She collected their money, blowing a kiss as she slipped a few generous bills into her tip jar. Then she turned and saw Owen.

"Hey, Earth Brother." She glided over to him, grabbing a beer and uncapping it and setting it on the bar in front of him with a single, effortless motion, like a dancer curtseying at the end of a ballet. "What's a handsome devil like you doing in a place like this?"

"I left my keys at home this morning," he explained, too tired to play along. "Can I borrow yours?"

Luna leaned on the bar, grinning. "Sure thing. I'm on break in twenty minutes—I can run next door and let you in. In the meantime, drink up."

He eyed the beer. "Is that for me?"

"Mmm-hmm. On the house."

"Thanks." He hadn't planned on drinking, but he'd learned that when it came to Luna, it was often easier to just give in. He wrapped his hand around the bottle, letting the cool condensation soothe his calloused palm.

Luna wiped the bar down with a rag until he could see his reflection in it, the hollows in his cheekbones and dark circles under his eyes. "You look tired, Earth Brother," she said. "Are you getting enough sleep?"

"Of course not." He looked up sharply. "I'm still having the dreams. Aren't you?"

She smiled. "Every night." Just mentioning them sent emerald flames dancing in her eyes, and he wondered for the millionth time if they bothered her the way they did him. She always spoke of the dreams as if they were sacred, in the same reverential tone she used to describe her childhood at the Children of the Earth.

He scratched at the label on his beer bottle, peeling it off in pieces. "Are the figures still there?" he asked. "Dancing around the fire?"

She held up a finger, signaling for him to wait while she poured a shot of tequila and handed it to a salivating goldfish of a man with round, sallow cheeks. Then she was back, leaning forward so their faces were level, her eyes mirroring his. "Are they still there for *you*?" she shot back.

He sighed. All he wanted was a straight answer, and he was too tired to play her games. "Yeah," he said dully. "And I'm starting to remember their faces."

He couldn't admit the terror that each reveal struck in him, the fear that paralyzed him as the figures turned, one by one, to show the faces that had always eluded him upon waking. Now they haunted him well past dawn and all through each day: The sharp chins and bony noses, the cheekbones like broken glass and the eyes, always green, always slanted, always an eerie mirror to his.

The eyes that now, on Luna, lit like fireflies. "But that's wonderful," she exclaimed softly. "You'll know them when they come."

"They're coming?" Her words made him go as cold as the beer bottle in his hand.

"Of course." She rolled her shoulders back, tilting her head to the side. "Don't you see? It's the rest of us, our Earth Brothers and Sisters. He's calling them here, just like he did with us."

"*Who's* calling us here?"

"You know who. Our father." She smiled like lava boiling inside a volcano. "The God of the Earth."

Owen stood hastily. "You don't really believe that crap," he said. Of her many quirks and eccentricities, Luna's steadfast insistence that their conception was a mystical ritual instead of a skeezy orgy in the woods was the most irritating.

But her gaze still sent a cold knife of panic slicing through him, a steel-bladed reminder that he hadn't come to Carbon County to hang around chasing enigmatic girls on an oil rig. He could have been touring the country on his bike, pocketing first-place winnings every weekend. But he was here, driven to the desolate valley by a voice in his dreams.

"It's not crap—and you believe it, too, Earth Brother."

"I don't believe anything," he said. As the words left his lips, he could almost hear the horrible, raspy voice in his head, the one that had woken him in a tangled sweat from countless nightmares. He couldn't deny that the dreams were real. The only question was where they were coming from—and why.

"You will soon." Luna's voice wrapped around him like a many-tentacled beast, moist and quiet in the din of the bar. "When the rest of us arrive to lead our army."

"*What* army?" Owen wanted to reach across the bar and grab Luna by her dreadlocks, to shake her until she started to make sense.

She smiled coyly. "You're looking at them." She spread her arms wide to indicate the prospectors downing beers and exchanging off-color jokes all around them.

"These guys?" Owen looked around the bar in disgust. "An army?"

"*Our* army." Luna's eyes gleamed. "I'm gathering them for him, getting them on our side. You'd be surprised how easy it is to manipulate guys like this. Guys with no other purpose in life but to get rich quick."

"You're going to manipulate them into becoming your *army?*" Owen asked sarcastically.

She gave him a long, withering look. Then she backed away slowly, the tree on her back shimmying as she oozed to the other end of the bar, every head turning to stare longingly.

She leaned over the polished bar top, close to a man with shaggy yellow hair and an unapologetic gleam of lust in his eye. Her teeth glinted as she smiled, and her bare shoulders gleamed in the light.

"You look like you could use a drink," she purred. His head jerked up and down like a puppet, his eyes fixed desperately on the taut, proud stretch of her collarbone.

"I think you want a Coors . . . and I think you want to pay double for it. Is that right?"

"Yessss," he hissed, reaching for her with trembling, yellowed fingernails. "Whatever you say."

She spun away from him, fetching a beer from the fridge under the bar, his cheeks sinking with loss as she disappeared momentarily from his line of sight. As she slapped the bottle on the bar in front of him, her eyes alighted on Owen's, holding them in her gaze.

This is how you do it, her eyes seemed to say.

25

THE WEDDING WAS THE NEXT day, the sky an endless, earnest blue, cloudless as a dream. The temperature stayed at an obedient 73 degrees Fahrenheit, and the birds of paradise took turns sailing through the air, gliding effortlessly on a faint breeze before alighting in the trees at the edge of the Varleys' property on Elk Mountain.

Janie, delighted that the birds had stayed in town, had made them the centerpiece of her wedding, and the coordinator, thrilled with the tropical color palette and Vince Varley's wide-open wallet, had transformed the mountaintop construction site into something worthy of *Western Bride* magazine.

From their "dressing room" inside an empty construction shed, Janie and her bridesmaids watched the guests swoon over the lavish decorations: the fuchsia feathers trailing from flower arrangements in vases the size of pickle barrels, the vast parquet dance floor surrounded by tables that glittered with crystal and silver, and the cerulean satin aisle runner embroidered with Doug and Janie's initials that led to an arch of flowers at the edge of the cliff, overlooking the great, gaping valley below.

"I think this is the fanciest wedding this town has ever seen,"

Madge said to Eunice as the two old ladies accepted glasses of tropical lemonade from a server in a shiny blue tuxedo.

"I expect we'll start seeing a lot more fancy things now that they've got that rig up." Eunice adjusted the fake lilacs on her hat and smiled broadly, revealing a blur of lipstick on her front teeth.

"Yes, but this will always be the first," Madge said authoritatively. They bobbed away, Eunice's lilacs trembling with every step.

"Did you hear that?" Janie turned to Daphne, flushed through her mask of foundation. "The fanciest wedding this town has ever seen—and it's mine!"

"We'd expect nothing less of you." Behind them, Hilary fanned herself with one of the programs, Doug and Janie's senior prom picture grinning from the cover. "You think we can get those caterers to bring some champagne back here, or what?"

Janie ignored her and went back to peeping through the shed's tiny window. When she turned she reminded Daphne of a snow globe, her belly big and round in a formfitting white dress that glittered with sequins. A fluff of feathers lined the scooped neckline and longer plumes trailed from the train, shivering like a winter snow squall whenever she moved. "Oh, Pastor Ted is here!" she bubbled. "He looks so good—am I glad I got him that suit!"

"This I have to see." Hilary crowded in next to her, the pink taffeta on her bridesmaid dress rustling. Her curls had been shellacked into place and secured with a fascinator of teal and fuchsia feathers—identical to the one that sat awkwardly atop Daphne's head, jabbing into her scalp and threatening to fall off whenever she turned her head.

But the fascinator was nothing compared to Daphne's bridesmaid dress, which poked at her ribcage and flared out from her waist in a stiff A-line that ended mid-thigh. The first time she'd tried it on, Janie had burst into tears and sworn that Daphne looked as elegant as a model. But Daphne had written it off as pregnancy hormones. When she looked in the mirror all she saw was a long, gangly pair of legs and a farmer's tan from her long days on the rig, the muscles in her arms taut and strong from lifting and hauling. She looked like someone who would always be more at home in a hard hat than a bridesmaid dress—and she was perfectly happy to stay that way.

"Dude, Pastor Ted looks like an Elvis impersonator," Hilary guffawed. "You got his suit to match the blue on those birds, huh?"

"I got *everything* to match the birds," Janie reminded her. "When something this beautiful shows up, you don't just ignore it!"

Hilary shifted back and forth on her high heels. "Especially if you need a theme for your gazillion-dollar wedding," she said.

Outside the shed, the buzz of arriving guests grew louder. The band, a six-piece country-western ensemble, struck up an enthusiastic tune, and the birds of paradise chirped along merrily. There was a knock on the shed's door, and the wedding coordinator poked her head in, her dyed-red bun pulled so tight the corners of her eyes slanted toward her temples.

"Five minutes to the ceremony." She quickly surveyed the room. "So bridesmaids, start lining up. Oh, and put some powder on the bride." She turned to Daphne and handed her a compact. "We don't want her to be shiny in the pictures, do we now?"

"Five minutes!" Janie's smile quavered as the bridesmaids bustled around her, collecting their bouquets and fixing their lipstick. "It's so soon."

"Come here." Daphne fumbled with the compact. As she patted powder onto Janie's face, she noticed that her cousin had gone pale.

"Are you nervous?" she asked.

"No!" Janie said. "I mean—maybe?"

"It's okay to have some jitters." Daphne swiped the powder over her cheeks. "It's a big day."

"Yeah." Janie's eyes were far away. Her hand shot out suddenly as a pinball and gripped Daphne's, the skin around her fingernails white.

"Daphne?" she whispered. Her blue eyes were huge, her lashes trembling.

"What?" Daphne was caught off guard. She'd been looking for a place to put the compact, and wishing for the millionth time that the bridesmaid dresses had pockets. How did girly-girls manage to carry all their stuff?

"I'm doing the right thing, right?" Janie whispered. Her eyes, so full of laughter and excitement ever since she'd come home from Cheyenne wearing Doug's engagement ring, looked like the aftermath of a storm at sea, dark and turbulent.

In the space of ten seconds, Daphne thought of a dozen possible answers, none of which she could have said out loud. Of course she didn't think Janie should marry Doug—seventeen seemed too young to marry anyone, let alone a verified slimeball. But it would be wrong to say that just minutes before Janie walked down the aisle. At that moment, her cousin needed her support more than anything else.

"Of course you are." She hoped she sounded convincing, that her face didn't reveal the way she really felt. "You're doing the right thing for your baby, and that's what matters."

"I guess." Janie let go of Daphne's wrist, but she still looked troubled. "But what if Doug doesn't get better? What if he hurts me . . . or the baby?"

The skin on the back of Daphne's neck prickled. "Has he threatened to?" she asked.

"No." Janie's eyes were dark. "Well . . . not really. But he's been drinking so much since Trey died, and he raised his arm once like he was going to hit me. Sometimes I just don't know."

Daphne took Janie's hand in hers, holding it tight. "It's not too late to back out, you know," she said. She couldn't help picturing

Jim's tomato-dark face as he pummeled her mother, Myra cowering and sobbing against the kitchen cabinets. Just the thought of Doug's abuse turning Janie into a sniveling shell of a person like her mother made her quake with rage. "If you really think he's going to hurt you, you shouldn't marry him."

Janie's lip trembled as she looked out at the assembled crowd. It seemed like most of Carbon County had turned out for the wedding, their festive clothes bright as lollipops under the cerulean sky.

She turned back to Daphne. "I can't," she said. "They're all here. It's about to start."

"You *can*," Daphne insisted.

But the storm in Janie's eyes had already turned to steel. She took a great, heaving breath and collected herself, fixing Daphne with a determined smile.

"Don't even listen to me," she said as the first strains of Pachelbel's Canon filled the air. "You were right—it's just wedding-day jitters."

She leaned in and gave Daphne a hug that smelled like powder and hairspray and flowery perfume.

"Thanks," she whispered in her ear. "And please—forget everything I just said."

"If you insist." Daphne squeezed her back, then knelt to arrange her train. She knew she could never forget what Janie had just told her. She was still shaking at the confession, the thought of Doug threatening her cousin sending livid rivers of rage through her veins. She wanted to grab Janie's ankles and force her to stay, to run out in front of the crowd and tell them all that the wedding was off. But the first bridesmaids had already begun their journey down the aisle, stepping in careful time to the music as the sea of heads in the audience bowed and murmured.

Daphne took her place behind them, her palms slippery around her bouquet as she counted slowly to ten just like the coordinator had instructed at the rehearsal dinner the night before.

Right before she took the first step, she turned and snuck one last glace at her cousin. Janie's head was high, and the smile shellacked onto her face belied any evidence that there had ever been a storm in her eyes.

↔

"We are gathered here today to witness the fruits of young love in bloom." Pastor Ted's smooth cheeks were pink against his blue suit, so that he almost looked like one of the birds of paradise himself. "The couple before me, Douglas James Varley and Janice Patience Peyton, may appear at first glance like any other young couple in love—perhaps *too* in love."

He nodded at Janie's belly, and the crowd tittered. A droplet of sweat trickled down Daphne's back—in addition to everything else she hated about the bridesmaids dresses, the stiff fabric was about as breathable as being mummified in saran wrap.

She watched her cousin's face closely, but every sign of the indecision that had ravaged her just moments before was gone. Janie looked rapturous: The color was high in her cheeks, and her smile, as much as she tried to contain it, kept leaking out as she gazed into Doug's eyes.

Even though Daphne hated him more than ever before, she had to admit that Doug cut a handsome figure in his tuxedo. He towered over Janie and the rest of the wedding party, his shoulders wide and square, a well-placed bowtie making his oversized head look less like it had been slammed haphazardly onto his shoulders. With the entire town's eyes on him, he looked down at Janie with such loving, tender affection that it seemed hard to believe he'd spent the past several months calling her a cow and hitting on her cousin. The magic of the crystal and flowers, the magnificent view, and the birds of paradise gliding overhead had wiped the past clean, so that Trey's death, Doug's dark moodiness, and Janie's growing fear of him seemed nothing more than the dim memory of a dream.

"But this is no ordinary couple!" Pastor Ted was clearly in his element, the tails of his new suit flapping in the breeze. "And the child growing in Janie's womb is no ordinary child."

A stillness blanketed the crowd. They leaned forward, barely daring to breathe. Even the birds of paradise stopped singing in the trees.

"I've had a feeling there was something special about this baby since the moment Janie walked into my church and confessed her pregnancy." Pastor Ted lowered his voice conspiratorially. "Something more than special—something *holy*. Do you believe?"

"I believe," the crowd murmured.

"And there have been signs. Since the child was conceived, God has sent us trumpets from the heavens and oil from the earth. And now, He has sent these beautiful birds to grace our skies."

Sweat flew from Pastor Ted's forehead, and his eyes blazed bright as butane.

"They are a gift, a sign from the Lord our God who resides in Paradise. My friends, when I look at these birds, I don't just see birds of paradise. I see a stork: a stork come to deliver a very special child. Do you believe?"

"I believe!" The words burst from the crowd like a bunch of balloons released to the sky. Even Daphne, caught up in the moment, felt herself mouthing along. Janie and Doug had torn their eyes away from each other to give Pastor Ted their full attention, Janie's mouth hanging slightly open, her teeth pearly behind layers of rose-colored lip gloss.

"For this will be no ordinary baby," Pastor Ted said firmly. "I believe with all of my soul that this child will be a prophet." He paused for dramatic effect. "Perhaps even the next messiah."

Janie gasped. Her hands went instinctively to her belly.

"Yes, Janie." Pastor Ted touched her gently on the shoulder. "And Doug." He raised his other hand to rest on his arm. "Together, you have a great responsibility—far greater than the bond of marriage, or even the sacred duty of parenthood. Together, you will be parents to a holy child."

Daphne snuck a glance at the first row of chairs, where the Peytons and Varleys sat side by side. Her aunt Karen was weeping openly, fat tears of joy rolling down her face and splattering the blue crepe front of her dress. Floyd had one arm around her shaking shoulders and was staring at his daughter and future son-in-law with a look of pure pride in his eyes. The Varleys merely looked shell-shocked.

"Janice Patience Peyton." Pastor Ted's voice was grave. "Are you ready to accept not only the great responsibility of marriage and motherhood, but also serve as the Lord's servant as a vessel for the messiah who may one day lead us through the Great Change and into Eternal Heaven?"

Janie blinked slowly, her false lashes sweeping dramatically. "I am," she said somberly.

"And Douglas James Varley, are you ready to love and cherish this young woman, and to raise your son in the spirit of humility and piety befitting the next Son of God?"

Doug stood taller. "I am," he said.

"Then may I please have the rings?" Pastor Ted held out his hand as Bryce, Doug's best man, stepped forward.

Daphne watched Janie's face closely as the couple exchanged

rings and vows. In a matter of moments, Pastor Ted's speech had transformed her from a girl playing at staging her dream wedding to something deeper and more mature. Where before her glow had been that of a princess in a fairy tale, it now reminded Daphne of the medieval paintings she'd seen once on a class trip to the museum, as if a light had been turned on inside of her that poured from the thin membrane of her skin and surrounded her head like a halo.

When Doug slipped the ring on her finger, instead of squealing or jumping up and down like the old Janie would have done, she simply smiled beatifically, as if their bond was a foregone conclusion ordained by the Lord.

"I now pronounce you man and wife," Pastor Ted's words drifted triumphantly to the sky. "You may kiss the bride."

Doug and Janie embraced in a flurry of feathers and sequins as the crowd rose to their feet, roaring their approval and sending the birds of paradise rising from the trees in a mosaic of color, flapping their wings and chirping joyously.

The band launched into an ecstatic march, and the couple disentangled themselves and practically skipped down the aisle, clutching hands and grinning with amazement. Daphne automatically fell into step after the bridesmaids, doing her best to smile at the blur of flushed faces and candy-colored finery as she passed.

As the crowd pressed in to congratulate the couple, a cool hand landed on her arm. She turned, startled, and found herself staring straight into a pair of deep green eyes.

"Owen!" she gasped. "What are you doing here?"

He flashed a mischievous grin. "I didn't want you to be the only bridesmaid without a date."

"What if *I* wanted to be the only bridesmaid without a date?" Her indignant tone sounded fake even to her. In truth, Owen's face was a welcome surprise among the sea of Carbon County locals, friends and family of the Varleys and Peytons who had all known each other since birth. He looked strong and lean in his slim black suit, his once-pale skin bronzed from a summer on the rig.

"The thought never crossed my mind," Owen said mildly.

She gaped. "So you just crashed the wedding?"

"I prefer to think of it as paying a surprise visit."

She sucked in air sharply. "Doug'll kill you if he sees you."

"I'll lay low—but don't kick me out yet." He wiggled his eyebrows. "I brought you a present."

He held out a brown paper bag, a red ribbon tied clumsily around its handles.

She narrowed her eyes. "You didn't." She peeked inside the bag, and a laugh boiled up from deep inside her, bubbling forth so fast she had to clap a hand over her mouth.

"This is *exactly* what I wanted," she admitted, pulling out the pair of beat-up black Chuck Taylors she kept in her cubby at work. "My feet are killing me. How did you know?"

"Hmmm . . . maybe because you've been complaining about

your wedding shoes all week?"

"That's not true!" she protested. But she was already fumbling with the buckle on her strappy heels, nearly losing her balance as she tried to perch on one precarious stiletto.

"How about you hold on to me," Owen suggested.

"No, I got it," she said, almost toppling onto a table piled high with cheese puffs and miniature hot dogs.

"Whoa, careful!" Owen caught her, his hands gentle but firm on her upper arms. The heat from his palms seeped into her bare skin, sending her pulse skittering. "Now, what were you saying about your perfect balance?"

"Okay, fine," she grumbled. He held her for a moment longer, making sure she was steady before he let go. Resting a hand on his shoulder, she slipped off the dreaded stilettos and quickly laced her sneakers.

"That's better," she said, trying to wiggle the circulation back into her toes.

"You're three inches shorter," he observed. "But you still look amazing."

"I look like a flamingo," she corrected.

"Hottest flamingo I've ever seen." Owen grabbed a pair of champagne flutes from a passing waiter and handed her one.

Her cheeks burned from the compliment. She turned away, hoping he wouldn't notice, and watched the sun start to set over the valley, trailing veins of rose-tinged gold through the sky. The reception was in full swing: The band, dressed in matching pink-and-teal western shirts and cowboy boots, played country renditions of Janie's favorite pop songs as dozens of wait staff circulated with silver trays of miniature tacos and Dorito nachos that the caterer had whipped up in Janie's honor.

"So can I get a *cheers*, or what?" Owen's voice was soft and playful behind her. She turned back to find him holding out his champagne flute.

"I don't know." Daphne watched the tiny bubbles rise to the surface. "What if Janie needs me for something?"

"If the new holy Madonna of Carbon County needs you to do anything, it's to celebrate her wedding." Owen clinked his glass against Daphne's. "May Mr. and Mrs. Doug Varley and their kid, the Second Coming, live long and prosper."

"Well, here's to Janie," Daphne agreed. She took a tentative sip, and then another. The champagne was crisp and heady, and the bubbles fizzed tantalizingly in her throat. The only other time she'd had champagne was when someone at work had snuck a bottle of Andre into the back room on New Year's Eve. There, the cloying sweetness had given her an instant headache. But she felt like she could drink this all night.

"C'mon—let's go check out the rest of this party." Owen took her arm and steered her through the crowd, past the gift table piled high with presents in pearly paper and the carving station where chunks of beef and ham sat waiting to fill peoples' plates. She knew she should tell him to let go of her, that he should go home before Doug realized his number-one rival had crashed his wedding. She would, in just a minute she decided, taking another sip of her drink and realizing it was nearly gone. She'd demolished it in a couple of gulps.

"You want another?" Owen asked.

"I shouldn't." The champagne was already making her loosen her grip on her senses, preventing her from telling Owen to leave.

"Sure you should." Owen steered them toward the bar for two fresh glasses. "It's a wedding. Everyone's celebrating. It's okay for you to have fun, too."

With a new flute fresh in her hand and Owen's arm through hers, she watched the people of Carbon County celebrate. The way they clustered in circles and then spun off into new formations in their bright summer wedding clothes reminded Daphne of plastic jewels seen through the end of a kaleidoscope, an ever-changing pattern of color and light. But she was at the other end, looking in. The realization was sudden and bittersweet.

She turned to Owen. "I've been here for almost three months now," she said softly. "And I still feel like an outsider."

His eyes met hers, dark and serious. "I know what you mean," he said. "I've always felt that way, my entire life. Maybe it was not really knowing where I came from, or wanting to win more than anyone else. But it always felt like I was on the outside, looking in."

"Even on the rig?" she asked. It was where she felt most at home in the world, the tough work and long hours uniting the crew in an easy camaraderie. On the rig, it didn't matter who you were or where you came from, whether you were running away or hiding something from your past, as long as you were willing to work.

"Even on the rig," he nodded. "I like everyone, but I don't really feel a connection to anyone. Except you."

The sky darkened as the sun sank behind the mountains in a blazing tangerine orb, and fairy lights twinkled on one by one.

"You mean, because we're friends," she said uncertainly.

"No." His face was a shadow in the velvety crush of night. "I mean—"

"Ladies and gentlemen, it's time for the first dance!" The wedding coordinator's shrill voice drowned in a screech of microphone static from the bandstand. "I'd like to announce, for the first time ever, Mr. and Mrs. Douglas Varley!"

The crowd erupted, and Daphne reluctantly drew her eyes away from Owen and to the center of the dance floor. Janie stepped forward, glowing like a Madonna. She seemed to glide without touching the floor, as if suspended in a golden web of well-wishes. Doug shuffled behind her, flushed and proud. The first strains of "From This Moment" drifted around them like tendrils of smoke. He took her hand, their bodies coming slowly together, the bulge of

Janie's stomach keeping them a safe distance like two sixth graders at a middle school dance. But their eyes were locked together, their faces bright and alive with love.

Daphne wondered what it could be like to feel that way about someone: so intoxicated, so in love, that you could overlook the bad stuff and only see the good. She had never understood her cousin's attraction to Doug—had never understood any woman's attraction to any man—but with her cousin swaying slowly on the dance floor, her friends and family dabbing at their eyes with Kleenex, and Owen by her side, she thought that maybe, just maybe, it could be nice to feel that way too.

One by one, other couples trickled onto the dance floor, holding each other tight. Bryce spun Hilary under a spotlight, Vince guided Deirdre Varley in a stiff waltz, and Floyd whispered something in Karen's ear that made her smile through her tears.

"Come on." Owen tugged at Daphne's arm. "Dance with me."

"No." She was terrified of how it might feel to be that close to him, to have his arms around her and her body pressed against his.

"Yes," he insisted. The world went soft as he took her hands and led her gently to the edge of the dance floor, his eyes locked on hers.

"I don't even know how to do this," she said, a last-ditch effort to change his mind.

"It's easy." He lifted her arms and arranged them around his neck, the softness of his thick black hair brushing her wrists. Then he laced his arms around her back, drawing her into the heady world of leather and metal and grease that lived under his skin, in his veins.

Her body went tight, a shield against the sudden, unaccustomed contact. She realized she was trembling.

"It's okay," he murmured in her ear. "You don't have to be afraid. It's just dancing."

She looked up at him, their noses nearly brushing. "But I am," she said.

"Why?" His voice was fierce and serious now, his breath warm on her cheek. "I know you want this too."

He held her tighter, trying to still her shivering. Pinpricks of heat exploded inside her as she felt herself respond, pressing up against him, craving the touch of his skin. She knew she was too close to the edge, in danger of giving up everything she'd worked so hard to protect. But she wasn't sure she could resist anymore. He was right—she did want this. And his lips were just millimeters from hers.

She closed her eyes, succumbing to the night, to his touch, to the threat of a kiss building between them. And then the song ended in a sudden, strangling cacophony of applause.

"And now it's time to cut the cake!" The wedding coordinator grasped the microphone, scarlet wisps from her bun unraveling around her head.

Still trembling, Daphne disengaged herself from Owen's grasp. She couldn't believe she'd come so close, let things go so far. The world dipped and swerved around her, and she realized with disgust that she was getting drunk.

The caterers wheeled out a cart the size of a small sedan, draped in a bone-white tablecloth. It took five of them to maneuver it into place, and as they made their way to the center of the dance floor a series of *oooohs* and *aaaahs* arose in their wake. Once they'd skirted the crush of people, Daphne saw what all the fuss was about.

The cake was a perfect scale replica of the Varleys' future house.

Candied stairs led up to a grand entrance etched in fondant, and the peaked windows were made of crystal-clear spun sugar. Frosted shingles and caramel gables sprouted from every surface, and it was surrounded by an elaborate English garden rendered in a dozen shades of frosting.

Janie approached the cake, laughing, Doug at her side. As the knife slid through the round turret at the top, Daphne realized with a sick shock that the elaborate celebration around her, the caterers and the champagne and the band that the Varleys had shelled out for so graciously, had nothing to do with their son's marriage. They were celebrating their new wealth, their renewed status in town, and their ability to show off and throw fancy parties. Her cousin was nothing more than an excuse.

There was a sudden whoosh, and a mass of teal and magenta feathers plummeted from the sky, landing with a sickening splat on the peaked roof of the cake. Janie screamed and leapt back, the knife still in her hand. Frosting and feathers flew everywhere: into Janie's eyes and down the front of her wedding dress, onto Doug's suit and the band's sheet music and the wedding coordinator's sleek black skirt suit.

"What the—" Vince cried angrily. "Did that damn bird just dive-bomb our three-thousand-dollar cake?"

Janie dropped the knife and wiped frosting from her cheeks. Tears sprung from her eyes. She backed away from the cake, a look of horror on her face.

"It's dead!" she sobbed, just as another bird plunged from the sky and into the center of the table closest to Daphne, breaking the oversized vase and spraying blood and water, glass and flowers across the tabletop.

Daphne stood glued to the spot, staring at the bird's corpse as everyone around her scrambled back, screaming and cursing and knocking over chairs in their hurry to get away. The bird's body was limp and cold, crisscrossed with lines of blood from the broken glass. A single onyx-colored eye stared back at her, unseeing, lifeless. Dread churned in her stomach, clashing noxiously with the champagne.

More screams rang out as another bird fell from the sky. And then another. They splattered onto the parquet dance floor, scattered the musicians, and plopped indiscriminately onto tables and chairs, each hollow thud more horrifying than the last.

"My chapeau!" Daphne heard old Eunice cry as a mass of pink feathers impaled itself on the spire of fake lilacs sprouting from her hat. Madge reached out a trembling hand to help, but a herd of children running full-tilt and terrified away from the rainbow hailstorm of dying birds knocked the two ladies to the side. Snot and tears streamed from the childrens' scrunched-up, scarlet faces, and their voices pierced the evening with a heart-rending wail.

It was as if the birds' sudden deaths had broken the kaleidoscope, the colors running together and falling, breaking apart. The wedding guests rushed from one end of the property to the other, shouting and shoving, desperate to get away from the birds of paradise falling thick and fast from the sky, as if shot down by a malicious band of poachers with deadly aim. The dance floor became slick with blood, the air a riot of colored feathers, the scent of fear and destruction sharp and pervasive in the velvety night.

Daphne couldn't make her legs work. Owen draped a protective arm over her shoulders as she stood dumbly, watching the birds fall in a rainbow blur before her eyes, watching her uncle Floyd whip off his fancy new suit jacket and cover Madge and Eunice's heads, rushing them to the relative safety of the porta-potties. She watched Doug kick the dead birds away, swinging his fists like he was trying to punish them for dying on his wedding day, to punch them out of the sky. And she watched Janie crumble, sinking to the ground in a pile of tears and tulle, her opulent wedding dress streaked with a hideous tie-dye of scarlet blood and green frosting.

The sight snapped Daphne into action. She threw Owen's arm from her shoulders and rushed to her cousin, her rubber-soled shoes mercifully sure on the slippery parquet. She felt her foot sink into something soft and gooey, one of the corpses, but she forced herself to ignore it and push on until she was at her cousin's side, crouched next to her in a puddle of blood and feathers as the last of the birds hurtled to its final resting place in the curved, brass bell of the tuba abandoned on the bandstand.

Janie's shoulders were trembling, her arms above her head in a bomb-shelter pose. Weak mewling sounds came from beneath her veil, like a kitten crying for milk.

"Janie." Daphne wrapped both her arms around her cousin and felt the cold from her bare skin, the trembling residue of her fear. "It's over now. It was just a freak accident. It's going to be okay."

Janie lifted her head. Her face was red and puffy from crying, her perfect, professional makeup job smeared across her face in thick, black streaks. "That was no freak accident." Her voice was a guttural whisper, her eyes dark with terror. "That was a sign."

26

IT WENT WITHOUT SAYING THAT Doug was pretty hungover the day after his wedding. The whole thing had been god-awful, ever since his folks got that bee up their bungholes about him proposing, and then his mom wanted to plan the whole thing and his dad wouldn't stop griping about the expense, being all "Why can't Floyd put his money into his own daughter's wedding instead of betting on this one-horse town?" and Janie was always bugging him about flowers or vows or whatever. Then there was the whole waste-of-time day itself, the parade of aunts who smelled like old carpet gurgling congratulations in his ear, the speeches about the responsibility of fatherhood (which, not that anyone asked, he was *so* not ready for), and then the icing on the cake—literally—those pain-in-the-ass birds dropping dead out of the sky.

Forget a honeymoon in Cancun, which was apparently not possible if your new wife was about to pop, or even getting a little wedding-night action. By the time they got to the presidential suite at the Holiday Inn, Janie was such a hot mess that all he could do was get her into the shower, trying to tell her it would all be okay and chugging Maker's Mark from the bottle he'd cadged from the wedding's bartender until she sobbed herself to sleep next to him on the bed.

Dropping her back at her parents' place and coming home was a freakin' relief. All he wanted to do was shut himself up in his dark room, nurse his hangover with grape Gatorade, and have a little peace and quiet to wonder where the hell his life was going.

But then that lawyer showed up, all gung ho about getting Floyd to sign that contract, insisting Doug come along to remind the Peytons they were all family now, and next thing he knew the three of them were piled into his dad's new Buick that smelled like old people and horse farts, eating donuts from the Cruller Corner and driving down that dusty, potholed road to the Peytons'.

"If I may," Elbert said as they approached the trailer. He folded his Cruller Corner napkin in half, then into quarters, then eighths, like some OCD freak. "Perhaps we can approach Mr. Peyton at the rig, instead of in his home. I've noticed those women surrounding him have a tendency to, er . . ."

"Meddle?" Vince finished for him. He'd been hitting the scotch at the wedding pretty hard, and he looked as rough as Doug felt. "Stick their noses where they don't belong?"

"I suppose that's an appropriate analogy."

"Hell yeah," Vince agreed. He lay his foot on the gas, and they sped by the trailer. "Good thinking, Elbert. This is why I pay you the big bucks."

"Actually," Elbert reminded him. "You haven't paid me a cent yet."

Vince pulled the car to a stop in front of the misshapen circle of trailers by the rig. The roar and chug of machinery pounded at Doug's headache, and the thick scent of petroleum made his stomach lurch when he opened the car door.

A chain of roustabouts rushed by, shouldering lengths of heavy pipe. Doug spotted that nasty cocktease Daphne in filthy jeans and a black-splattered T-shirt, her face streaked with grime and oil. The frigid bitch probably thought she was so tough, working on the rig with the boys. He'd show her what *tough* really was—if he could ever get her alone again.

"And which trailer do you think we might find him in?" Elbert wrinkled his nose at the dirt and noise, gripping his briefcase like it was the last bastion of civilized society.

"This one, I suppose." Vince approached a trailer with a small, hand-lettered sign that said *Admin* on the door. He rapped twice and a tangle of male voices grunted something unintelligible within. Pushing it open, they found Floyd sitting with a couple of idiots in hard hats and chambray shirts.

"Vince!" Floyd looked unsettled. "And Doug. What a, uh, nice surprise." There was something haggard in his face, the lines in it heavier, his eyes tired and dull. Even his eyebrows, which usually danced until it drove Doug crazy, drooped low.

"Hello, Floyd." Vince nodded at the other men. "Got a minute?"

"We were wondering if we might have a word." Elbert stepped in next to him, and Floyd's face fell even further, his smile scrambling to stay upright like a rider about to take a spill off his bike.

"I suppose so," Floyd said heavily. He turned to the other men. "Boys, can you give us a second?"

Floyd gestured for them to sit as the men brushed past them and out the door. The trailer wasn't much to look at: fake wood paneling, a few dinged-up filing cabinets, indecipherable charts and diagrams scotch-taped to the walls. The air reeked of burnt coffee.

"What can I do you for?" Floyd tried for joviality but fell short. Even his voice sounded tired.

"Well, now that we're all family," Vince began. He looked proud of himself for pulling the family card, and Doug knew why. Family was practically all Floyd ever talked about, family and God. And now the old fart was his father-in-law, he reminded himself. As if being stuck with Janie for the rest of his life wasn't bad enough, he had to get her cuckoo parents in the bargain.

But Floyd barely managed a smile. Vince cleared his throat and started again. "Now that we're family—and we're extending our home to the young couple and their child and all—I thought it might be time to make our business relationship official. Elbert here has all the paperwork. Nothing's changed, and it's still all boilerplate. All you've gotta do is sign."

Elbert snapped open his briefcase and extracted the contract and a thin, silver pen with his initials monogrammed on the side, sliding both across the table to Floyd.

"I'm not sure if you've had a chance to look at it," he said. "But if you read it over, I'm sure you'll find it's abundantly fair to both parties. No more or less than the verbal agreement Mr. Varley tells me the two of you entered into, so to speak."

Floyd looked at the thick pile of paper without moving. The silver pen sat untouched, gleaming in the trailer's fluorescent light. He looked up at Vince, his face sagging, as seconds ticked by on the lawyer's expensive-looking wristwatch.

"Vince, I don't know," he said finally. His voice was a sigh.

Vince struggled for breath. "But Floyd—we're family now!" he tried again.

"Exactly." Color rose in Floyd's cheeks, and a hint of life returned to his eyes. "We're family now, and families trust each other. They take one another at their word."

"Sir, if I may," Elbert began.

"You may not!" Floyd thundered. Doug looked up, startled; in all the time he'd known him, he'd never once heard Floyd Peyton yell. "Vince, I made you a promise, and I fully intend to keep it.

You know I'm a man of my word. But you and this lawyer of yours have been trying to push these papers on me since the second we shook hands, and I'm starting to think that the money is more important to you than trust or family or the good this oil can do for the community."

Doug couldn't believe what he was hearing. Floyd Peyton, pulling a bunch of holier-than-thou crap when he'd been out of work for months and only struck oil through pure, dumb luck? That was rich. A look of disgust crossed Vince's face.

"Now, Floyd, I think you have the wrong idea," he began.

"I know what I saw, and I know what I believe," Floyd said softly. His eyes were steely with resolve. "Last night, I saw you throw the fanciest party this town's ever seen. I don't know how much it cost, and frankly I don't want to know. All I know is that you thought of everything, and invited everyone—except God."

"Oh, for fuck's sake!" The words were out of his mouth before Doug could stop himself. Of course Floyd would have to bring up God, when his dad was just trying to make a deal, fair and square. That's what they got for dealing with someone who actually took Pastor Ted's nutjob ideas seriously.

"That rig out there," Floyd ignored him and pointed a finger at the trailer's door, toward the roar of the derrick beyond, "is for putting good people to work and getting our town in the black again. It's for keeping our schools open and giving good old-fashioned American entrepreneurs a place to build a business and thrive—not for throwing frivolous parties and building ridiculous palaces. It's a gift from God, a blessing. And the more I think about it, the more I think God is testing us with this gift, to see if we're worthy of the *real* gift he has in store for us."

"And what might that be?" Elbert drew his fingertips into a peak under his chin.

"Why, the Second Coming, of course." Floyd's eyes widened as he looked from Elbert to Vince to Doug and back again. "He didn't tell you?"

Doug shook his head, embarrassed to even be there. He knew Floyd was a few cards short of a full deck, but did he really have to go spouting Pastor Ted's bullcrap?

"I can't say he has." Elbert said in a voice choked with stifled laugher.

"There's a prophet coming to Carbon County," Floyd explained. "Our pastor believes it'll be our grandchild, and I tend to agree with him. But now that we have this extra responsibility, I'm frightened for Carbon County—and I fear for our children, and our grandchild. If we learned anything yesterday, it's that God can take away just as quickly as He gives. He gave us this oil as a gift, a blessing. It wasn't meant to blind us with riches, or eat away at our trust so a man can't even be taken at his word."

He shook his head slowly. The fatigue had returned to his eyes, and the lines in his face ran as deep as rivers. Elbert's mouth was a tiny pink Froot Loop of surprise.

"Vince, I'll be honest," Floyd continued. "It's become pretty clear to me that you'd rather spend this money on yourself than your community. I was troubled by what I saw yesterday. Those birds dying in the middle of our celebration: I saw it as a sign from God Himself. He thinks we're getting too big for our britches, and he sent those poor birds to their death to warn us. Didn't you wonder that the first one fell in the middle of that cake—a ridiculous, overpriced tribute you had built to a ridiculous, overpriced mansion? I didn't, Vince. And I think if you dig deep in your heart, you'll agree with me. But in the meantime, I won't sign your papers."

He pushed the contract back across the table. The pen wobbled and rolled off, clattering across the surface with a thwack-thwack-thwack and falling from the edge to land in Elbert's outstretched palm.

Floyd's gaze stayed steady on Vince, steel and unwavering in a face that looked ravaged with time. "I'm a man of my word, and I meant it when I said we'd split this oil money," he said. "But my word won't go further than a handshake, Vince. You'll just have to trust me on that.

"After all," he finished bitterly, "we're family now."

↔

Back at the Varleys' house, Deirdre poured coffee from the high-end machine she'd ordered online, and served doily-shaped cookies.

"Those Peytons," she sniffed when her husband filled her in on their conversation with Floyd. Disgust flared in her eyes. "You'd think owning an oil rig would make them act like civilized people, but no. Once trash, always trash, I suppose."

Vince turned to Elbert. "So what do we do?" he asked.

"An excellent question." Elbert placed his half-eaten cookie precisely in the middle of his cocktail napkin, getting all OCD again. "As I see it, we gave Mr. Peyton a more than ample chance to sign the contract, and he ignored it. Now I think it's best we proceed with the lawsuit."

Deirdre and Vince sat forward, and even Doug found felt himself leaning over the coffee table. He'd never been part of a lawsuit before. It sounded kind of cool.

"I've been looking into their claim to the land, and, unfortunately, it truly is airtight," Elbert continued. "Thus, I think our clearest path is to claim that Floyd and his family are unfit to control the oil—and that you, as next of kin thanks to Doug and Janie's marriage, are next in line."

"I like it!" Deirdre squealed.

"If I were on the jury, today's little conversation would be all the evidence I'd need," Elbert added. "The man believes that his unborn grandson is a prophet. Have you ever heard anything more ridiculous?"

"Well." Deirdre looked troubled. "Pastor Ted did say so. And the whole town seems to agree."

Across the coffee table, Elbert choked on his cookie.

"Are you all right?" Deirdre rushed to his side with a glass of water.

"Quite," Elbert assured her, coughing his crumbs discreetly into a napkin. "Regardless, I think it will be easy to prove that the family is mentally unfit to control the oil. In addition to Mr. Peyton's religious beliefs, I took the liberty of having a private investigator check up on the family's history."

"And?" Deirdre hovered at his side like a dragonfly.

"I'm afraid that beyond some rather significant credit card debt, I couldn't find much on Floyd's immediate family," Elbert said. "But the extended family—that's another story. He has a niece, I believe . . ."

"Yeah, Daphne." Doug shook his head.

"That girl in the trailer that day, who wouldn't let him sign the contract," Vince added.

"I see." Elbert smiled thinly. "So she's living with them, then? That's even better."

Deirdre sniffed. "Nobody really knows what happened to her parents—kind of fishy, if you ask me."

"I'll say." The lawyer looked pleased. "So they've been lying to you—to everyone, I suppose. Because I have something on Daphne, something good. She killed a man—and from my interpretation of the court records, she isn't sorry in the least."

"That bitch killed a guy?" Doug asked gleefully.

His parents scolded him for his language (still—even though he was a real man now, married and all), but he ignored them. It all made sense. No wonder Daphne was such a frigid bitch—she was a man-killer, *literally*. It would explain why she'd kneed him in the nuts that night he tried to get to know her, which was too bad because he'd been really sure she was into him from the way she averted her eyes whenever he looked her way.

He'd like to see her try blowing him off again, with the dirt he had on her now. Next time they found themselves alone in the dark, she'd have no choice but to give in—not unless she wanted everyone in Carbon County knowing her secret.

Elbert started yammering again, going on and on in his nasal legalese until Doug was practically drowning in his own boredom. Finally he just got up and went upstairs, his parents so into whatever the prissy-ass lawyer was saying that they didn't even notice.

It was typical shit. They were acting like Doug didn't exist, like he hadn't just laid his entire damn future on the line for them, thrown his life away to marry Janie just so they could get their hands on a little extra dough. They'd put him up for sacrifice like a goat, dragging him to jewelry stores only to have Deirdre pick out a ring, orchestrating some farce of a perfect romantic dinner for him to propose, even calling the restaurant themselves to make the reservations, not once asking him what *he* wanted, whether *he* would choose to be tethered to Janie forever and ever just because he wanted to try it without a condom a few lousy times.

Rage rushed in his ears, nearly blurring his vision as he remembered yet again that he was trapped. Rage at his parents, at Daphne, at Janie, at her family and the church and Pastor Ted for making fatherhood sound even more terrifying, as if being a dad at eighteen wasn't scary enough. Now everyone was saying he'd be a dad to freakin' Jesus Christ Jr. It was enough to make anyone want to polish off a bottle of Maker's.

He stumbled into his room and shut the door, glad to be away from the whole dumb world. Lying down on his bed in the semidarkness, he crossed his arms behind his head and stared up at his football trophies and girlie calendar and the old watermark on the ceiling. The anger lay down with him, covering him like a blanket.

He hated everyone, and he didn't know what to do about it. All he knew was that someday, somehow, he'd figure out a way to get them all back.

27

DAPHNE'S KNIFE SANK INTO THE plump flesh. It gave way beneath her, soft and pliant, yielding. Red juices spurted into the air, and she brought the knife down again and again, her movements precise and merciless, quick and efficient.

Karen looked over from where she was grating cheese at the opposite counter. "Those tomatoes look perfect, honey," she said. "Just toss them all into the pan and give them a good strong stir, okay?"

It was nearly dinnertime, and the trailer was steamy with the scent of frying garlic and onions, a pot of noodles boiling merrily on the stovetop and a news anchor chattering away on the television, his hair as motionless as one of Aunt Karen's Precious Moments ceramic figurines. Janie sat on the couch, wrapped in an afghan, watching the news. She'd been jumpy since her wedding, always looking over her shoulder, her hands resting protectively over her belly more often than not.

Daphne stirred the tomatoes in with the onions and garlic, watching the sauce bubble and pop on the stovetop. Karen was teaching her to make her famous lasagna, the one she'd always demanded seconds and thirds of when she was a child. Daphne found herself wishing that Myra had taught her to cook—or had ever bothered to cook herself. Her childhood had been an endless parade of boxed mac 'n' cheese and Chinese takeout, the oven in their apartment used so seldom that Daphne started hiding her toys there so Jim wouldn't break them when he was drunk.

"Holy guacamole," Janie said from the couch, pointing a pink-tipped finger at the TV. "Is that Pastor Ted?"

Daphne and Karen rushed to the living room. Pastor Ted's familiar face grinned from the small projection television, where he stood next to a female newscaster with bright coral lips. They were in front of what looked like a construction site, and the text beneath them read: *Carbon County Miracle: Ancient Tablet Found.*

Karen nodded, her mouth hanging open. "Turn it up!" she urged.

Janie found the remote and turned the volume up as high as it would go.

". . . an unequivocal miracle, a true sign from God!" Pastor Ted was saying. His face had been heavily powdered, but there was no mistaking the wonder in his eyes. "We've been seeing a lot of miracles in Carbon County lately, but this is by far the most thrilling yet."

The camera panned out to reveal a hole in the earth wrapped in caution tape. It sat on top of a hill, surrounded by construction vehicles and bags of concrete fill, a shadowy valley visible in the background.

"Is that Elk Mountain?" Daphne asked.

"It is—that's where I'm gonna live!" Janie exclaimed.

"Do you think it's real?" the newscaster was asking Pastor Ted.

"I believe with my entire heart and soul," Pastor Ted assured her. "I've believed my whole life that God has special plans for Carbon County, and today He's sent us a special message. The wheels are already in motion, and the Great Change is coming—so folks, hold on to your hats!"

The newscaster tee-heed politely and turned to address the camera. "The tablet, which appears to be stone, was found during a construction excavation."

An image of the tablet appeared in a box behind the newscaster's head. Daphne was able to make out a few of the words (*fire, children, divide*) before it flicked off the screen.

"And what language is that?" the newscaster asked, her voice chipper.

"It's ancient Aramaic," Pastor Ted confirmed. "Which is truly a miracle, since nobody has ever been known to read or write in that language in the vicinity of southern Wyoming."

Daphne's head swam. Aramaic? But she'd just been reading it—the words on the tablet had appeared as clear to her as plain English. She flashed back frantically to the image of the tablet, trying to remember if she'd noticed the letters. She couldn't recall:

It had filtered through her brain as quickly as a message on a billboard. She silently begged for them to show the image again, but the newscaster was wrapping up her segment.

"Archeology and religious studies experts, currently gathered at an annual conference in Bethlehem, will be traveling to the area when they return to evaluate the tablet's authenticity and, if it checks out, translate the message. Until then, remember you heard it here first. Now back to you, Frank."

The male anchor's head filled the screen, rigid and jovial. "Thanks, Patricia—there's been a lot of big news coming from that little town lately," he burbled. "And now the weather . . ."

Daphne turned to her aunt and cousin. "Did you—" she began, meaning to ask if they'd also been able to read the ancient text.

"The sauce!" Karen cried. Acrid black smoke filled the trailer's small kitchen as the tomato sauce Daphne had been so carefully stirring bubbled over, and the next few moments were lost to a flurry of pan-removing and window-opening, fanning the air and adding water to the sauce.

"I think it'll be fine," Karen said once they had the situation under control. She rummaged in a cabinet for her lasagna pan and began laying out noodles. "And who can blame us for losing track with news like *that* on the TV? Can you believe it—an ancient tablet right here in Carbon County? It truly is a sign from God, don't you think?"

"I hope it's a good one," Janie fretted, patting her tummy. "Me and baby don't want any more bad news."

Daphne bit her lip. As uncomfortable as talk of God still made her feel, she had to admit that some pretty strange things had been happening around Carbon County lately. She still couldn't shake the image of the birds falling from the sky, raining down on the wedding as if flung from the heavens.

Then again, what if it was a hoax? In Pastor Ted's own words, nobody had ever read or written Aramaic in Carbon County, and it was suspicious that the tablet had been found at Elk Mountain. What if Doug had placed it there just to be a jerk, to get the town's believers even more riled up so he could boost his ego tearing them down, or as a kind of twisted revenge for the chaotic death scene at his wedding? She had trouble imagining him pulling something like that off, but it wasn't impossible.

"What do you think it says?" Daphne asked, feeling the situation out.

"Oh, I surely don't know," Karen clucked. "That ancient Aramaic just looked like squiggles to me."

"Maybe it's more about how my baby will be a prophet," Janie said hopefully. "It would be nice if it said something about no more dead birdies, too."

A hard shiver shuddered through Daphne's bones, and she had to take a break from arranging noodles in the pan to grip the edges of the counter with both hands. Her head felt heavy and murky, like she'd been spinning in circles. So the language really hadn't been legible to anyone else—Karen and Janie hadn't seen the words in it that Daphne saw, the symbols spelling out *fire, children, divide.*

Either she was going crazy, or she could read Aramaic.

↔

Shortly after one a.m., Daphne snuck out of the trailer and across the road to the Global Oil equipment hut, her heart thudding in her chest. As exhausted as she was, sleep had eluded her, the image of the tablet flashing endlessly through her mind as she tossed and turned. Finally, she gave up. She had to see the tablet, to try reading the message with her own eyes.

Guilt snapped at her heels as she lifted the keys for one of the Global Oil jeeps from its hook. She'd never so much as bent the rig's rules, but with the image of the tablet looming huge in her mind, she saw no alternative but to borrow a company vehicle. It would take all night for her to walk to Elk Mountain and back, and the sound of his truck starting right outside his window would certainly wake Uncle Floyd. She was trying to save up for a car of her own, but between insisting on paying room and board to the Peytons and secretly sending checks home to her mother, the money wasn't accumulating very fast.

It was a clear, moonless evening as Daphne turned the key in the ignition, the stars hard and faraway, unblinking. On the radio a female pop-crossover star with a big voice and bigger hair assured Daphne she was *doin' better off without him, and thank you very much for askin'.*

She turned onto Elk Mountain Road, and the stars disappeared behind the overhang of trees. The mountaintop construction site was deserted and silent as a graveyard, and when Daphne cut the engine and stepped out into the night, she could almost feel the ghosts of everything that had happened there: the opulent wedding and her awkward not-date with Trey; a dozen beer-fueled parties around the bonfire pit; Janie losing her virginity to Doug; a sleepy team of lumberjacks clear-cutting the land; Vince Varley's great-grandfather arriving on a covered wagon and surveying the valley below with a look of wonder; a Native American tribe consecrating the mountaintop with a tribal ceremony shrouded in mist; and long, long ago, in another time, a man in a rough-hewn robe standing with his arms aloft, bathed in a golden beam of light, accepting an urgent message from the heavens . . .

She shook her head and the visions cleared like cobwebs, leaving her skin clammy and cold. She was on a mission, and the night wasn't getting any younger. She flicked on her flashlight and ran its beam over the deserted landscape. A construction crane threw towering shadows across the ground, and something scurried away from her and into the underbrush, sending her heartbeat skittering.

The tablet's location was easy enough to find. It was back behind the main foundation, where the contractors had begun digging a decorative pond, and was covered in a blue tarp. Orange safety tape surrounded it, along with signs that read *No Trespassing* and *Authorized Personnel Only*. The flashlight jiggled in Daphne's hand as she approached, sending the scene into a wavering underwater dance.

She reached, trembling, for the edge of the tarp. Her fingertips brushed the surface, which was slick and frigid with dew, and the darkness crouched closer. Gripping the tarp firmly, she pulled the corner back, bracing herself at the plastic crackle that shattered the night's silence. A large black spider, disturbed in its nocturnal activities, ran across the back of her hand, eight tiny feet tickling her flesh. She shook her arm hard, sending it flying, and instantly felt guilty: The spider had been minding its own business, doing what spiders do. *She* was the one trespassing.

She ducked under the tarp and trained her beam around the earthen pit until she found the tablet. It was an expanse of bone-colored stone about the size of an encyclopedia, its edges worn and rounded from years spent buried in the earth.

Seeing it, Daphne gave a small sigh of dismay and sank to sitting, the cold ground freezing her thighs through her jeans.

Because even though the tablet was carved in ancient characters, even though her entire knowledge of foreign languages began and ended with two years of high school Spanish, even though she'd never been further east than Ohio, even though she didn't believe in God and only went to church to be polite, she could read every word.

She clutched the flashlight with trembling fingers, ignoring the cold gravel poking into her legs and the wind whistling through the pines. She read the tablet once, then again, and again, the words clashing like thunderbolts in her head as she struggled to decipher the meaning.

When the true Prophet reads this message, the tablet said, *the era of the Great Divide is at hand. For on the eve of the Great Battle, seven signs and wonders shall come to pass, each in turn and none without the others. And these shall be:*

Clarion

Blood

Fire

Plague

Relic

Death of a Firstborn

Prophet

And yea, once these seven signs and wonders appear, there shall be a Great Battle between the Children of God and the Children of the Earth.

The Children of the Earth shall sow evil and discord wrought from the pits of Hell, while the Children of God turn to the heavens for strength from the One True Deity. The victor shall rule the land and the sky, the earth and the heavens, and forever hold dominion over the soul of humankind, and the loser shall be cast out forevermore into Eternal Nothingness—while those who fail to choose sides shall perish. Heed, for when this warning is uncovered and the true Prophet comes to light, the era of the Great Divide is at hand.

She read it once and then again, a fifth time and then a sixth, struggling to decipher its meaning. Only one thing was clear: that if it was a hoax, Doug hadn't planted it. The language was too sophisticated, the nuances too delicate, to have emerged from his thick skull.

Another thought poked at her, unwelcome yet persistent. What if, in spite of everything, the tablet was real?

The ghosts of Elk Mountain swirled around her and came to rest on the man in the rough-hewn robe, an image blurred and indistinct as a watercolor: a golden beam of light streaming down from the heavens, a bearded man with a rock and a chisel receiving the urgent message from above.

Daphne climbed hurriedly from the pit, brushing the earth from her jeans as she tried to chase the vision away. She was careful to shake out each wrinkle from the tarp as she drew it back over the hole, to leave it looking exactly as she'd found it.

The message haunted her as she started up the truck and went rattling down Elk Mountain Road. Pastor Ted had mentioned a prophet, and so did the tablet. Were they related somehow . . . and did that mean that the prophet on the tablet was also Janie's unborn child? Was the Great Divide on the tablet the same as the Great Change that Pastor Ted was always talking about in his sermons?

I sound like Janie, she thought with a wry smile as she parked the truck in the Global Oil lot and returned the keys to their hook. She was making wild assumptions, seeing signs and omens where there had to be a logical explanation, and practically taking Pastor Ted's sermons as fact. If she kept this up, she'd be greeting everyone in town with "I believe" before she knew it.

She fell into bed, the words from the tablet still thundering in her head. But as soft as the pillow was under her head, and as much as her body ached for sleep, it still wouldn't come. The message blared in her mind, incomprehensible and disturbing. As she tried uselessly to untangle its meaning, four little words played over and over in her mind, a drumbeat underscoring her thoughts:

What if it's real?

28

THE MOTOCROSS TRACK BUZZED WITH Friday-night activity, bikes zooming and leaping over the jumps and berms, careening around curves and kicking up great plumes of dirt until the riders were brown from head to toe. Dust and exhaust hovered in the floodlights like striations on a layer cake, leaving a thin coat of grime on Daphne's jeans and the tang of metal and grease on her tongue. High above them, a crescent moon grinned a pale and sickly smile.

"Who are all these people, anyway?" Janie asked, looking out at the dozens of riders dipping and churning around the track as even more waited on the sidelines, pawing the dirt with leather boots. Even the bleachers, which had once belonged strictly to Janie and her friends, were scattered with stubble-cheeked men cradling forty-ounce beers and smoking Marlboros, politely trying to blow the smoke away from the ladies.

"Uh—you noticed the giant new oil rig in town, right?" Hilary set down her half-empty can of Coors Light. "'Cause, trust me, these guys aren't here for the culture and nightlife."

"I guess you're right." Janie was bundled in an old fleece pullover of Doug's, the sleeves bunched in her hands to ward off the evening chill. "Maybe they came to see the tablet, though. I don't know."

"Yeah, like old Vince would let them anywhere near it," Hilary scoffed. According to the rumors whirling around town, Vince Varley had installed a twenty-four-hour guard to protect the tablet, which he was planning to get authenticated and sell for millions to the highest bidder. But despite all of Hilary's prodding over the past few days, Janie refused to admit whether the rumors were true.

"I just wish those experts would hurry up and finish their conference," Janie sighed, snuggling deeper into the fleece. "I'm dying to know what it says."

"It probably says, *Haha, suckers, this thing is as fake as Deirdre Varley's Louis Vuitton handbag*," Hilary said.

Janie gave her a sharp look. "How can you even joke about it? It's another sign from God. Personally, I think it's going to tell us all about how my baby will lead us through the Great Change so we can get our Eternal Reward."

Hilary shrugged and picked up her beer. "It is weird, I'll give you that. Especially with all the other stuff that's been happening around here." She turned to Daphne. "What do you think it says?"

"I think we should wait and see what the experts say," she replied coolly. It was her standard answer, the one she'd given to her coworkers, Uncle Floyd, and just about everyone else who asked. She wasn't ready to admit that she could read the tablet, or to share its strange and disturbing message.

A roar came from the track, and the girls leaned forward, watching a rider below emerge from the knot of color and noise. He coasted off the jump with air to spare and kicked his legs out behind him, grabbing the back of the seat so he looked like Superman flying through the night. A cheer floated up through the dust as he landed smoothly back in the saddle, wheels as straight as if he'd never left the ground.

Hilary let out a long wolf whistle. "Who was that?" she asked.

"Owen," Daphne replied automatically. She'd been following his red bike frame and glossy black helmet, marveling at the fluid way he took each turn and jump, like a fish darting effortlessly through water. It was clear to her that even with the influx of newcomers, he was still the best rider on the track—and equally clear that he wasn't doing a great job of not showing off in front of Doug and his friends.

"Oooooh!" Hilary nudged her in the ribs. "Look who's been checking out the new guy."

Daphne blushed. "We're just friends," she insisted.

"That's not what it looked like at the wedding," Hilary teased. "Before . . . I mean, never mind. Crap." She snuck a sidelong glance at Janie, who had drawn the fleece up over her chin like a turtle retreating into its shell. Talk of the wedding still made her eyes go dark with terror, and despite the Varley's prompting she still refused to open her gifts or look at any pictures from the day, insisting they all reminded her of God's terrible sign.

From the top of the bleachers, a voice like tarnished silver bells called Daphne's name. She turned to see Luna descending the bleacher stairs like mist, trailing the jagged ends of a moss-colored robe. Beneath it she wore skintight leather shorts and a cropped macramé top, revealing a glowing moonstone that seemed magically embedded in her bellybutton. She carried a hula hoop over one arm, wrapped in blue and silver tape that was worn away in places.

"How's it going?" Luna flopped down next to Daphne, swinging the hoop around to rest on her knees. Daphne felt every pair of eyes on the bleachers clinging to Luna's back, could almost taste the prospectors' longing through the dusty night.

"Fine," Daphne croaked. Luna must have been aware of their gazes, but she ignored them and turned to the cluster of girls, fixing them with her sea-green stare.

"I'm Luna," she said.

"Of course you are," Hilary muttered, loud enough for Luna to hear. But instead of shrinking into herself or finding an excuse to leave like Daphne would have, Luna opened her mouth wide and laughed like a pocketful of change falling to the floor, her teeth sharp and white.

"You got me," she admitted. "Hippie chick, hippie name. Who's winning?" She squinted at the riders zooming around the track.

"It's just a meet," Janie explained. There was something hard in her eyes that Daphne had never seen before, a new line of distrust across her forehead. Daphne wondered if it was simply that her cousin didn't like having another girl on her turf, or if there was something else about Luna that made her uneasy, some quality radiating off of her that made her normally bubbly cousin cagey and territorial. "They're just messing around and stuff—it's not a competition."

"Gotcha." Luna leaned forward, eyes sparkling with interest. "Which one is Owen?"

Daphne pointed him out, amazed that Luna had never bothered to watch him ride. They'd arrived in town together, were sharing an apartment, but beyond that their relationship was inscrutable as tempered glass.

Janie reached over and gripped Daphne's knee hard. "He's going for it," she said through clenched teeth. An engine thundered below, accompanied by encouraging bellows from the crowd, and a rider in a green helmet approached the high jump.

"Doug?" Daphne asked.

Janie's head bobbed. "That trick Owen did earlier—he's going to try it. I can just tell."

Doug yanked hard on his throttle, sending a cloud of exhaust billowing behind him as he gathered speed and roared toward the jump, gunning over the lip. At the height of the ascent, he launched his body behind the bike, kicking his legs like a novice swimmer trying to make it back to shore, determined to emulate Owen's Superman move.

But his weight and inexperience made the bike wobble dangerously, dragging the rear wheel down. He'd waited a moment too long—gravity was already pulling him back down to earth.

Doug realized his mistake in midair and flopped frantically, trying to flail his way back into the saddle. Both he and the bike tumbled to the ground, rolling in opposite directions until they came to a stop in two identical mounds of dirt.

Doug was on his feet in an instant, brushing billows of dust from his jacket and staggering to his bike. Janie's hand still gripped Daphne's knee, fingernails dug in like a claw. She made a small mew of distress, and Daphne put her own hand over her cousin's in a belated gesture of comfort.

"It looks like he's okay," she ventured.

"I hope so," Janie said, shaken.

Doug righted his bike and scrambled into the saddle, crossing the track in a plume of dirt and injured pride.

"He the one who did that to you?" Luna asked Janie, pointing at her stomach.

Janie gave her a look that suggested the question wasn't worth her time and turned to Daphne. "Should I go see if he's all right?" she asked.

"I wouldn't," Daphne replied. The riders were already back in action, swerving around corners and jiggling over the whoop, engines whining like a pack of wolves. "I doubt going down there would be good for the baby," she added.

"I guess you're right," Janie pouted. She cupped her chin in her hands, her lower lip drooping. "I just hope he gets over it quick."

"I'm sure he will," Daphne said, not sure at all.

They watched the rest of the meet in relative silence, interrupted only by Hilary's sarcastic asides and Luna's gleeful exhalations. As the moon crawled higher in the sky, the guys tired and dropped off the track one by one. Bryce swung by the bleachers to grab Hilary, and eventually Doug, red-faced and scowling, appeared for Janie. Luna went off to find a beer and never came back, and before long Daphne found herself alone in the bleachers, watching the final rider swing around the track in dazzling circles.

It was Owen, of course. Alone on the track he rode like a dark horseman on the wind, whipping through the curves and flying over jumps. He torqued and spun, levitated off the seat and gripped the handlebars with his toes, guided the bike in swoops and swirls until it seemed like he'd be airborne forever, like his wheels would never touch the ground. Back in the parking lot the party blossomed, squeals and laughter underscoring a driving rock song, the bonfire twisting knotted columns of flame into the sky. But Daphne barely registered any of it. Alone and unwatched, she no longer had to stop herself from staring at Owen. She could bask in his untamed energy and let her imagination roam as freely as his bike on the track, to a place where she didn't have to keep pushing him away.

Eventually someone turned off the floodlights, plunging the track into a silky darkness punctured only by Owen's headlight and the silver sparkle of the stars. Owen turned his bike toward the trail, and Daphne listened to his motor putter up the hill and disappear into the party's cacophony. She stood, surprised at the stiffness in her knees, and headed toward the party. She'd been watching him for longer than she realized.

↔

The party filled the parking lot and spilled out into the scrubby trees beyond. Smoke from the bonfire mingled with the tattered vapors floating from dozens of cigarettes, and the night was ripe with cheap beer and liquid courage, electrified by the influx of prospectors and rig workers who liked to play as hard as they worked.

Daphne noticed Janie and Doug clustered by the tailgate of Doug's truck in a tight knot of Carbon County locals. They were outnumbered, she realized, surrounded by prospectors and guys from the rig. It was true that the track was no longer just "their" place, and the harder she looked the more she could see the sadness and confusion hovering in a cloud over their group.

The newcomers, on the other hand, seemed pumped with energy, larger than life. They'd formed a loose semicircle around the bonfire and were greedily watching Luna dance with her hoop, sliding it across her chest and undulating her hips to meet it, rolling it over her shoulders and around her waist, her lips parted and glistening. Her robe lay in a heap on the ground, and firelight danced on her skin, giving her a molten quality that burned lava-red from deep within. Her eyes flickered over the crowd, and she flashed a wicked smile.

"Is she for real?" Daphne overheard one of the floorhands ask another.

"I dunno," his friend grunted. "But if she's not, I sure as hell don't want to wake up."

Even the Carbon County locals were entranced. Still huddled together, they crept closer to the fire, a cluster of cautious curiosity clutching sweating beers. Doug had his arm around Janie, but Daphne could sense him straining toward Luna, his desire permeating the air like cheap cologne. Janie nestled herself closer to him, reaching up to twist his wedding ring, reminding him of where he belonged. The line of distrust ran even deeper in her forehead, and her eyes were narrowed as if Luna was a too-bright light that she couldn't bear to face head-on.

Daphne felt a dark presence moving through the crowd. Her skin tingled as Owen appeared on the other side of the circle, arms crossed over his chest and a bemused half smile on his lips. His eyes weren't fixed on Luna and his mouth wasn't hanging open like the rest of the men around him. He seemed to be scanning the crowd, looking for something—or someone. For her.

The song drew to a pounding crescendo, and Luna flung her hoop high in the air. It formed a silhouette against the starry blanket of sky and seemed to hang for just a moment from the tip of the moon. Then the song was over and the hoop plunged back to earth, where Luna caught it neatly around her shoulders, arms outstretched as she dropped a falsely innocent curtsey amid applause and catcalls. Guys surrounded her the moment she threw her hoop aside, and she tossed offhanded commands that sent them scurrying to pick up her robe, fetch her a beer, build up the fire, and get her a nice place to sit. The hardened prospectors tripped over themselves like puppies as they hurried to fulfill her demands, their eyes never leaving her body.

Luna's silvery laugh rang out above it all, inviting and taunting and teasing. She sought Owen in the crowd and curled her finger, beckoning him.

"What do you want?" He was still high from his long solo ride on the track, the adrenalin buzzing through his veins. He wanted to take Daphne aside, to finally finish what he'd tried so many times to start. But Luna was between them.

Luna accepted a beer from a prospector with a deep scar along his cheek. "Are you ready?" she addressed Owen. "To do your part?"

He shook his head, irritated. "I don't know what you're talking about. You always talk in riddles."

She shrugged her robe over her shoulders, the ends swirling around her feet. "And you always take things too literally. The rest of us are almost here. I know you know it. You've seen them in your dreams. You have to welcome them, to help them learn the truth."

Across the bonfire he saw Daphne back away, fading into the shadows. He didn't want to let her slip through his fingers yet again.

Luna followed his eyes. "You really want her, don't you?" She raised an eyebrow.

He kicked at the ground, frustration rising in his chest. "It's more than just a want."

Luna's smile was slow and thick. "So take her," she said. "Take her for us. We can use her."

"For what?" Owen exploded. He could see Daphne moving in the shadows beyond the flames, talking to some of the guys from the rig.

"For the battle, of course." Luna shook her head gently, the charms in her dreadlocks clinking. "For the God of the Earth."

Owen paused, staring through slit lids at the girl who may or may not have been his half sister. The firelight reflected in her eyes, giving the green irises a mad, red gleam, and her teeth were sharp behind an off-kilter smile. She looked spookily beautiful, like an inmate in a Victorian asylum. She looked insane.

This was a girl who'd been raised on a commune and grown up believing its lies, who had created a twisted fantasy world out of a few bad dreams. Now she was drunk with her power over the prospectors, delusional for seeing the attention from a few sex-starved men as something more than it was.

"You're letting a few dreams drive you crazy," he hissed, his face close to Luna's. "There is no God of the Earth, and you know it. You're just trying to make yourself feel better because your dad was a piece-of-shit hippie who abandoned you, and you grew up not knowing shame."

Luna's face hardened, the fire smoldering in her eyes. She laughed bitterly. "You'll see," she began. "You'll see how wrong you are."

But Owen had already turned from her and was half-striding, half-running through the crowd. Between the carousing clusters of prospectors and the glowing yellow tips of their cigarettes, he caught fleeting glimpses of Daphne, her long, dark hair and narrow limbs, the cautious purse of her lips that always made it look like she was guarding something.

He cut around someone's parked Jeep Cherokee and caught her, his hands brushing the butterfly softness of her wrist.

"There you are," he said.

She turned, eyes liquid.

But Doug stepped between them.

He towered over Owen, a thick-necked mountain, face dark with rage and broken blood vessels snaking red across the whites of his eyes. Janie cowered behind him, surrounded by their friends—none of whom looked like they wanted to be there.

"I thought I told you not to come around here anymore," Doug snarled.

"Do you own this track?" Owen tilted his head so he could look Doug in the eye.

Doug sputtered, his neck turning a deep scarlet.

"Listen, I just want to ride," Owen continued. "I didn't come here to steal your thunder or your friends or any of that, and I'm happy to stay out of your way if you stay out of mine. But I live here now, and since this is the only track in town, how about we learn to share it like gentlemen?"

"You're no gentleman," Doug spat.

"Maybe not." Owen's smile was calm and measured. "But I'll agree to act like one if you do, too."

Doug continued hovering, conflicting emotions crossing his face like cars zooming through a busy intersection. Daphne sensed that he knew he was pushing his luck: A few of the rig workers had already drifted toward the confrontation, and now they surrounded Owen from either side, forming a larger and tougher-looking crew than Doug's small group of nonplussed locals. Owen was popular on the rig, a steady worker who never copped attitude or turned down extra tasks, and it looked like it had paid off. When it came down to it, his friends had his back.

"I don't like your attitude . . ." Doug started to say. But Daphne was tired of Doug's bullying. Janie may have been afraid of him, but she wasn't. She knew that beneath the bluster and bravado, he was just a sad, spoiled child. She stepped forward.

"Hey, this is a party, right?" she addressed the crowd.

Heads around her nodded, and there were several enthusiastic *yeahs.*

"So let's act like it," she urged. "Can we get some music going here? Maybe we can all just chill out and have a fun Friday night."

The crowd murmured their assent. Someone went to the speakers, and soon the familiar chords of that summer's top pop anthem blared out, the singer urging everyone to *have a drink, or two, or three, or four, then drop it low so it hits the floor.*

The music cut through the thick tension, dissipating it like a bad smell, and Janie took advantage of the break to grab Doug by the hand. "C'mon, baby, let's go get you another beer," she cooed. "I've got a nice six-pack cooling in the truck."

"Okay," Doug relented. But as Janie led him away, he glanced back at Owen one last time. Hatred blazed in his eyes.

"Doug's got issues, huh?" Owen asked, his voice mild with amusement.

"That's one excuse," Daphne agreed grimly. She could still feel Doug's eyes on them, dark and accusing, from the tailgate of his truck.

"You want to go somewhere else?" Owen asked.

She could hear the subtext in his voice: *somewhere else* meant somewhere away from the rest of the crowd, somewhere they could be alone. She knew she shouldn't go with him; she was getting worse at saying no to him, at ignoring the heat that spread through her body whenever he was close.

But she was tired of fighting, exhausted from building walls only to have him tear them down like they were made of paper with a single look. "Okay," she agreed. They turned and began walking toward the track, away from the fire and the noise and the people.

"You want a beer or anything?" he asked before they left the party behind.

Daphne declined. Already, her head buzzed with something clearer and stronger than any intoxicant, and a buoyant, fizzy sensation had begun to rush through her veins.

They left the party behind and started down the trail in the darkness, their eyes slowly adjusting to the dim moonlight. He felt for her hand and grasped it, guiding her over roots and rocks. She could feel the strength in his wiry muscles, and smell the metallic mixture of motor oil and leather on his skin.

It was easier to see in the open expanse of the track, the packed dirt features pale and spectral as an alien landscape in the wan moonlight. They walked the course silently, the only noises their quiet breath and the party's faraway buzz, until Owen paused at the lip of the high jump.

"It's either stop or turn back at this point," he said. "Unless you want to risk the jump."

Daphne joined him at the edge, and her stomach dropped. It was higher than the roof of the Peytons' trailer, with nothing but air underneath. It looked so much taller from there than it did from the bleachers.

"I think I'd rather keep my legs intact, thanks." She sat, letting her feet dangle over the side, and Owen joined her, close enough for her to feel the warmth of his thigh through their jeans. The stars gazed down at them impassively, high and cold as ice chips in the heavens.

"So . . ." they said at the same time. They turned to each other, surprised, and then they were laughing softly, voices clear in the vast, empty space.

Daphne's mind raced with all of the things she wanted to know: where he'd come from and why he'd left, how he'd gotten to Carbon County and why he'd stayed, the secrets behind his bizarre relationship with Luna and what he made of the strange events that had been occurring in town. But she didn't know where to start.

"Luna's pretty talented," she said, just to break the ice.

Owen laughed. "She knows how to work a crowd," he admitted.

"How did you guys meet, anyway?" Daphne asked.

Owen paused, and the air around them seemed to thicken.

"It's kind of a strange story," he said.

"Everything around here is kind of a strange story."

He studied her closely, drinking in the clean lines of her silhouette against the night, the gold flecks in her amber eyes and the arc of her legs dangling into the empty space below. As much time as they'd spent together on the rig, there was still something mysterious about her, a secret that she carried like an egg, protecting it from breaking.

"You don't have to explain—" Daphne backpedaled, but Owen cut her off.

"I want to."

Maybe if he opened up and told her everything, the whole crazy story about the dreams and the voices and the surreal trip across country, she'd be willing to tell her story, too. The desire to know her secret burned inside him like the familiar urge to win—but he knew he'd never get it out of her if he didn't open up first. She was too guarded for that.

"I turned eighteen a few months ago," he began, his arm brushing hers, "and that night I had the first dream. They always start out with fire, and that's all I see: big, orange flames in every direction, anywhere I look. I get closer and I realize it's not wood in the flames, but stacks of human bodies."

Daphne thought of the blood on his hand when he touched the oil and the dark glow of his skin the night Trey died. She shivered, wondering if they were somehow related to his dreams, but said nothing. She didn't want to stop his story before he even began.

"There are people dancing around," he continued, "going in a circle to these strange, dull drumbeats, really getting into it like they're at a ritual or a rave. I can't see their faces: They're all just these dark shapes against the fire, and something about them is completely terrifying.

"But at the same time, I feel like I *have to* see their faces," Owen continued, "like something even more awful will happen if I don't. So I go closer, even though I don't want to. I'm sweating bullets, and I'm so scared I want to throw up, but I don't. I keep going closer, and everything smells like singed hair, and they're dancing even harder, practically throwing themselves into the fire, but I still can't see their faces."

Owen took a deep breath and gazed out over the barren landscape. Daphne could smell the fear in his sweat, the pure terror that came from even remembering the dreams. He turned to her, his strange green eyes holding hers. "That first night, I woke up before I saw any of them. Right before I came out of it, this huge growling voice whispered *find the vein*. I woke up tangled up in my sheets and sweating so hard I was actually scared I'd wet the bed."

He ducked his head, suddenly bashful. "I can't believe I just told you that part," he said quickly. "I mean, for what it's worth, I didn't."

"It's okay," Daphne laughed, glad for the small wedge of light in his strange, dark tale. His story had left her feeling cold and frightened, as if his fear was airborne and had somehow gotten into her lungs.

"That first night I tried to write it off as just some stupid nightmare, maybe some weird coming-of-age anxiety dream about turning eighteen. But it kept happening, and before I knew it I was having the same dream every night: the bonfire full of bodies, the voice, and the dancers."

"Did you ever see their faces?" Daphne asked.

"I started to, yeah. I've seen all of them now. They're all different, but the weirdest thing is . . ." he broke off, unsure if he should go any further. When he discussed it with Luna, it all made a twisted kind of sense, but he had never talked about it with anyone else.

"Is what?" she asked softly.

Owen ducked his head. "You're going to think this is crazy."

"Try me."

"Okay." He took a deep breath and continued. "The weird thing is, they all have my eyes."

Understanding dawned on her with dazzling force. "Like Luna," she said.

"Yes," he replied.

"You saw her in your dream before you guys even met?"

He nodded, telling her about his wanderings across America and the festival where they'd met, how they'd been born on the same commune and even though he had never laid eyes on her before, he instantly knew who she was.

"And here's the really creepy thing," he concluded, "it turned out, she'd been having the exact same dreams."

A shiver tickled its way across Daphne's limbs, leaving a raised bed of goose bumps in its wake.

"You're cold." Owen's voice was husky. He decided not to share what Luna thought of the dreams and instead shifted closer and draped his arm over her shoulders. The heat from his body was molten, like a furnace, seeping into her skin and igniting something beneath. "And I've been talking about myself this whole time. What about you? What's your story, Daphne?"

His voice was so open, so sincere, that for a moment she considered telling him everything: about her miserable life with Myra and Jim and the violent way she'd put an end to it, the trial and her escape to Carbon County. But when she opened her mouth, the words wouldn't come. The secret had been lodged too deep inside of her, for too long. Extracting it would be as impossible as removing a ship from a bottle—and she was scared that if she tried, she might somehow break herself, too.

"There's not much to tell," she said finally. "I'm pretty boring."

He drew her closer, his hand hot and firm on her shoulder. "That's not what I keep hearing. They say there were trumpet sounds the day you arrived, and that even with all these prospectors looking for it, you're the only one who found oil. Sounds like the opposite of boring."

He found her eyes and held them. "I think you know it, too. I think you're just scared to let people know how amazing you really are."

She dropped her eyes, watching their feet dangle over the precipice. "Well, there is something kind of weird about me," she confessed softly. "I don't know if it's special, exactly—but I don't think it's normal, either."

He raised his eyebrows. "Why don't you let me be the judge of that?"

"Okay." She took a deep breath. "But this is going to sound crazy."

"Crazier than meeting someone from your dreams who has your exact same eyes?"

She laughed softly. "Kind of on that level, yeah."

"Tell me," he insisted.

She took a deep breath. "You know the tablet that they found up at Elk Mountain, the one written in ancient Aramaic?"

He nodded. "It was on the news. Why?"

"Here's the crazy thing." Even though they were completely alone at the top of the jump, she found herself lowering her voice to a hoarse whisper. "I can read it."

Owen sat back, his eyes wide. "How?"

"I don't know," she admitted. She told him about seeing the tablet on the news and realizing the words made sense only to her, her solo trip up Elk Mountain in the dead of the night, and the bizarre and troubling message she had read.

"I can't remember all of it," she finished. "I wish I had taken a picture. There was all this stuff about a Great Divide and a battle between the Children of God and the Children of the Earth, and then there were these seven signs and wonders."

As she listed the few she could remember, she felt Owen's hand grow cold in hers. The temperature had dropped a few degrees, she realized, and the wind had picked up, wailing through the pines like a lost child.

"You saw the tablet on the news, right?" she finished.

Owen nodded, his face pale.

"Could you read any of it?" she asked.

"No." He shook his head slowly. "It just looked like scribbles to me."

"Darn." She felt a wry smile cut across her face. "I hoped I wasn't the only one."

Owen shook off the spike of dread that had pierced him when she mentioned the Children of the Earth. He wouldn't let his fear ruin the moment, their first real time alone together since they'd met. "There's some pretty crazy stuff going on in this town," he said.

Daphne looked out over the motocross track, at the pines beyond and the dark outline of mountains far away. "Do you think it's something about this place?" she asked. "Some reason these things keep happening and we both ended up here?"

"I don't know." Owen took his hand in hers, sending a spark sizzling up her arm. "All I know is that the voice in my dreams, the one telling me to *find the vein*? It stopped when I got here. Now it's telling me that the vein is here."

She turned to him, embers of excitement in her eyes. "So we were both drawn here," she said. "And Luna, too. You guys had your dreams, and I just had this—well, a *feeling*. Like if I didn't come here, something bad would happen. Like there wasn't any other choice."

She sat back, contemplating the stars. "Maybe Pastor Ted's right," she mused. "Maybe there really is a great change coming, and we're supposed to be here for it. Maybe he's not as crazy as I used to think."

"You mean, like, God brought us here?" Owen bit his lip.

His words deflated her. "God wouldn't want anything to do with *me*," she said, dropping her head.

"Why not?" Owen leaned into her, forcing her eyes to meet his. The gold flakes in her irises stood out in the moonlight, floating on a troubled amber sea.

She shook her head. "There's too much bad in my past."

So she was still hiding a secret. It made her even more alluring, a puzzle he was always one piece away from solving. He scanned her face for clues but saw only sorrow, sorrow that ran strong and deep.

He moved closer and wrapped his arm around her, pulling her close. Her eyes met his, a liquid cocktail of confusion and need, and her lips glistened in the moonlight.

Then he was kissing her. One hand pressed against her back and the other brushed her cheek, tangling in her hair, and she was responding, finally, her lips soft and pliant under his. He knew, then, that she hadn't just been playing hard to get, that she'd been as attracted to him all summer as he was to her, that by fighting him she was fighting her own inner demons. But waiting for her had paid off. He felt tied to her by something more than the kiss, their fates lashed together in an uncertain future.

He broke away from her, his breath ragged. "I just want you to know," he murmured, "that whatever happens, you don't have to go through it on your own."

Daphne felt something unclench inside of her. She'd been alone, and afraid, her entire life. Now someone was here—and he was holding her, seeing her, and not letting her go.

"I know," she murmured, leaning in for another kiss.

29

THEY DIDN'T SAY ANYTHING ELSE. They didn't need to. Their lips had finished talking and were busy discovering each other, his hands warm on her back and her arms around him, grasping his shoulders and running up and down the ridges of his arms.

Being this close to someone had always seemed strange and frightening, the very opposite of Daphne's instinct to cower and run whenever a guy approached. But Owen had unlocked something inside of her. She was consumed with desire, aching for his lips and tongue, the soft stubble on his cheek and the heady scent of motor oil and shampoo and the musky tang beneath all of it that must have been simply *him*, his own need responding to hers.

"I've wanted you," he whispered in her ear, kissing her cheeks, her neck.

She planted a hand on either side of his face and dragged his lips back to hers.

She wanted to kiss him all night, forever. She lost all sense of time, was on top of the world and deep in the ground, floating in the heavens and digging to the center of the earth, far below where the oil sluiced and bubbled.

And then they heard the scream. It was wild and haunting, a silver arrow piercing the night.

Daphne shot upright, her hair loose around her face. Her cheeks were flushed, her clothes askew.

"What was that?" Owen joined her, a steadying hand on her back.

The scream came again, louder, terrified.

Daphne leapt to her feet, the beautiful warm haze of the kiss in tatters. She knew that voice.

"Janie," she breathed. "I have to go."

Blades of cold air slashed her face as she raced back down the jump, stumbling on the rough terrain of the track and righting herself and stumbling again. She dimly sensed footsteps a few paces behind her and knew that Owen was following, but she couldn't afford to wait.

Something had happened to Janie, something horrible. Another scream came, agonized and full of fear and pain. What if she'd fallen somehow, or burned herself on an ember from the fire? What if Doug had lost control and was hurting her, savagely shoving aside anyone who tried to intervene?

I never should have left her alone, Daphne cursed herself as she dashed up the trail, dew from the overhanging trees falling in rivulets down her face. She burst into the parking lot, calling her cousin's name.

"There you are!" Hilary grabbed Daphne's arm as soon as she emerged into the firelight. She dragged her through a circle of onlookers, elbowing them out of the way. They parted like strands of hair, shuffling with nervous coughs and murmured apologies, letting them pass.

Janie lay in the center of the circle, on a bald patch of earth. She clutched the ground with one hand and her belly with another, her face streaked with dirt and makeup and slick with sweat. A steady trickle of moans poured from her mouth, ululating through the quiet night, and for one terrible moment Daphne wondered if she was possessed, if by somehow finally finding her own faith she had unleashed the devil on her cousin.

Then Janie's eyes met hers, and they were still Janie's: big and blue, surrounded by thick, dark, eyeliner, and utterly terrified.

"What's wrong?" Daphne rushed to her side. Kneeling in the dirt, she put an arm around her cousin's trembling back.

"Gggggguuuuuuuuunnnnnnnnnnghhhhhh!" Janie howled. The circle of partygoers took a hurried step back. Daphne noticed Doug in the front row, an empty beer can crushed and forgotten in his hand, eyes bulging with horror as he gazed, paralyzed, at his wife.

Janie clung to her belly, panting and sobbing. A puddle of water began to form beneath them, seeping into the ground and spreading in a radius of sopping tendrils. A terrible thought dawned on Daphne as she watched it.

"Janie." She cupped her cousin's chin and gently forced her to eye level. "Is it the baby?"

"I think so," Janie whimpered. "I think . . . he's coming."

Daphne glanced from the growing puddle on the ground to the clammy sheen of Janie's face to the crowd still huddled around them like extras in a movie scene gone wrong.

"Did anyone call an ambulance?" She whipped around to face the partygoers. They shook their heads, bashful and reticent.

"They'll bring the cops," someone said.

"Are you fucking *kidding me*?" Daphne screamed. "She's going into labor five weeks early, and you're worried about your stupid party getting busted? Someone call an ambulance *now*!"

"They said they'd shut down the track if—"

"*Now*!" Daphne repeated.

"I got it," a voice beside her said. She turned to see Owen standing apart from the crowd, already punching the numbers into his phone, and a horrible déjà vu swept over her. She could almost see Trey's charred remains silhouetted in the firelight.

The only sounds as Owen spoke to the operator were the bonfire crackling and the wind whispering and Janie's jagged, panting breaths.

"They're on their way," he said, hanging up the phone.

The words dropped on the party like a bomb, everyone exploding like shrapnel toward their cars. Feet pounded by them, people running in all directions, barking hurried instructions and frantically calling for their friends in the confusion. A howl of feedback ripped through the speakers as someone's music player was hastily unplugged, and a half-empty beer can rolled clumsily toward them, kicked over in its owner's hurry to split the scene.

Truck engines roared to life one after another, headlights throwing cones of illumination through the swirling dust. They drove away like wasps being smoked out of their nest, the buzz of their motors angry and urgent. One sped by close enough to kick a clump of dirt into Daphne's face. Dust and gravel whirled around them, stinging their eyes.

"Doug!" Daphne called. In the middle of all the chaos, he stood frozen, rooted to his spot at what had once been the edge of the crowd. His whole macho act had been stripped away, and he looked lost and scared. "We have to get her away from this—help me get her to the bleachers."

Doug's mouth hung open, uncomprehending. His eyes were cloaked in a haze of fear. Slow as a zombie emerging from the dead, he shook his head.

"Come *on*," she urged.

"I—can't," he croaked. "I'm sorry."

Janie looked up, stricken. She opened her mouth to call his

name, but a contraction shook her body like an earthquake and she doubled over, wailing.

Doug took a slow step back, then another. If Daphne didn't know him better, she could have sworn she saw true regret in his eyes, a genuine desire to stay and help even if he didn't know how. But he was Doug: creepy, violent, arrogant Doug, who never cared about anyone but himself. It was no surprise to her when he turned and started running, each foot hitting the ground like a ten-pound sack of potatoes, heavy shoulders heaving as he hurried away.

"Daphneee!" Janie gasped, tears rolling down her cheeks. "It's—oh, God, it hurts."

Daphne's heart thudded in her ears as she looked around for Owen. He stood a few paces away, trying to direct traffic to keep the caravan of cars from running Janie down as they sped out of the parking lot. She called his name and he turned, taking in the situation with one quick glance. Then he was beside her.

"I'll get one side, you get the other," he suggested. They each wedged a shoulder under one of Janie's arms and lifted, carefully arranging her knees over their arms so they could carry her to the bleachers.

"Can someone please turn on the lights?" Daphne screamed into the chaos of the parking lot. Mercifully, someone must have heard, because soon they buzzed on, bathing the bleachers in a harsh fluorescent glow.

They lowered Janie, panting and moaning, onto the cold metal. Daphne squatted next to her cousin and smoothed back her hair, using her sleeve to wipe the sweat from her forehead. "You're going to be all right," she assured her. "The ambulance will be here soon, and they'll take care of you."

Janie's eyes were round as peaches, her breath coming in short, desperate puffs. "I don't know if I can wait," she gasped. "It's really coming. Like, now . . . *ooooooooww!*" Her head snapped back, and the howl shuddered through her body, turning her into something feral and frightening, a bright-hot conduit of pain.

Daphne looked helplessly at Owen. "You don't know anything about delivering babies, do you?" she asked.

"Only what I've seen on TV. I know we need boiling water and towels, and that's about it."

"We don't have either. This will have to do." Daphne ripped off her hoodie and laid it under Janie's writhing torso. The night wind whipped against her bare arms and went screeching away through the trees, but as hard as she listened, she still couldn't make out the wail of an ambulance.

Janie flopped back and forth on the hoodie, contorting herself and clawing at her underwear. As Daphne bent to remove them, she realized with a shiver that they were soaked in fluid and already spattered with blood. Janie was gasping for breath, growling low in her throat.

"Don't forget to breathe," Daphne reminded her. She forced herself to take an exaggerated deep breath and blow it out through her mouth, like it had said to do in one of the baby books she'd brought home from the library. "Breathe with me. Good. You're going to be okay."

Rivulets of sweat poured down Janie's face, which was as pink and strained as a pimple about to burst. It soaked her hair and dribbled into her mouth, making her gurgle and sputter even as she cried out a prayer.

"God," she panted, eyes rolled back to address the heavens, "please watch over us and deliver my baby safe and sound. Please, God, that's all I ask."

Her prayer ended in an agonized yelp as her body contorted violently, shaking the bleachers.

"I think he's crowning," Daphne said. The blood was coming thick and fast, soaking her hoodie and running like rivers down the grooves in the bleachers, but through it she thought she could see a shape emerging, the round top of the baby's head. A sudden and unexpected wonder surged in her chest: Life was beginning before her eyes, and a tiny miracle was about to enter the world.

"Push," Owen urged. He had ripped off his shirt to wipe the sweat from Janie's eyes, and the muscles in his chest twitched as she crushed his hand in the throes of another contraction. Another small section of the baby's head emerged, and Daphne noticed with growing astonishment the tiny curls of hair on his scalp. The whole time Janie had been pregnant, she'd thought of "the baby" almost as an abstract concept, an object that lived inside her cousin's belly like an extra organ.

But as she watched the head emerge centimeter by centimeter, as Janie grunted and screamed and Owen stood by her side reminding her to push and breathe, assuring her that she was doing great, that it was almost out, Daphne truly understood for the first time that the baby was a real person, someone with a unique personality who would develop his own habits and dreams and ambitions and fears. He was someone with a soul.

Pastor Ted had claimed the baby would be a miracle, a prophet sent by God to lead the people of Carbon County through the Great Change, and now that she knew about the tablet and Owen's dreams, she may have even believed it. But whether the child was a prophet or just an ordinary kid who burped and pooped and smiled, he'd still be a miracle. Every soul on earth was.

Daphne held out her hands to catch him as Janie's son made his way into the world, into the light. Janie gave one final push, Owen urging her on, the contraction so strong she nearly levitated off the bleachers. There was a rush of blood that soaked Daphne's arms all the way to the elbow and spilled out in a lake of red, and then Janie was lying back in a soft pile of exhausted flesh, and the baby was in Daphne's hands.

She used Owen's shirt to wipe the blood from his face,

revealing wisps of hair softer than corn silk, a nose no bigger than her fingertip, and eyes the color of cornflowers staring up past her, way up into the sky. He was perfect. Each of his limbs, all ten of his tiny fingers and toes, were flawlessly formed, as if sculpted by the greatest artist who ever lived.

But there was something wrong.

He wasn't crying.

His eyes, so blue and serene, saw nothing. His flesh, still warm from Janie's body, grew slowly cold in her arms. She put her hand to his chest, but there was no heartbeat.

And when she bowed her head to listen for his breath, there was nothing but the mourning keen of a siren still half a dozen miles away.

"Can I hold him?" Janie groggily propped herself up on one elbow, wisps of hair framing her face like a halo. "I want to hold my baby."

Daphne just looked at her, tears flowing down her face for the first time since she was a very young girl, unable to speak the horrible truth: that there on the cold, dusty bleachers at the Carbon County motocross track, with nobody around to bless his soul, Janie had given birth to a baby boy who was perfect and beautiful in every way . . . but would never take his first breath.

The child in her arms was stillborn.

30

THE COFFIN WAS NO BIGGER than a shoebox.

Pastor Ted stood above the grave, his suit black and his face, normally pink with piety and passion, the dull gray of regret. It matched the late-afternoon sky above them, a solid blanket of drabness as endless as their grief.

The world was gray. Mourning.

No longer able to keep up the tough exterior that had protected her since childhood, Daphne let the tears fall as the tiny coffin was lowered into the ground. The rage that had flowed through her blood for most of her life was washed away, replaced with a bleak hopelessness that fell in endless tears from her eyes. She'd been crying off and on since the baby went cold in her arms. In those horrible few minutes before the ambulance came, the words from the Aramaic tablet had blared in her head: *Death of a Firstborn.*

Her tears flowed through the ride with Janie in the ambulance to the hospital, dribbling down her face while she sat under the bleak glare of the waiting room lights until Floyd and Karen burst in. Seeing her cry for the first time since her father died, they understood what had happened without having to be told.

Karen's face went white, and her knees seemed to give out from under her. She nearly hit the floor before Floyd caught her and, clinging to one another, they made their way to the intensive care unit. The night passed in a long blur of hushed conversations and IV drips as Janie was treated for blood loss and dehydration and the words on the tablet echoed over and over in Daphne's mind like the chorus to a terrible dirge: *death of a firstborn, death of a firstborn.*

The baby was officially pronounced dead at one eleven a.m., and Daphne sat helpless next to her aunt and uncle as the doctor solemnly explained that funeral arrangements needed to be made.

The Varleys arrived sometime after two, Deirdre's un-made-up face like a pile of chalk dust. Her hand shook as she placed a bouquet of hastily cut begonias from her garden in a vase by Janie's bedside.

"We couldn't find Doug." Vince's voice was coiled tight as a spring. "Tried calling, texting—no answer. I don't suppose you've seen him."

"No." Daphne thought of Doug's slow headshake when she asked him for help, the terror in his eyes before he'd turned tail and run clumsily away. "Not since the meet."

Uncle Floyd's face, already the color of day-old dishwater, darkened, but he said nothing. It was dawn before they were able to take Janie home, bundled in a hospital blanket and shivering. She hadn't spoken since her son had been pronounced dead, and her eyes stared unseeingly out at the world, as empty as a grave.

Pastor Ted had no sermon. There were no lessons in the death of the child, a holy child who he'd believed with all of his heart would lead the Children of God through the Great Change. He merely opened the Bible and read.

"Thessalonians 4:14," he recited, his voice hollow with grief. "'For since we believe that Jesus died and rose again, through Jesus God will bring with Him those who have fallen asleep.

"'For the Lord Himself will descend from heaven with the sound of trumpets. And the dead in Christ will rise first. Then we who are left will be caught up together with them in the clouds to meet the Lord in the air, and so we will always be with the Lord. Therefore, encourage one another with these words.'"

The congregation was silent. Their faces, the sky, the entire day and all the days beyond seemed gray. Uncle Floyd blew his nose into a handkerchief, Aunt Karen wept openly, and the rows of folding chairs were a sea of sniffles. Shoulders shook and sopping tissues were crammed into pockets and purses, the steady shuffle of grief broken by the occasional wet sob.

Only Janie sat silent. Her face was stony and white as a marble statue, her eyes unfocused and unseeing. She stared past Pastor Ted, not registering his words, unresponsive to the protective hand her mother laid over hers. She was somewhere beyond grief, in a place of shock as bleak and barren as the desert.

Across the aisle, Deirdre Varley dabbed at her eyes and Vince balled his fists tight in his lap, his face twitching. Doug sat between them with his hands on his knees, shoulders hunched over, refusing to look at anyone. His head had been down since they arrived, his skin colorless. He hadn't yet spoken to Janie, hadn't done so much as acknowledge her with a glance, and Daphne could tell that the fact that they weren't sitting together was raising eyebrows.

Pastor Ted knelt and sprinkled a handful of earth into the open grave. "We commend unto thy hands, most merciful father, the soul of this thy child," he chanted in monotone. "And we commit his body to the ground, earth to earth, ashes to ashes, dust to dust. Amen."

Sorrow spilled from his eyes as he stood and faced the congregation once more. "You may now proceed to the funeral home for the reception," he said quietly.

Daphne stood. As she turned to follow Uncle Floyd, she realized that Janie hadn't budged. She sat like a pile of earth, unmoving, as the crowd bustled around her.

"Janie." Daphne took her hand, which was as white and limp as a dead fish. "It's time to go."

The stiff beige drapes and overstuffed sofas in the funeral parlor's reception room felt oppressive. The stagnant air smelled of Lysol and egg salad, and the congregants moved slowly through the space, too shell-shocked to mingle freely. A rainbow of crudités and crystal bowls of dip sat untouched on a long table to the side of the room, small mountains of egg and pasta salad unmarred by anything but their silver serving spoons. Even the pyramids of brownies and lemon squares were intact. The occasion was too bitter for sweets, and the congregation had lost its collective appetite.

"Do you want a soda?" Daphne asked Janie as they made their way through the doors. Her cousin made a soft gagging sound, which Daphne took as a no. She fetched a clear plastic cup of water instead and watched Janie accept it passively, holding it in front of her like she didn't know what it was.

"Drink." Daphne placed her hands over Janie's and helped bring the cup to her lips. "The doctor said you need lots of fluids."

Her cousin's lips opened obediently, and her throat rippled as she swallowed. A small stream of liquid leaked down her chin, leaving a dark spot on the front of the dress Daphne had selected for her that morning while Janie sat catatonic on the couch.

Daphne looked around for her aunt and uncle, but they were on the other side of the room, surrounded by friends trying to console them as Karen sobbed and Floyd clutched her helplessly, for once at a total loss for words.

"Janie." Hilary was the first to approach them, dragging a reluctant Bryce by the arm. "I am so, so sorry for your loss. I don't even know what to say. There aren't any words." Her red-rimmed eyes crumpled and her nose scrunched up pink and translucent as a rabbit's, the skin around her nostrils bright and irritated from constant blowing. She reached out to hug her friend, but Janie's arms stayed stiff by her sides, and she stared blankly over Hilary's shoulder.

Hilary drew back, startled. "Are you okay?" she asked. "I mean, I'm sorry, I know you're not okay. What a stupid question. But, I mean, you'll *be* okay eventually?" The edge of doubt grew in her voice, buoyed by Janie's eerie, unresponsive staring. Realizing that her friend barely registered her, she shot Daphne a look of blatant concern. Daphne shrugged silently.

"Well, let me know if there's anything we can do," Hilary said, as much to Daphne as to Janie. "I'm the world's worst cook, but I'll totally bring over a casserole or whatever. As long as you don't mind if it's burnt."

Daphne thanked her as she drifted back into the crowd. One by one, Janie's friends and fellow churchgoers stepped forward, choking up awkward platitudes and offering limp pats on the back, embraces that were met with the same stiff-armed detachment.

Daphne could barely believe that the blank-eyed zombie next to her was her cousin. The Janie Daphne knew cried over dog food commercials, but since the death of her own son, she hadn't shed a tear. It was like someone had gone in and flicked a switch to *off*, leaving only the shell of her body behind.

When Pastor Ted finally made his way to them, Daphne felt a guilty relief at being able to hand her cousin off. She needed a break, if only for a couple of minutes. She found Owen at the edge of the crowd and wanted to collapse in gratitude as he brought her in for a tight embrace, surrounding her in the dusky, mechanical scent that simultaneously spiked her pulse and calmed her growing panic. When they parted she saw that there were dark circles beneath his eyes, and his face was unusually pale.

"Are you all right?" he asked. She hadn't seen him since she'd left with Janie in the ambulance, and she hadn't realized until that moment how much she'd missed him.

"As much as I can be," she said. "What about you? You—don't look so good."

"Thanks." He smiled wryly. "You sure know how to flatter a guy."

The brief glimmer of humor was tantalizing as a jewel in the oppressive afternoon. For the briefest moment, she let herself grin back.

"I'm sorry—I just meant . . ."

"It's okay. I've been working like a dog, and I have to leave in a minute to go home and change for the afternoon shift. But I haven't been able to get anything about that night out of my mind. That tablet . . . you said it said . . ."

"I know," she interrupted, her voice low. "The death of a firstborn. What if it was talking about this?"

The words knocked her tears loose again, and a fat, gleaming drop rolled down her cheek.

Owen brushed it away with the back of his hand. "We can worry about that later," he murmured. "How's Janie doing?"

"Not great," Daphne admitted. They both looked over at Janie, who was sitting on the couch with Pastor Ted. She gazed past his head with the vacuous eyes of a doll, clearly not processing a word.

Daphne lowered her voice to a whisper. "I've never seen her like this," she admitted. "She's not even crying—she's just acting like a zombie. Honestly, I'm really scared."

"Has Doug talked to her?" Owen asked.

Daphne shook her head. Doug was on the other side of the room, leaning against the wall with a cup of coffee in his hand, staring stubbornly at the pattern on the funeral parlor's carpet. "He seems almost as out of it as she is."

Owen sighed. "Look, as much as I dislike the guy, he may be what gets her to snap out of it. He's the father—whatever she's going through, he's going through, too. It might help if they go through it together."

"I don't think he wants to talk to her," Daphne said, hating Doug more than ever.

"Someone should make him," Owen muttered. "I'd try, but I'm not exactly his favorite person."

Daphne looked back at Janie. Her mouth hung open slightly, and her shoulders slumped as Pastor Ted read to her from a pocket-sized Bible. She looked like she needed to be propped up, like she could slide down the couch and onto the floor at any moment.

"Maybe I should talk to Doug," Daphne said. Her stomach contracted at the thought of it, but she'd suck it up if it there was even a possibility it could help Janie.

"It's up to you," Owen replied.

But Daphne had already made up her mind. "I will," she said. "I'll go do it right now."

"Good luck." Owen squeezed her hand tightly before letting go.

She crossed the room to Doug and planted herself in front of him, overriding the nausea that swelled in her stomach whenever they were close.

"Hey, Doug," she said, struggling to keep her voice friendly.

He dragged his eyes up from the pattern on the carpet. "Hey, Daphne," he said tonelessly.

"Are you doing all right?" she asked, hoping to start on neutral ground.

"Am I *doing* all right?" Doug's eyebrows flattened into a low, straight line. "I dunno, Daphne—my wife's a basket case, and my kid's dead. How do you *think* I'm doing?"

He laughed a hard, sarcastic laugh and slammed his fist into the wall, causing several heads to turn sharply in their direction. Daphne realized too late that Doug's detachment and indifference, the antisocial way he'd walled himself off from the rest of the mourners, wasn't boredom or sadness at all. It was rage—a rage that he'd been trying to keep a lid on by staying well away from everyone, a rage that she'd just brought to the surface.

"Doug, I'm really sorry . . ." she began.

"Sorry?" Doug drew himself up to his full height and advanced on her, making the blood cower in her veins. "My son is *dead*, Daphne—dead because you thought you could play doctor and deliver him at a friggin' motocross track. And all you can say is you're *sorry?*"

He bellowed the last word, stopping all conversations in their tracks. The crowd stared openly at them, waiting to see what Daphne would say. It was as if Doug had taken a sword and sliced straight through the thick haze of emotion in the room, severing it so that he landed on one side and Daphne on the other.

"It wasn't like that." Her throat was dry. "She was going into labor. Someone had to do something."

"Yeah—someone with a medical degree," Doug snarled. "Not you."

She stepped back, surprised.

"I was just trying to help," she explained.

"Sure—big help *you* turned out to be." Spit flew from Doug's mouth and landed on her cheek. He was towering over her, his face purple with fury.

Daphne looked around at the congregation, appealing for help. Surely someone would realize that Doug was being unreasonable, that he was going too far.

But the faces staring back at her were blank, offering no glimmers of protection. Nobody stepped forward to intervene. They stood suspended as the chunks of pineapple in Eunice's Jell-O mold, watching, waiting to see what she would say.

Their silence, the sudden unreadable sheen of their faces, unsettled her. "It wasn't my fault," she tried to insist—but her voice wavered, unsure. *Wasn't it?* a voice in the back of her head taunted. *Once a killer, always a killer. Why would Janie's child be any different?*

Doug cocked an eyebrow, taunting her. She felt the mood in the room shift, the gears in the group mind turn, and the mechanisms of blame click slowly into place. They'd read the weakness in her tone, latched onto her own nagging insecurity and seen it as an admission of guilt.

"I was trying to help her!" she tried again, forcefully. These were the people who hailed her as the finder of oil, the bearer of good fortune. So many of them had been at the motocross track when it happened—they'd seen Janie go into labor with their own eyes! Could they really blame her for being the only one who stayed?

"Or maybe you just wanted to play hero," Doug said bitterly. "You've been pretty high on yourself ever since you supposedly found that oil—maybe now you thought you could deliver a baby with no medical training, too."

Daphne recalled the look of terror on Doug's face when she'd begged him for help, the way he'd backed away like Janie was a dangerous animal before turning and running into the night. What if he was covering up for his own cowardice, blaming her for having the courage to stay when he had fled? If so, there was no way she'd let him get away with it.

"I begged you to help, and you ran," she reminded him, sure the crowd would see it her way.

"Yeah, because I'm *not a doctor*," Doug said condescendingly, his voice wound with tightly controlled fury. "I don't think I'm God's gift to everything and go taking babies' lives in my hands."

A murmur of assent wafted through the room. Daphne realized with a shock that people were nodding—they were actually *agreeing* with Doug!

"Daphne." Pastor Ted stepped forward, arms crossed over his long black robe. "Did you try to deliver this child?"

She felt like she was on trial. She flashed back to the courtroom in Detroit, back in another lifetime, with the prosecutor asking her point-blank: *Daphne, did you kill this man?*

The answer was the same. She could no more lie here in front of Pastor Ted and the congregation, her friends and family, than she could after swearing to tell the truth in a court of law.

"Yes," she said quietly. "But I *had* to. The baby was coming."

"You couldn't have waited ten minutes for the ambulance?" The voice was high and shrill: Deirdre Varley's.

"Yeah," someone in the crowd agreed, and the chant was taken up: *Yeah, you couldn't wait? Ten minutes? Really?*

Daphne looked around incredulously. The people of the town that had taken her in, the first place she'd ever truly felt safe, were accusing her of something so awful that just thinking about it made tears spring to her eyes—she, who had never cried until that night, not since the day she'd learned that her father was dead. The funeral parlor blurred as she struggled to keep the tears from spilling.

"There wasn't any time," she insisted. "I *love* Janie—she's like a sister to me. Why would I try to hurt her baby? What could I possibly stand to gain?"

"Power." It was Doug again, commanding the room with a sinister sneer. "My son was going to be a prophet, but you wanted that power for yourself, just like you've wanted everything for yourself since you got here. So you killed him. And that bastard Owen helped."

"It's not true!" Daphne shouted. There was no stopping the tears—there were too many brimming behind her eyelids, pushing to escape. They poured down her cheeks and the crowd glared, seeing them as a confession and admission of guilt. The white-hot cloud of their fury choked the airless room, and she could see the malice in their narrowed eyes, in the grim set of their teeth. They had turned on her. "I wanted that baby to live more than anything. I tried to save him. Why would I lie?"

"*Because you're a liar!*" Doug thundered. His eyes flashed fire as he took a step toward her, and a horrible premonition made her shrink back, chilling her blood. He was going to say the most awful thing yet, something that would turn the town against her for good. And she was powerless to stop him.

"You lied about everything," he spat, "who you are, why you're here, what you did back in Detroit."

"No," she whispered. Her heart, her blood, her breath all slowed to a stop as the cold hard truth of Doug's accusation detonated inside her. He had found out. Somehow, impossibly, the person who most wanted to destroy her had discovered her terrible secret.

Doug's neck cracked as he gazed triumphantly around the room, staring everyone down, daring them to contradict him. "There's something you should all know about Daphne," he said, "a little something she sort of forgot to mention when she arrived. She may have told you that her stepfather's dead, but I bet she didn't tell you why. It's *because she killed him.*"

A gasp snaked through the crowd. Daphne's knees turned to liquid; she fought through layers of gravity to stay upright.

"Oh yeah," Doug laughed, his eyes fireballs of hate. "Straight through the heart with a knife. You can look it up in the papers if you don't believe me . . . but unlike Daphne, I have no reason to lie."

A shocked silence blanketed the congregation. Daphne felt it tug at her from the inside out, sucking her up like a vacuum, the pressure in her chest threatening to make her implode. Her worst nightmare had come true, and there was no waking from it. She'd been exposed for exactly what she was.

"Is this true?" Pastor Ted asked gravely.

"It . . ." she stammered. "I . . ."

"She's lying!" Doug screamed before she could form the words. "She lies about everything: She's a murderer and a liar!"

With that, the crowd seemed to erupt.

"Murderer!" a cracked female voice called from the back of the room.

"Liar!" someone answered, like a twisted game of Marco Polo.

"Baby-killer!" someone else howled.

The accusations flew thick and black as a flock of ravens, swooping in hysterical arcs from one side of the room to the other. Daphne felt like the words were physically attacking her, clawing at her skin, pecking at her eyes, goring a hole in her stomach from the inside.

"Please!" she cried over the noise, her hands above her head as if they could deflect their horrible words. "It wasn't what you all think, it was in self-defense. The jury acquitted me!"

"Liar!" they screamed, mouths twisting around the word like rubber Halloween masks, fists in the air. Through the shouting and the chaos, the angry words hurled at her like rocks through a glass window, bruising her harder than any stone ever could, Daphne saw Uncle Floyd and Aunt Karen huddled together, looking small and weak and overwhelmed. Betrayed. She had meant to tell them the truth someday. Now she was too late.

But it was Deirdre Varley, not Floyd or Karen Peyton, who came barreling at her across the funeral home. "You killed my grandchild," she wailed over the din. She staggered forward, skinny hands outstretched in anger, ready to close around Daphne's throat. "My holy grandson, the prophet—you brought the devil to this town, and you killed him with your bare hands!"

Her kitten heel caught on the carpet and she went pitching forward, arms windmilling in a frenzy of black boucle and crepey white flesh. She sprawled on the ground at Daphne's feet, too overcome with grief and anger to stand, beating her puny fists on the floor and calling Daphne a baby-killer over and over again, her voice scraping at Daphne's last tiny shred of self-control.

Vince pushed through the crowd to help her up, and she collapsed in his arms, wailing. He tried to drag her away, but she turned, narrow lips spewing recriminations. "I see you for what you are!" she crowed. "You're the work of the devil—and my grandson's blood is on your hands."

"But it was on the tablet!" Daphne cried. She felt surrounded and trapped, hunted like an animal, ensnared by their hate. "I could read it, the Aramaic, all of it! It said there would be seven signs and wonders, and one of them would be the death of a firstborn."

Her words cut a swath through the chaos, trailing silence behind.

"The tablet?" someone asked.

"From Elk Mountain?" another echoed.

"The ancient Aramaic?" a third intoned.

"Yes!" she sobbed, hands open in supplication before them, an offering, a plea. "I don't know how or why, but I could read it. It said there would be the death of a firstborn, and a whole bunch of other stuff: a plague, a prophet, a battle between the Children of God and the Children of the Earth. I didn't know the firstborn would be Janie's—if I had, I would have tried to do something, I swear!"

"You could read the tablet?" Pastor Ted asked doubtfully.

Daphne nodded. She felt the disbelief radiating off of the crowd in waves, acrid contempt scenting the air, and she wished she'd said nothing. Across the room, she saw Uncle Floyd staring at her, bushy eyebrows high on his forehead. For a moment, there was the old glimmer of affection in his eyes, the tiniest trace of the admiration she'd earned by helping discover the oil and landing a job at the rig. He looked like he wanted to believe her. But he was the only one, and in his bereavement and confusion, his last gasp of faith wasn't enough.

"I doubt they teach that in Detroit," Vince Varley sneered.

"She's a filthy liar," Doug cut in, "just like I said."

The congregation nodded, simmering, pumped up on coffee and fury, the storm of accusations a potent outlet for their misplaced, unprocessed grief. They shook and sneered, lashing at her with their eyes and words, a pack of wolves surrounding their prey.

Pastor Ted took stock of the situation. He approached Daphne cautiously, like a cop about to put down a rabid dog. "I think it's best you leave," he said solemnly. "This is a delicate time for our congregation, and we'd appreciate it if you left us alone to take care of our own." His eyes were the coldest blue, and somehow his gentle, tactful authority hurt more than all their brutal name-calling combined.

"You're asking me to leave?"

His nod was short, curt, the message unsaid but clear: *not asking. Telling.*

"And don't come back!" someone shouted.

"And take your dirty baby-killing boyfriend with you!" another shrilled.

"Go away!" the crowd chorused. "Go away! Leave us alone! Don't come back!"

Her eyes, blurred with tears, searched the angry faces and landed on the Peytons. They clutched each other, trembling, staring at her with looks of hopeless shock. She met their eyes and raised her eyebrows slightly, a question, a plea. But it was too little, too late. Karen buried her head in Floyd's chest, her shoulders shaking, and after a moment Floyd, too, forced himself to turn away.

She had no other choice. The community she'd begun to think of as hers, the town she had started to call home, the family she'd become a part of, were all rejecting her, throwing her out the door like yesterday's trash.

"Okay," she said simply.

She turned and walked out the door, her back to everyone and everything she'd come to love.

31

MILK. SHE WAS FULL OF milk, drenched with it from the inside. It felt like milk had replaced all the liquid in her body, her blood, sweat, and tears. Sweet milk, white milk, inside of her, everywhere.

Milk filled her chest, pulsing inside her breasts until they were sore. It leaked from her nipples, leaving slick white trails inside her bra, leaking through until it felt like she was swimming in it, drowning in it, immersed in a pale white sea.

It was for him, but he wasn't there.

Where was he, her son, Jeremiah, the prophet? She'd given him a good name, a Bible name, a name worthy of the burden he'd bear, the light he'd bring to the world. She had carried the name along with him in her body for months, knowing she had to see him first to be sure.

She'd seen him. She'd been sure. But where was he?

She'd seen him emerge from her body, into the world, Jeremiah, her son, the prophet. But he was gone, hiding somewhere, taken from her, leaving her full of milk, bursting.

She ached for the feeling of his tiny mouth suckling at the nourishment she had to offer, the secret formula of motherhood.

Without his mouth her body was wasted. Her arms should have been holding him, so there was nothing to do with her arms. Her lap should have been rocking him, so there was nothing to do with her legs. Her mouth should have been kissing him, so there was nothing to do with her mouth, no words to say, no reason to speak, not until they brought her baby back to her. Her ears, listening for his cries, heard nothing else. Her eyes, watching for him, were empty to any other sight.

Her mind was an open wound. Her son, her baby, gone.

There were rooms full of light and rooms full of darkness, people speaking to her and dressing her and holding her hand. There was a needle in her arm and then there wasn't, there was a blanket around her and then there was dawn. There were nurses and a doctor, her mama and daddy and Daphne, all crying. There was her own bed, there were phone calls, there was a ride in a long black car, and then they were all outside, sitting in rows, and Pastor Ted was speaking, but nobody was saying, "I believe."

There was a wooden box, no bigger than a shoebox, that they buried in the ground.

Something was wrong, but it didn't matter. What mattered was that they bring her baby back to her, that Jeremiah empty her of her endless supply of milk. Where was he? Where was her son?

There had been yelling, accusations, harsh words flung back and forth across a room that was all beige. So much yelling. She couldn't understand, and she didn't care, not unless it would bring Jeremiah back. After the yelling they'd taken her home, her mama and daddy, silent, shaking, gray. She had sat somewhere, looking at something, for a few minutes or a few hours, heavy, liquid, bulging with milk, and then Doug was there.

"Everyone's hanging out up at the house," he said, standing in front of her, his father's elk head belt buckle level with her eyes. "So get yourself together. Let's go."

A flannel shirt above the belt buckle, his thick neck, a scowl. Doug. Jeremiah's father. Did he know where their baby was?

"I said, let's go. C'mon. Don't you want to do your makeup or whatever?"

Her body remembered a motion from what felt like long ago. Like moving a pile of rocks, she shook her head: one turn to the left, one to the right.

"Okay, well, whatever, the gang's already up there. They said to come get you. We're drinking in memory of—well, you know. So let's go."

He wanted something: Doug, the enormous body before her, the thick shoulders and hot neck, the body she knew so well. He wanted something, and she wondered what she could give. She had nothing to offer. Nothing but milk.

"Janie, honey." Her mama, sitting on the couch next to her, took up her limp hand in both of hers. She smelled like face powder and apple-scented soap. "Doug wants to take you out to spend time with your friends. Do you want to go?"

Out. Friends. The words had meanings, but they were confused in her head, swimming like little lost fish in a big white ocean, an ocean of milk. She felt her mouth go slack as she tried to understand, her lower lip heavy and wet. She was supposed to do something, for Doug. Doug needed something from her. He was in front of her, simmering with impatience, but somewhere deep under all that flesh and anger, he was as lost and confused as she was. As lost as their baby. Their Jeremiah.

She stood, slowly, keeping her body upright so she wouldn't spill.

"Great," Doug sighed in exasperation and relief.

"Take good care of her," she heard her mama say to Doug as she stood swaying on the carpet, trying to remember which direction was out.

"I will," Doug replied. But he was already out the door, heading to his truck. She pulled her body through space, wanting to be close to him, wanting him to hold her so hard she became part of him, the two of them melded together with just enough space left for an infant. She wanted him to touch her, take her hand, float with her on a sea of milk where neither of them had to think or feel or talk. But he just started the truck.

Darkness. Headlights. They rode roughshod over the potholes, her breasts bouncing painfully, leaking. The truck's cab smelled like smoke and musty Slim Jim's, and Doug's mouth was a tough, straight line.

"I wish you'd snap the fuck out of it," he said.

Her head was heavy. Keeping it above the sea of milk, up where there was air, was hard. So hard. She let herself tip sideways until her head rested on the broad, flat expanse of his bicep, the flannel soft against her cheek, the Abercrombie smell of him a small, sweet comfort.

He jerked his arm, sending her head arcing in the other direction until it smacked against the passenger window. Stars exploded around her temple, pretty little sparkles of pain.

"I mean, it was my kid, too. You don't see me walking around like the living dead."

She rubbed her head. A small bump was beginning to form. But at least she still had milk—she could feel its warm pressure inside of her, the slow dribble into her bra. She still had milk for Jeremiah.

"You gonna say something, or just sit there like a stupid cow?"

Like a cow. So he understood. The corners of her lips did something, pulling toward her ears.

"What the hell are you smiling about? What is *wrong* with you?" Doug shouted.

She didn't like shouting. She cowered away from him, slumping against the door. She watched the trees out the window, branches brushing the glass, waiting for it to stop, for him to go back to being the pillar of Doug-flesh who had poured himself into her so many times, molding them together, begetting life.

Doug muttered something she couldn't hear and lit a cigarette, opening the window, the cold rush of air and smoke an unwelcome surprise on her face. Did Doug smoke? She couldn't remember. Everything from before was blurry, painted over in white. She'd bought baby clothes. She'd gone to the clinic. She'd given birth. But where was the baby?

They pulled up to the house on top of Elk Mountain. It was beginning to take form, rising from the earth like a big steel daddy longlegs climbing out of the foundation. There were sleeping construction vehicles and piles of sandbags and sheetrock, a big blue tarp on the ground surrounded by signs saying *Do Not Enter*. Something important was under that tarp, something with an answer. But she couldn't remember what, and it didn't matter. Nothing mattered with Jeremiah gone.

There were parked cars and a campfire, their friends huddled around it, coolers full of beer. One of the cars was pulled up close to the fire, doors open and lights on, a pop anthem blaring from the speakers. *Have a drink, or two, or three, or four, then drop it down low so it hits the floor.*

"Janie!" her friends said. She stepped out of the truck, feeling her way with her feet, trying to remember how to stand. They rushed to her, hugging her, taking her hand, asking if she was okay.

"Have a drink," Hilary said, putting a can of something red, one of those alcoholic energy drinks that tasted like strawberries, into her hand. She hadn't had a drink in nine months. "You look like you could use one."

She put the can to her lips.

32

DAPHNE RAN OUT OF THE funeral home and into the endless gray of the afternoon. The world was blurred and distorted through her tears, the road a ribbon of concrete flying by under her feet. Her shoes rubbed at her heels and broke the skin, blood seeping through the thin canvas, but she didn't notice. All that existed was the searing ache in her heart, the panic of having her life torn up by the roots and flung at her feet like a handful of weeds.

Why had she lied? Surely the Peytons would have taken her in if she'd told them the truth: that she'd killed a man in self-defense, after years of fending off his unwanted advances. The Peytons were good people, godly people who would have taken her at her word, who would have been happy to give her a fresh start. If only the truth hadn't stuck in her throat when they asked, gagging her with its repulsive magnitude. If only she'd trusted them enough to let them into her past.

But she hadn't, and now she was paying the price: a price that stung so bitterly it caught her with a sharp jab and she doubled over, gasping by the side of the road.

A truck blew by, flashing silver in a cloud of dust. Several feet ahead it squealed to a stop and then slowly backed up, flashers blinking red around a Kansas license plate.

"Daphne!" Owen opened the door and leapt out, his suit replaced with jeans and a T-shirt, his work clothes. He wrapped his arms around her, and she sobbed into his chest, ear against his heartbeat. He held her tight, stroking her hair. "What happened?" he asked.

She pulled away and found his eyes through her tears, shocking green against the dingy sky. With another jolt of misery, she realized he didn't know—he'd left before she approached Doug, before everything had crumbled around her like a pillar of ashes. He didn't yet realize that the girl standing before him was a murderer and a liar—but he'd find out. Even if she said nothing, if she tried to stretch the charade a few more hours, the news of her deceit would travel through Carbon County at the speed of gossip, eventually reaching his ears. And he was implicated in it, had been there when the baby slid lifeless from her cousin's body, was as reviled by the town as she was.

"Tell me," he urged, wiping the tears from her cheeks.

She couldn't bear the gentleness of his touch. She removed his hand from her face and placed it at his side, then took a step back. Hurt and confusion clouded his eyes.

"They found out the truth about me," she said flatly, forcing the words to come. "I killed my stepfather and lied about it so the Peytons would take me in. Everyone knows. And now you do, too."

She braced herself for him to turn and leave. She was ready to taste the dust from his tires, to drink in one last look at the back of his head riding away from her forever. A great gulley of hurt opened inside her, knowing there would be no more kisses, no more bursts of happiness so intense she couldn't breathe.

But Owen didn't move.

"I know that's not the whole story," he said. He cupped her chin in his hand and tilted her face up to meet his eyes. "What really happened?"

He didn't understand. "That is the truth," she insisted. "I stabbed him. End of story."

Owen shook his head, refusing to believe. "Why?"

Her voice was as small and hard as a cherry stone. "He was trying to rape me. At knifepoint. I got the knife out of his hands and used it on him instead."

She could still recall with sick precision the soft wetness of the blade slicing through his flesh, the spongy surprise of his organs. Nausea welled up at the memory, but Owen stopped it with a kiss. The shock of his lips on hers cut through the panic, slowing her heart and washing her with a quiet calm.

"Killing a man in self-defense doesn't make you a murderer, Daphne," he said when they pulled apart, his palm still resting on her cheek. "Anyone else would have done the same."

"It's not true," she shook her head. "I'm bad. Everyone thinks so. Even the Peytons. Even Pastor Ted."

"You can't listen to them," Owen said firmly. Anger sparked in his eyes. "They're upset and grieving. They need a scapegoat."

She shook her head, her face still burning with shame from the confrontation in the funeral home. "They think I'm in league with the devil, that I killed Janie's baby on purpose, and that you helped. I tried to defend us, but I couldn't—everyone was talking all at once, they said if we really wanted to save the baby we wouldn't have delivered him ourselves. The Peytons—you should have seen them. They looked so betrayed. I can't stay here anymore. I have to leave town."

"You don't have to go anywhere," Owen said immediately. He paused, inhaling sharply. "If you want, you can stay with me and Luna for a while, and we'll figure things out."

She shook her head sadly. "I can't stay here and bring more disgrace to my family. I've done enough damage already."

"You can't leave." Owen grasped her hand tightly, the fervor in his voice approaching rage. He brought his lips to hers, and she returned his kiss with a furious need. It sealed their bond, a pact between two outsiders who had found one another at last, a secret agreement of commitment and gratitude and desire. More than any words they could say, it united them against a world that had grown to despise them. It steeled them for what was to come.

"We'll go to your place and get your things," Owen said when they were done. "And I'll tell Dale I need the afternoon off. He'll be pissed, but he'll get over it."

Daphne nodded. Maybe if they hurried, she could clear out before the Peytons got home. As much as she wanted to say goodbye, she didn't want to cause them any more pain with her presence. She had already hurt them enough. "But then there's something I have to do," she said. "Something important."

Owen turned off Buzzard Road, past the Global Oil sign and down the chewed-up gravel road to the rig. "What's that?" he asked.

She bit her lip as they rounded a bend and the oil rig came into focus. "I have to get another look at that tablet."

33

THE DRINK IN THE RED can was bubbly and tart and impossibly sweet. Janie gulped it down, and the bubbles tickled her throat and swam into her head and danced there like fairies, whispering at the inside of her brain, making her laugh at everything and nothing. Loud music, aggressively fun, pumped from the parked car, urging them to drink, to kiss, to live.

To live. After the second can, it was all she wanted to do. She wanted to live larger and louder than anyone, to live away all the death and pain, to live until there was only laughter and never loss, until everything was pink and sparkling and perfect. Talk flew around the campfire in spirals, old tales from the motocross track polished and exaggerated until they shone like chrome, trashy celebrity gossip and drinking stories, each brighter and more boisterous than the last. They talked as if their voices could chase away the sadness, to scare the horrible events of the last few days into the bushes, to make them run away and never come back.

And, oh, she wanted them to! She wanted the sparkling red drink to power-wash the milk from her glands, the music to sweep the thoughts of death and loss and longing from her brain. She drank in their voices, their stories, trying to make each thing they said the only thing in the world, trying to focus on the things that were now, the things that were close and real and alive.

She was doing better, maybe even doing good. She saw it in Doug's eyes, the way he relaxed against a cooler and smiled at her, putting his hand on her knee (the first time he'd touched her since it happened, and oh! His touch felt so good!). She could see the darkness inside him loosen as he downed beer after beer, sending another joke around the fire, bragging about his new bike and reaching into the cooler for another. Always another.

It had bothered her before, she remembered that. In the weeks and months before The Thing happened, his drinking had set her skin on edge and made her clutch her belly protectively, trying to keep their unborn child safe from his moods, his words, the giant ham hocks of his fists that she always feared might start swinging. But now she understood. The bright red can in her hand made the bad go away, made everything sweet and bubbly and bright. She was laughing and they were laughing with her, pink and blurry in the firelight, they were glad to see her happy, smiling, and she was glad to be with them, the same old Janie again: Janie who was the life of the party, Janie who knew how to have a good time.

The parked car blasted out a new tune, and she stumbled to her feet, her grin big enough to split wood. "I love this song!" she slurred, and then she was dancing, making big circles with her butt and waving her hands in the air and reaching toward the fire.

The fire was an even better dancer than she was. It leapt and twirled, jumped and cartwheeled high into the sky, embers like a million tiny sequins on a ballroom dancer's skirt. They were dancing together, she and the flames, twisting and swaying to the beat, the fire anticipating her moves, seducing her like a lover, begging her to come forward, reaching for her body with scarlet fingers.

She danced closer and it was hot, ooooh, so hot, and the heat leapt into her veins and pumped life through them, a bigger and brighter and faster life than before. She was ready to be its partner—in dance, in life, forever. She spread her arms to caress the flames, ready to be stroked by their flickering fingers, to succumb to their torrid embrace. One more step and she'd be inside the ring, engulfed in the feverish dance that could bring her into something even larger and better, greater than any life she'd ever known . . .

"Janie, what the hell!"

A shadow tackled her, back and away from the flames. It grasped her arms, yanking them behind her back until her shoulders cracked and a vicious, miserable wind rushed her body where the delicious heat had been. She cried out like an animal, struggling against the brutal arms that were wrapped around her waist and refusing to let go. She flailed, kicking up dust, trying to squirm away.

"What is *wrong* with you?" Doug hissed in her ear.

"The fire . . ." she tried to explain, still wriggling in his grasp, the red drink sloshing her head sideways and then back again. "We were dancing together."

"Are you fucking retarded?" Doug spun her around and grasped her by the shoulders, shaking her like a rag doll. His fingers dug into her skin, and she whimpered, realizing she'd done something wrong, something to make the darkness inside of him come rushing back.

"I was just trying to have fun," she pouted. Doug could be so impossible, so unfair. First he wouldn't bring her baby back, and then he wouldn't let her pretend there had never been a baby at all. "That's what you wanted, right? For me to have fun and forget it ever happened, just like you."

Doug's eyes narrowed. His face went dark as a bruise. "You think I forgot?" he snarled. "I'll never forget."

"Never forget what?" she taunted. The drink had loosened her tongue, and now she wanted him to say it, to face head-on what they'd all been dancing around. That their son was gone. That he wasn't coming back. That God was punishing them for indiscretions she couldn't understand, that He had deserted them just when she needed Him the most.

Doug drew himself up like a viper about to strike, reminding her of the snake that had sprung hissing from her laundry back in the spring, what felt like a lifetime before. Deep red blood vessels forked across the whites of his eyes, the capillaries raw and open from drink. "That you let our son die," he hissed.

Janie recoiled. The words were poison, rotting her blood, paralyzing her flesh. Words disintegrated on her tongue.

"You let that rotten cousin of yours deliver him, you trusted her when you knew you shouldn't have." His hands were clamped on her shoulders, fingers hard as iron.

But he was wrong, that wasn't how it had happened. She tried to find the memory, to explain, but it was like trying to read a paper that's been drenched in mud: sodden, illegible, buried. "But . . ." she tried.

"You didn't even want it in the first place, did you?"

"Huh?"

Doug sneered out a laugh. "You didn't want a baby any more than I did. You were just afraid of losing me, so you did the only thing you could think of to keep me."

The words crashed against her like a battering ram, bruising her heart. "What are you talking about?" she gasped.

"Don't play coy with me, Janie. I see right through you. You were going to give him up for adoption, remember?"

Janie shook her head fiercely. It had been a TV commercial, nothing more—a thought she'd entertained only once, when Trey was dead and Doug was angry all the time and she didn't know where else to turn. A thought that Daphne had put in her head.

Doug wasn't finished. "You never even cared about having a baby in the first place. All you wanted was to tie me down so I could never leave or be with someone else or have a goddamn life. Admit it: That's the truth, right?"

"No!" Janie hiccupped. How could Doug's version be so twisted, so different from her own? "I never asked you to marry me. You were the one who proposed, remember?"

"Oh, that." Doug laughed meanly. "You really are even dumber than you look. You think I wanted to marry you? My family made me, because they wanted to make sure your stingy-ass dad kept his word about the oil money. If it weren't for that, no effin' way would I have proposed. I'm eighteen years old, you think I want to be stuck with *you* forever?"

All of the bubbles inside her, the bright playful happy bubbles from the drink in the pretty red can, popped at once. She felt herself melting into her feet, the popped bubbles dripping through her in thick slicks of sickly red gloop, the sugar crystals dissolving and clinging to her organs. She wanted to sink down to the ground and then through it, to disintegrate into the earth and become the lowly brown dirt she suddenly felt like. The only thing holding her up was Doug's grip like claws on her shoulders.

She looked for the Doug she'd fallen in love with, the big silly vulnerable guy who always put his arm around her in the school cafeteria and touched her breasts as reverently as if they were ancient icons, the Doug who had proposed to her with a diamond ring on top of a slice of chocolate cake. But that Doug was gone, and the one in his place was a red-eyed monster, a roiling volcano of hate. He could have grown fur and fangs, have sprouted horns and branded her with a tongue made of molten iron, and she wouldn't have been any more frightened. She whimpered, the sound of a lost child.

"You're pathetic." Doug abruptly let go of her shoulders, and she collapsed, slamming to the ground. She lay there in a pile of herself, sniffling, leaking tears and milk and down there, between her legs where it had flowed like a river after the baby came, blood. "And you know what?"

Her eyes were level with his ankles, bulging and hairy above dirty green sneakers.

"What?" she whimpered.

"I'm gonna divorce you," Doug announced. "Once we're done suing your family for that oil money, I'm not gonna have anything to do with you anymore."

Divorce . . . suing . . . she wished she didn't understand what Doug was saying, that she could go back to the world of pure white emptiness, the world where all she thought about was milk.

But the words were real, and she knew what they meant. They meant that her heart was useless, a once-shiny toy that her love had discarded when it was no longer new. They meant that all of her happiness, the joy that she'd held in her palms just days before, had slipped through her fingers and shattered.

She looked up at him, past the hairy ankles and the faded, sagging jeans and the elk head belt she'd unbuckled for him so many times. Above the burly expanse of his chest, above his creased and scarlet neck, above the curl of his lip like a wolf just after ripping into its prey, she found his eyes.

"I thought you loved me," she whispered.

She was speaking to the other Doug, the old Doug, the Doug who had once filled her womb with a holy child. But his eyes didn't change. They stayed red, and dark, and cold.

"I did once," he said flatly. "Not anymore."

He turned and strode back toward the fire, his heels and the wind kicking dirt into her face, leaving her in a pile of empty, useless flesh on the ground.

She put her cheek to the earth and wept.

34

THE SKY WAS THE COLOR of graphite, the air thick with the pent-up electricity of a pending storm. A stiff wind blew the branches on Elk Mountain Road into their windshield, scraping the glass as Owen's truck climbed the narrow driveway. Inside they were silent, Owen concentrating on the road through the growing mist, Daphne fixated on the tablet.

She could feel it drawing her in, calling her closer, its strange carvings like a force summoning her home. When she closed her eyes she could almost see it, the message dancing and shifting in flashes of light and darkness. She prayed that this time the meaning would click into place, that she would finally understand.

They pulled into the parking area. "There are cars here," Owen said, surprised.

Daphne's shoulders tensed. "That's Doug's truck." She spotted the lightning down the side of his bright green pickup. "Are they seriously having a party *now?*"

"Looks like it." Owen cut the engine, and the cab filled with the raucous sounds of a throbbing dance beat. "What do you want to do?"

She wanted to leave, to turn and put as much distance between themselves and Carbon County as possible, to drive fast through the night, pretending the town had never existed. But the clawing need in her gut wouldn't let her. She had to have one more look at the tablet, to try one last time to put the pieces together before she gave up on Carbon County forever.

"I want to see the tablet," she said firmly, one hand already on the door handle.

A howling wind ripped through their bodies the moment they stepped outside. It nipped at their ankles, sending small tornadoes of dust swirling around them and lifting Daphne's hair from the back of her neck, tangling it behind her as she pulled her hoodie closer, trying to ward off the ominous chill. The trees around them shrieked and struggled, leaves clinging to their branches with tenuous fingers until the force was too great and they broke loose, somersaulting through the sky.

Beyond the row of parked cars, they heard yelps as the fire leapt one way and then the other, blown into a vortex by the wind.

"My eyes!" someone cried, and Daphne could feel the thick, acrid smoke stinging her own retinas, rubbing the already-raw skin on her cheeks.

"Let's go," she whispered to Owen. They snaked through the parked cars, cold metal brushing Daphne's back and making her shiver through her sweatshirt until they stopped at the edge of the parking area, hovering in the shadows as Daphne tried to calculate their next move.

The partygoers were clustered around the campfire, skin like brass in the flickering light. They'd pulled up camp chairs and coolers and opened the back of someone's SUV to pump tunes and lounge on the tailgate. Empty beers and large red cans littered the ground around them, and a big bottle of rum was being passed from hand the hand, its gold liquid sloshing. Their voices were loud, their laughter shrill and frequent, but underneath it there was something grim and hard, a fierce determination to forge through their sadness with reckless, defiant partying.

Daphne instinctively looked around for Janie, but she couldn't see her. Her heart constricted as she pictured her cousin at home with her parents in the dim circle of light from the living room lamp, catatonic on the couch, mourning. Of all the things that hurt about the past few hours, losing her cousin stung the most.

Doug was there, though, standing with his hands on his hips in front of the fire, anger radiating around him like a blistered halo. The hulking black of his silhouette sent a cold finger of nausea creeping up Daphne's gullet. She clenched Owen's hand tighter, reminding herself that not all guys were terrible.

She turned and met his eyes, and Owen nodded. Tiptoeing, they crept around the shell of the house, its steel beams looming over them like sentries. The pit that had been dug for the decorative pond was still roped off, the *Do Not Enter* signs around it faded by sun and rain. The shack that had been set up for Vince's security guard was mercifully abandoned: Doug must have bribed him to take the night off.

A gust of wind whirled by, rippling the tarp and sending a cacophony of plastic percussion toward the campfire. Daphne and Owen froze in their tracks, the sound like gunshots in their ears.

But the crowd by the campfire seemed oblivious. They were in the midst of a countdown, voices raucous and uneven, as someone chugged from the bottle of rum, followed by a long, loud belch that echoed dankly through the night.

Daphne and Owen ducked under the ropes.

"Are you sure you want to do this?" Owen whispered. "We can still turn back."

Fear and need pounded through her. She knew that seeing the tablet again could reveal truths she didn't want to see. Its meaning had been cloudy and incomprehensible the first time, the words mere echoes in her head. Back then it had spoken in riddles. But now, with the death of a firstborn, everything had changed. The tablet had hinted at a terrible event, and she couldn't ignore its power any longer. She couldn't keep pretending that everything was a coincidence. As reluctant as she was to believe, she knew it meant something more.

A tentacle of lightning split the sky, turning the landscape around them the silver of tinfoil. Owen tensed, and gasps came from the campfire, underscored by tipsy, nervous giggles. In the sudden burst of light, Daphne reached down and yanked back the tarp.

He followed her into the pit, the ancient rock glowing like moonstone in the darkness. The lines and squiggles that were gibberish to the rest of Carbon County leapt up at her, the words so clear they hurt her brain. She turned to Owen, her pulse racing.

"Are you sure you can't read it?" she asked, hoping against hope that she wasn't the only one.

He shook his head. "But you can."

"All of it," she admitted.

Thunder rumbled in the distance, and the sky blackened, storm clouds sweeping low across the mountaintop and blotting out the tops of the trees. As Daphne squinted to make out the letters, Owen reached into his pocket and whipped out his phone, illuminating the tablet in an eerie, electronic blue.

"Read it to me," he urged.

A draft clawed at her face as she bent in close, reading the prophecy out loud.

"When the true Prophet reads this message," she recited, "the era of the Great Divide is at hand. For on the eve of the Great Battle, seven signs and wonders shall come to pass, each in turn and none without the others. And these shall be:

"Clarion

"Blood

"Fire

"Plague

"Relic

"Death of a Firstborn

"Prophet—"

She broke off and turned to Owen, her face the ghostly gray of a spirit.

"The signs," she said slowly, the shape of the words still in her throat. "They all happened. And they all happened *here*."

"Are you sure?" His brow was a furrow of concentration as he looked from her to the tablet. "Let's go over them again. You said 'clarion.' Do you even know what that means?"

"No." She bit her lip. "I was too freaked out to even look it up."

He bent over his phone, pushing buttons. A moment later, his head snapped up. "The dictionary says it's a medieval trumpet with a shrill, clear tone. Does that mean anything to you?"

"The trumpets," she said slowly. "The day I got here. Everyone kept saying they were a sign from God, but I thought they were nuts—that there had to be a logical explanation."

He directed his light back to the tablet, allowing her to read the next word.

"Blood." Their eyes met over the ghostly stone. "When you touched the oil that day . . ." she began.

"I knew it wasn't a cut," he finished grimly, confirming the fear she'd had all along: that there was something otherworldly about Owen, something that turned oil to blood.

She turned, shivering, to read the next word. "Fire."

"The rig?" Owen guessed. "That explosion in the flare stack?"

"Or Trey." Her voice dropped, his name almost lost to the screeching wind as the memory licked at her mind like flames: the burning bush. The bike igniting. Trey's body twisted and blackened in the white-hot embers.

She forced her eyes back to the tablet, to the augur that had told her story centuries before she was born to live it.

"Plague," she recited. "I don't get that one. Nobody's been sick."

"What about the birds?" Owen's voice was toneless.

Icicles of doom tickled the back of her neck as she remembered the birds of paradise falling from the sky, raining down on the wedding party in a hailstorm of destruction. "They died so suddenly," she agreed. "Janie said it was a sign. I didn't believe her then, but the tablet already knew."

"Read the next one," Owen urged. "It says they all have to happen in order—*each in turn, and none without the others.* What comes after that?"

The word *relic* floated up to her in the gloom. "That's something old," she thought out loud, "a piece of something bigger that was left behind."

They both looked at the tablet.

"This."

Owen's skin glowed pale as Daphne continued. "They found it right before Janie gave birth. Her child was supposed to be the prophet."

He nodded solemnly. That brought them to the next sign, the most horrible of all. The death of a firstborn. Grief brimmed in Daphne's eyes.

"I should have told someone," she said, a tear rolling off her cheek and onto the tablet, where it filled one of the carvings like a tiny lake. "I should have put the pieces together. Maybe I could have done something to stop it, made her go to a hospital or—"

"No." Owen took her by the shoulders. "This isn't your fault. According to the tablet, it was all preordained. It would have happened anyway, no matter what you did."

"Preordained," she repeated quietly. "So every word on it will come true?"

"I don't know." He shook his head. "But so far, it's seven for seven. What's next? In that big block of text?"

A loud thunderclap sounded overhead, rattling the tarp. Struggling to keep her tears at bay, Daphne turned back to the tablet.

"And yea, once these seven signs and wonders appear," she read, "there shall be a Great Battle between the Children of God and the Children of the Earth. The Children of the Earth shall sow evil and discord wrought from the pits of Hell, while the Children of God turn to the heavens for strength from the One True Deity. The victor shall rule the land and the sky, the earth and the heavens, and forever hold dominion over the soul of humankind, and the loser shall be cast out forevermore into Eternal Nothingness— while those who fail to choose sides shall perish. Heed, for when this warning is uncovered and the true Prophet comes to light, the era of the Great Divide is at hand."

Like a candle being suddenly snuffed dead, the blue light disappeared. Owen stumbled back, away from her and the tablet, as if trying to escape the words.

"No." His voice was low and tortured, his breath ragged. "It has to be wrong."

"What?" The word echoed across the pit. The passage she'd just read was opaque to her, as baffling as the seven signs and omens were clear. Pastor Ted called the churchgoers of Carbon County the Children of God, but everything else was a mystery.

"What if she was right?" Owen moaned. Her eyes began to adjust to the dimness, and she could make him out in the corner, his back heaving and his hands clenched into fists.

"What if *who* was right?"

"Luna." The word ripped from his mouth in a guttural growl. "She knew about this all along. She's been gearing up for it, gathering an army. And I thought she was crazy."

Daphne went to him, placed a gentle hand on his arm. She felt him trembling beneath her palm. "Are you saying she knew why we were all drawn here? For this battle between the Children of God and the Children of the Earth?"

Owen's only answer was a long, jagged breath.

Fear percolated in her chest as a memory prickled at the edges of her brain. "Luna called you her Earth Brother," she said, her voice suddenly sharp. "What did she mean?"

A bitter laugh escaped his lips. "That commune I told you about? Where Luna and I were born? It's called the Children of the Earth."

Daphne took a step back, the words buzzing through her like a swarm of bees. "Maybe it's just a coincidence," she suggested. "Aren't all commune names, like, *Planet This* or *Earth That?*"

"It's no coincidence." Owen paced back and forth across the pit, pounding a fist into his palm. Between heaving breaths, he told her the story of his birth, of Luna's insistence that the God of the Earth had called them to Carbon County to fight a great battle in his name.

Daphne leaned against the wall, the pit's earthy loam soaking the back of her hoodie. "So you're one of them," she said when he was done. "One of the Children of the Earth."

"I guess." Owen sounded hollow, broken.

"And the voice that drew you here," she continued, putting the pieces together, hating the picture they formed, "it wasn't God. It was . . ."

He turned and faced her, the green of his eyes glowing unnaturally bright. "The opposite," he said darkly.

Daphne felt the world slipping around her, everything she'd always known and believed in flying away from her on a swift, cold gale. "But we were both meant to come here," she whispered, her lips cold. "Does that mean I'm evil, too?"

It would explain everything: why she had killed a man, how she could never bring herself to have feelings about someone until Owen, who was evil just like her. A noxious stew of self-loathing bubbled within her, threatening to spill over. Pastor Ted, the angry mob at the funeral parlor, even her own mother: They had all been right. She wasn't just a bad person. She was pure evil—and nothing she did, no matter how hard she tried, would be able to change that. It had been written in stone.

"No, Daphne," Owen said sadly. "Read the first line again." He trained his light back to the top of the tablet, forcing her eyes to the very first sentence, to the lines and squiggles that seared themselves into her head and hers alone.

When the true prophet reads this message.

A great crack of thunder shook Elk Mountain, and electricity crackled around them. Daphne felt it surge through her, touching a hidden reserve of power and unleashing it screaming into the night, zinging out from her fingers, making her hair stand on end. Even as fear exploded in her chest, she knew that the power was there. It had been there all along, hiding, waiting for someone—or something—to release it into the world.

Owen grasped her shoulders and gazed at her with deadly intensity, his eyes the color of the storm. "You've got it all wrong. They all did. Pastor Ted was right that there was a prophet coming to Carbon County, but it wasn't Janie's child."

His voice dropped to a murmur, a breath.

"It was you."

35

THE THUNDERSTORM CAME SCREAMING DOWN on her as she dashed from the pit, drenching her head with cold sheets of rain while thick mud sucked at her feet. She barely felt the downpour battering her face and chest, barely heard the thunder crashing in the sky, was deaf to the sounds of cars starting up and the partygoers at the campfire fleeing the storm, their headlights shattering curtains of rain as hard and unrelenting as diamonds.

She raced around the few stragglers, their faces blurred like painted skeletons in a haunted house carnival ride as they hurriedly collected empty beer cans, the fire already doused by the torrents of water falling from the sky, its final tendrils of smoke choking the air.

A tree branch, knocked loose by the wind, hurtled past her, barely missing her nose, its bark slick and black as oil. It plummeted to the earth a few feet away and stuck in the mud like the mast of a sunken ship, heralding destruction.

She raced past the towering steel shell of the Varleys' future mansion, up the gentle slope where Janie and Doug had been married, the mud pulling at her ankles and seeping through her thin canvas sneakers, worming between her toes.

Her breath caught in her throat like shards of glass. The valley of Carbon County spread below her, the town battened down against the storm, its lights as muted and faraway as stars as storm clouds rolled silver and furious over the mountain range to the north. Pools of water churned and glistened in the flooded foundations of what would become new housing developments, bars, and shopping centers; off by the Peytons' trailer, the derrick continued to pump stoically through the downpour, dipping and rising from the earth in grim determination, making money, marking time, a blessing and a curse and an omen all rolled into one. Next to the foundation for the new, state-of-the-art Carbon County First Church of God, the makeshift steeple of the old church in the Pizza Hut grasped at Daphne through the deluge, calling to her, begging her to stay.

Carbon County needed her. The people who had taken her in, revered her and then rejected her, were about to face a struggle more dire than anything Pastor Ted had predicted, an influx of evil that only the Children of God could fight—and only with her help. As bitterly as their accusations still rang in her ears, as hurt as she'd been by their words, she knew she was the only one who could save them. And she had to. It was her chance to finally do some good in the world, to redeem herself from the fear and death that had stalked her for her entire life.

Footsteps splattered through the mud behind her. Soon Owen was at her side, coal-black hair soaked and clinging to his face.

"This is real. I *feel* it," she gasped.

She gazed out at the storm-whipped valley beneath them, the wind raking chilled fingers across her cheeks. "The rest of them— of you—of the Children of the Earth: Are they coming here, like the tablet said?"

"Yes." He stood next to her, shoulder to shoulder on the edge of the cliff.

"Will you recognize them when they come?"

She felt him nod. "From my dreams," he explained. "I've seen their faces now, all of them. I can feel them getting closer."

Daphne's heart splintered. "So it's true," she said bitterly. "We're on opposite sides. When this Great Battle comes, we'll be fighting against each other."

"No." Owen whipped around, his jaw hard. "I won't let this happen. I don't want it. I don't care what the signs say. They can't *make me* be evil."

A white flash of lightning sent him into sudden silhouette, hands on his hips and soaked shirt clinging to his chest. She wanted to believe him more than anything. But she couldn't ignore the signs. Now that all the pieces were laid out in front of her, she could sense the battle coming, could feel its magnitude drawing her in, preparing her to lead the way. Perhaps it was what she'd been feeling all along.

"But you just said it that it's preordained," she said. "The tablet's been right about everything else. Why do you think you can fight this?"

"Because I don't want it." He took her in his arms, and she gripped him tightly, feeling his heartbeat against her cheek. "And I never do anything I don't want. Daphne, I want to be on your side. I want to be with *you*."

She pulled back and drank him in, his face pale and sculpted as a marble statue, lips firm. "How do I know this isn't a test?" she asked suddenly, her eyes clouding. The sky around them had turned jaundiced, the brooding yellow of a bruise. "How do I know you're not deceiving me, that I'm not just seeing what I want to see?"

Owen grasped her hands as the last wash of rain swept the valley clean. "You're the prophet," he replied simply. "You see the truth."

She stepped away from him and gazed down at the valley as it transformed before her eyes, telling tales of what was to come. She saw visions of destruction and rebirth, of a great clash between good and evil that pierced the very center of the earth and radiated in fiery waves to the heavens. She saw the Children of God rise up against the Children of the Earth, saw the citizens of Carbon County—the citizens of the world—struggle between the promise of purity and the temptation of easy riches. She saw the flames of war and a million dark tornadoes of inner conflict, and she knew that out of it all, a victor would rise greater and more powerful than anything the world had ever known.

But her vision stopped there, the outcome as murky as the mist still swirling below them.

"I see it," she said as the images faded, leaving only the storm-swept valley in its wake. She turned to Owen, a new determination blazing in her eyes. "It's coming."

They stood, two pillars from opposite sides of an ancient rift, united on the mountaintop.

She knew, then, that she believed: not just in gods and prophecies, but in the quiet power within her and all humankind. It had guarded against her mother's rage and protected her from Jim's abuse, had bubbled out in Janie's laughter and washed over her in the peaceful glint of Floyd's smile. It had guided her, when her world was dark and unforgiving, to a family she loved and a town she could finally call home—and it had brought her and Owen together, piercing the iron shell she'd put up around herself and showing her the deep and solid core of good in a man who had been marked for evil.

She knew that to preserve what they had, to get them through the hardships to come, she had to keep that core of good alive in him, to be the light guiding them through the darkness. She had only her own power to rely on, power that was as small as her pounding heart yet as vast as the cosmos.

She turned and took his hand in hers, a fresh night breeze whispering in their ears of events to come. "It's almost here," she said quietly. "I just hope we'll be ready in time."

Acknowledgments

So many people went into making this book a reality: from friends and family to strangers who were thoughtful enough to post motocross and oil rig videos online.

First and foremost, I want to thank my wonderful editors at Razorbill, Jessica Almon and Ben Schrank, for believing so totally in this world and in my ability to bring it to life. None of this could have happened without your great ideas, astute character notes, and masterful plot manipulations.

My agent, Tina Wexler at ICM, deserves a medal for her gracious support, advice, and endless encouragement . . . even (especially) at nine months pregnant.

For helping *End Times* be so much more than words, I want to thank Anthony Elder for a cover design that took my breath away, Casey McIntyre for an inspired publicity campaign, and Sarah Chassé and Kate Frentzel for making sure each word was the correct one.

Thanks as well to all of my early readers (Pittacus Lore, Leah Konen, Jocelyn Davies, Danielle Paige, Jessica Khoury, Morgan Rhodes, and Nova Ren Suma) for your excellent feedback and kind words.

The road to becoming a published author is full of twists and turns. I've been fortunate to have navigation assistance from some truly phenomenal folks along the way, including Bennett Madison for helping me find my voice, Shani Petroff for telling me to just go for it, Micol Ostow for opening so many doors, and everyone in her YA fiction class for being there through the dark days. I also want to thank the Hearst Corporation for helping me buck the stereotype of the "starving writer" and my fantastic colleagues at Hearst Digital Media who make coming to work a pleasure every day.

It goes without saying that I never could have written a word without the early and constant encouragement of my parents, Zeke and Linda Hecker, who plied me with books and never doubted that I would grow up to be a writer.

Finally, eternal gratitude to my incredibly patient, intelligent, and handsome husband, Tim, for always having dinner on the table, acting like it's normal when I talk incessantly about fictional seventeen-year-olds, and personally DJing my one-person LED hoop jams when all I needed was a break. You are the osssssssssssumest.

Turn the page for a
SNEAK PEEK AT

CHILDREN OF THE EARTH,

THE SECOND BOOK IN THE END TIMES SERIES!

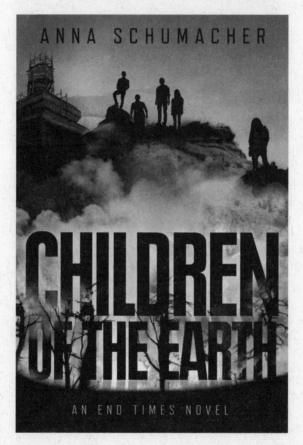

ANNA SCHUMACHER

CHILDREN OF THE EARTH

AN END TIMES NOVEL

1

DARKNESS HAD FALLEN OVER CARBON County by the time Daphne pulled her compact Subaru to the side of the dirt road. Up ahead she could make out strains of raucous laughter, and the acrid smoke of charred meat drifted down to her on a sharp breeze.

She pulled her boyfriend's worn flannel shirt around her shoulders, trying to ward off the early autumn chill, and double-checked that the doors were locked before slipping the key into her pocket. There wasn't much to steal in her car—after splitting her earnings from working the oil rig between her ailing mother in Detroit and the collection plate at church, she could only afford an ancient clunker with a perpetually jammed cassette deck. Still, she couldn't trust the drifters who had taken up residence in the abandoned motocross track parking lot. They were rough-and-tumble oil prospectors with not a lot going for them and even less to lose, and it was rumored that they'd steal the shirt off your back, if given the chance.

The night noises sharpened as she approached: gas generators hacking out watts of power, hot dogs sizzling on portable barbecues, and plastic tarps erected as haphazard shelters crinkling in the wind. The parking lot where the Carbon County locals had once come to race dirt bikes, drink beer, and swap bragging rights was now a makeshift village of weather-beaten tents and rusted pop-up trailers, the track itself shut down.

None of the locals had wanted to set foot there since the horrible night just three months before when Daphne had helped deliver her cousin Janie's stillborn baby on the cold metal bleachers overlooking the track. Too many of their own had died there: first Trey, who had wrecked fatally during a race, and then Jeremiah, the baby who never took a breath.

Now the gate to the track was permanently shut, its padlock caked with rust, and the parking lot was transformed into a drab tent city of desperados. Only one thing could send Daphne there almost nightly to pick her way through the narrow paths between tents, stepping over mud-caked work boots and pots still crusted with last night's beans. It drew her there despite the drifters' unsavory reputation, despite the rumors of their rough-handed, heavy-drinking ways. She went because beyond the gate, on the eroding hills and turns of the track itself, was the only place where she could meet her boyfriend, Owen, in secret.

Owen was the best thing that had ever happened to her, but also one of the worst. He was the last person she'd expected to find in Carbon County, a rural town in the Wyoming foothills where she'd taken refuge with her extended family, the Peytons, after an especially rough winter in Detroit. But instead of the peace and quiet she'd been craving, she found oil on her uncle's land and a strange ability to read the ancient Aramaic words on a stone tablet discovered beneath the earth, an ability that some said marked her as a prophet. She found all that, and she also found Owen, a green-eyed stranger who somehow wormed his way into her heart despite her general distrust of everyone, especially guys.

As soon as he arrived, it felt like Owen was everywhere: on the oil rig where she worked and at the motocross track, where he quickly destroyed the locals in competition, instantly making him the least-liked guy in town. It didn't help when Trey, a popular local boy, died in a race against Owen—or that later, he and Daphne were the only two present when her pregnant cousin, Janie, went into sudden, early labor, delivering a stillborn infant on the cold metal bleachers overlooking the motocross track.

Maybe it was because Owen was there at all the wrong times that the townspeople hated him, or maybe it was just because he didn't say much to anyone besides Daphne, didn't have the gift of small-town small talk that put them at ease. Whatever it was, she knew exactly what they thought of him . . . and what they would think of *her* if they knew he was her boyfriend.

Now, more than ever, she needed the townspeople's approval. She'd fallen from their graces once before, when her cousin's jerk of a baby-daddy, Doug, revealed that she'd stood trial for her stepfather's murder in Detroit. It had been in self-defense, after he tried to rape her at knife-point, and she'd been acquitted—but Doug didn't tell anyone that part. Instead, he'd accused her of not only killing her stepfather, but he and Janie's infant son as well. He'd implicated Owen, too, and the townspeople had rallied behind him, threatening to throw both Daphne and Owen out of town.

It was only after Pastor Ted learned that Daphne could read the Aramaic tablet and declared her a prophet that the townspeople grudgingly allowed her back in their good graces . . . but by then, it was too late for Owen. The town needed a scapegoat, and he was the most convenient target.

If it weren't for her aunt and uncle, Daphne wouldn't have cared what anyone thought about her personal life. But Uncle Floyd and Aunt Karen meant everything to her: They had taken her in when she had nowhere else to go and taught her the true meaning of family and faith, and she would rather die than upset them. They had never trusted Owen, and still believed that he may have had a hand in their grandchild's death—and until they had a little more time to heal, Daphne didn't want to upset them further.

So, to avoid suspicion, she and Owen met on the abandoned motocross track after sundown, where fear of the drifters kept the gossipy townsfolk away.

Gravel crunched behind her, and Daphne froze. But the path through the camp was deserted, the drifters gathered around a fire at the other end of the parking lot. An unsecured tarp scratched at the ground, echoing the sound that had made her panic. Exhaling in relief, Daphne turned and made her way out of the camp.

She slipped past the padlocked gate and onto the dark trail leading to the motocross track. Even when she wasn't sneaking out to meet Owen, their clandestine relationship made her jumpy and anxious, always looking over her shoulder and trying to wipe the traces of their secret from her face. If she could have resisted him, she would have. But their bond was too strong, too powerful, to ignore.

The dark drew itself around her, only the pale comma of a moon punctuating the sky, and she heard the crunch again, closer than before. But she wouldn't turn and look, wouldn't let her paranoia get the better of her.

Stones skittered across the path behind her, and the wind panted in her wake. Although it was too dark for shadows, she thought she saw something flicker across her vision. Her stomach clenched as she felt the sudden presence of a stranger behind her, his skin emanating a dank rot.

She whirled around, but it was too late. Yellowed nails dug into her shoulders, the force knocking her to the ground. She got in one good scream before his hand clapped over her mouth, filling her lungs with the sickening scent of decay. Adrenaline flew through her veins as she kicked the air, praying for her steel-enforced boots to connect.

The stranger covered her body with his, stilling her legs and pinning her to the ground. Greasy strings of hair fell onto her cheeks, and he laughed a grating chainsaw laugh, reaching into the folds of an oily trench coat to reveal a blade that turned the weak beam of moonlight to ice. The world pulsed, and terror screamed through her, her vision condensing into a single point of light. Her eyes rolled back in her head as power gathered in her stomach, spreading from cell to cell until she was charged like a battery, electricity fighting its way through her skin and making her writhe and quake under his weight. She looked straight into his eyes—one gray, one brown—and saw, with horror, their true intent.

She'd had a knife to her throat and a grown man's unwanted body on hers before. She knew what that man, her stepfather, Jim, had wanted: to force himself inside of her, debasing her body until it no longer felt like her own.

But this man didn't want that. He didn't care about her body. He wanted her life.

She jerked and seized beneath him, and the power rocketing inside of her forced her hands around his neck, choking off his windpipe with a python grip. For a moment, everything was black. Then she heard a voice in her head, and all she could see was fire.

The Vision of Fire

And yea, there will come a day
When ye stand before the derrick
That pumps oil from the earth
And a wall of flames consumes the sky.

These shall be no ordinary flames
But the hellfire of damnation,
Wild with hunger to destroy
All that is holy and good.

And ye shall see, as the fire approacheth
And crude oil boils inside the earth
And the heat peels trees from land
And skin from bone

Ye shall see a shadow
With shoulders wide as mountains,
Arms raised, fingers outstretched,
Coaxing the fire ever closer.

Slow as boulders forming
The dark figure turns

Until he looks down upon you
And you fall to your knees.
For this figure has a face you know,
A face you have touched.
You have seen these eyes,
Flash serpentine green.

These eyes have deceived you,
These hands draw down fire to burn the land,
This heart serves only the dark lord
And this soul is as black as the devil.

Your limbs shall tremble
And your heart shall tear in two,
For this is a face you know—
A face you love.